A Little Taste

USA TODAY BESTSELLING AUTHOR
TIA LOUISE

Copyright

This book is a work of fiction. Names, characters, places, and incidents are products of the author's imagination or are used fictitiously. Any resemblance to actual events or locales or persons, living or dead, is entirely coincidental.

A Little Taste
Copyright © TLM Productions LLC, 2023
Printed in the United States of America.

Cover design by Cover Design by Y'all that Graphic

"Love is the closest thing we have to magic."
—*Jay Ann*

To my readers, my friends, and Mr. TL,
a little pixie dust ✧

Chapter 1

Aiden

"Yep, he's a goner." Deputy Doug Hally straightens with a groan, holding the squashed cucumber out for my inspection.

I nod grimly, and Terra Belle throws up her arms in distress. "My entire pickle farm is destroyed! Who would do such a thing?"

We're standing in the middle of the two-acre field now riddled with large, circular ruts and damaged fruit still on the vine. The pattern of the tire tracks reminds me of that movie about the aliens making crop circles, but this damage was definitely done by a vehicle of some sort.

"My money's on them no-good Jones boys." My sole deputy tosses the damaged fruit to the side, lowering his brow in a knowing way.

"You think it was Bull and Raif, Dad? Are you going to arrest them? Can I go?" My son Owen blinks up at me, his seven-year-old eyes wide, and I hesitate.

If he weren't here, I'd say this looks more like asshole

teenagers who watched that movie and wanted to play a prank. The Jones boys were probably too drunk or high last night to do something this precise, but it's important to me to be a good role model, even when I'm tired.

Placing my hand on Owen's shoulder, I summon my dad, the former sheriff of Eureka's calm wisdom. I think about what he'd have said to me at Owen's age.

"It's not our job to decide who's guilty, son. We have to collect the evidence and make our best determination, then we'll get a judge to issue a warrant."

"Oh, you know it was those Jones boys." Terra drops to a squat, holding up a vine of crushed cuke after cuke—it looks like a sad party favor. "I'm tempted to gather up the rest of these and beat them to death with 'em."

"Now, Terra," Deputy Doug cautions. "Two wrongs don't make a right."

"Yeah, don't go there, Terra," I add. "Then I'd have to arrest you, too."

"So you *are* going to arrest them?" She stands quickly. Her dark hair is tied up in a red handkerchief, and she's wearing faded overalls and from what I can tell, nothing else. "This kind of vandalism can't go unpunished. It's trespassing, destruction of property, murder…"

With every charge she shakes the pickle vine at me, and I stand straighter, rising to my full six-foot-two height and lowering my voice. "Take it easy, Terra."

It's my standard way to diffuse tense situations, and sure enough, Terra deflates.

"What am I going to do about my existing orders?"

"You've got insurance, don't ya?" Doug squints as he walks to where we're standing.

"Of course I do!" she snaps at him, but I let it pass.

She's facing a pretty significant loss, which has her understandably emotional. I have no clue how long it takes to grow a crop of cucumbers, and Terra Belle's Pickle Patch is regionally famous, which I guess might make her a target. Of what, I don't know.

Exhaling slowly, I maintain my calm. "I'll head back to the office and get you a police report to send to the insurance company. Hopefully, that'll get you some money pretty quick." She starts to argue it's not enough, and I nod. "I know you want justice today, but I can't go arresting people without evidence. It'll just get thrown out, and that's not how we do things."

"Well, maybe it should be," she grouses.

I'm tired. I haven't had my first cup of coffee. The call to come out here had me out of bed before the sun even broke the horizon. Now it's climbing higher in the sky, and I'm ready to head to the office and possibly have breakfast.

"Doug, you finish up here, and I'll get Terra's report ready." I'm not sure the correct way to phrase my next question. "Before I go, do you have any enemies or rival… picklers?"

"Oh, I've got plenty of rivals, but no one would stoop to this level." She wipes a tear off her cheek. "Destroying my *babies*."

Pressing my lips together, I nod. I'm not good with tears, especially tears over "baby pickles," which in reality are called *cucumbers*.

"All the same, send me any names that come to mind, and take plenty of pictures. I'll have that report to you by lunchtime."

I whistle to my son, who's holding a squashed fruit with a stick and examining it. He drops it at once and takes off running to my truck. I let Doug drive the cruiser. In this town, I'm fine with a black Silverado and a light on the dash when necessary.

Terra can work this out with her insurance company, and I'll have Doug inspect every teenager in town's vehicle for traces of cucumber vines. It won't take long in Eureka, South Carolina. I'll include the Jones boys to cover all the bases.

We're halfway back to town, the radio playing some old country song. Owen's beside me, buckled in and bouncing Zander, his tattered, stuffed zebra on his legs. "Why would anybody drive a car in Ms. Belle's pickle patch?"

My hand is propped on the top of the steering wheel, and I think about it. "The older I've gotten, the less I understand why people do anything. I guess that's why towns need sheriffs."

"I'm going to be a sheriff when I grow up!" He smiles up at me, pride in his eyes. "Just like my dad."

My stomach tightens, and warmth filters through my chest. I'm generally considered something of a grumpy badass, but this little guy... He's a lot like I was at his age, thinking my dad was the greatest and wanting to grow up to be just like him.

I thought I'd have a chance to work right alongside him, but a heart-attack took him two days after I graduated from college. I've missed him every day since. Especially when life hits hard. Especially when I need advice.

I went from being a student, to being a Marine, to being a sheriff, and now Owen wants to follow in my footsteps.

"You'll be one of the best." I glance at him before returning my eyes to the road.

He sits straighter, lifting his chin, and I almost grin. I had no idea when he was born how much he'd carry me through the dark times.

He was barely old enough to remember his mom when she was killed four years ago on her evening walk. I'd mourned her and pledged to find the person who hit her and drove off without even looking back.

Then a year later, when I'd finally worked up the strength to go through her things, I found a box of love letters from Clive Stevens, who happened to live on the very street where she was hit.

He'd even had the balls to attend her funeral before he moved back to wherever he was from. It never occurred to me to be suspicious of her evening walks, but after that, I pretty much swore off anyone not related to me by blood. They're the only ones you can trust, and even then, it's good to keep your eyes open.

"Do you know what a zorse is?" Owen looks up at me,

bouncing Zander on his leg. "It's a cross between a zebra and a horse!"

"Is that so?" I park the truck in front of the courthouse, which houses the mayor's office and our headquarters.

"A group of zebras is called a dazzle. I wonder if a group of zorses would be called a zazzle?"

He looks up at me like I would know. "Forget sheriff, you should be a zebrologist when you grow up."

"That's not a thing!" He groans as he climbs out of the truck, slamming the door and trotting up beside me, slipping his little hand in mine.

It warms my chest, again almost making me smile. I don't smile often, and I definitely don't hold hands, but with Owen, everything is different.

"You can be the first." I scoot him through the glass doors ahead of me, hoping Holly, our secretary and dispatcher, ordered breakfast—or at least has a pot of coffee ready.

"Aiden, I heard you were at Terra Belle's Pickle Patch." I'm met at the door by Edna Brewer, longtime mayor of Eureka, and unfortunately my boss. "My intuition tells me something sinister is afoot."

"Terra would agree with you. She left her house without her wig on."

Edna's dark brown eyes widen. "You saw Terra's real hair?"

"She had a handkerchief around her head, and she was in overalls."

"Only something truly sinister would cause Terra to leave the house in such a state."

"I suspect it's nothing more sinister than teenagers." I start to walk past her, but she pulls me up short with her next words.

"Owen, your father is a good man, despite his lack of faith."

My jaw tightens. We were almost having a nice moment, and she had to go there. "I prefer sticking to the facts when doing my job."

"Magic has never let me down, Sheriff, which is more than I can say of people."

She'll get no arguments from me when it comes to people, however, "Where was magic when Lars needed it?"

Her eyes narrow. "What happened to my son-in-law was a tragic accident, but escapologists are not magicians."

Neither are you. The retort is on the tip of my tongue, but I don't say it. We're fighting old battles, and we only go in circles.

The Brewers and the Stones declared a truce after my father died, and I've done my best to honor it since starting as sheriff—as long as Edna keeps her hocus pocus to herself and out of my work.

Placing my hand on Owen's back, I give him a little pat. "Why don't you run see if Holly got donuts on her way in." He takes off with a little whoop of "Krispy Kreme," and I turn to the mayor. "I apologize for saying that about Lars. It was insensitive."

She lifts her chin. "I accept your apology."

"And I'd appreciate it if you didn't put ideas in my son's head."

"Your son is very bright, Aiden."

"Thank you."

"And children are very sensitive to spiritual things. Owen's fascination with zebras is a clear indicator. They're remnants of a time when the world was shadows and light."

"No." My tone is firm.

She waves her hands. "I'm not trying to start a fight. I simply wanted to let you know I've been monitoring this rise in crime lately, and I think we need to bring in some backup."

My brow furrows. "What does that mean?"

She starts for her office, and I follow. Edna is almost seventy, with silver hair that hangs in a bob to her chin. She's dressed in a white silk blouse and tan pencil skirt with matching pumps, and in this conservative disguise, you'd never know she's a former magician and matriarch of the town's resident band of carnies.

She believes in premonitions and psychics and *vibrations* as much as cold hard facts when making civic decisions. It drove my dad nuts, and it doesn't make me too happy either—particularly when she drags her "psychic" daughter Guinevere into the mix. Gwen is a real space cadet, and sneaky as fuck.

You'd think Edna would be ready to retire by now, but this crazy town keeps voting her back in office every time she runs. If the town of Eureka were a zebra, she'd be the black to my white—and I'm sure she'd say the exact opposite.

"Someone has been nailing messages on telephone poles for a month. Last week, Holly said three of her hens were stolen. Now Terra Belle's prized pickle patch has been demolished. I think we need someone with special training in this type of work."

Heat rises under my collar, and a growl enters my tone. "You're not to call in additional officers without consulting me."

"I'm consulting you now. Doug's pushing sixty, but even if he was younger, you know he isn't up to this type of work. You could use the help."

I'm annoyed she's right. Still, the last thing I need is some new person coming in, getting in my way, asking a bunch of questions—or worse, another kooky mystic reading tea leaves and being totally loyal to Edna.

"Who did you have in mind?"

"That's the best part." She claps, rising to her feet and smiling like she's about to pull a rabbit out of a hat. "My granddaughter Britt has been working in Greenville, training at the crime lab at Clemson. She's got the best possible credentials."

My stomach tightens. "Britt said she wasn't coming back to Eureka."

The last time I saw Edna's granddaughter—at her going away party, which my youngest brother tricked me into attending—she'd said she wanted to define her life outside this town and her family's reputation.

"Oh, poo." Edna waves her hand. "Guinevere will call her. She'll want to be back in her hometown with her best friends and family."

I'm not so sure of that. I'm also not so sure about her working with me. Britt Bailey is too young and too pretty, and on the night of her farewell party, things got a little too blurry on the back porch of her friend's home.

We somehow wound up out there alone, and we started talking about her life in Eureka, my time in the Marines, her dreams, my son. It was the first time I'd seen her as the only sane member of her family.

Our bodies had drifted closer until we were almost touching, and the conversation faded away. She blinked those pretty green eyes up at me, and the starlight shone on the tips of her blonde hair. She smelled like fresh flowers and the ocean, and her pink lips were so full and inviting. It had been so long since I'd lost myself in the depths of a beautiful woman...

Obviously, I'd had too much whiskey.

"I can tell by your pleased expression you like this idea." Edna nods. "I'll have Gwen call her today, and I'll let you know how soon she can get started."

"That wasn't what I was thinking." My expression was *not* pleased. "Is she even old enough to work here?"

"She's twenty-eight, Aiden. Don't be ageist."

Seven years younger than me.

"But this would be her first actual job as a crime scene investigator?"

"She's an experienced forensic photographer. You can get her up to speed on the rest. She's a fast learner." Edna picks up her phone, excitedly tapping on the face. "Trust me, once you have my granddaughter at your side, you'll wonder how you ever survived without her. The vibrations are shifting already."

I'm sure they are, and it's exactly what's putting me on guard.

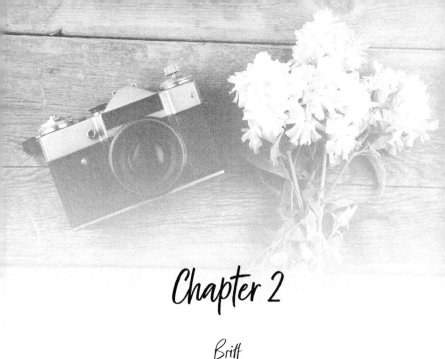

Chapter 2

Britt

"**T**HANK YOU FOR INVITING ME TO YOUR GROUP. I'M SO EXCITED to be here." I stand in front of a white marble fireplace with my hands clasped, doing my best not to fidget as I meet the eyes of the small group of elite females sitting on plush velvet sofas and chairs in front of me.

The Greenville Ladies Club meets in Keekee Waters's well-appointed living room once a month, and I've been invited for the first time by my new friend of two days Maylyn Evers.

We met in a "primal movement" fitness class at the Y, which I'd attended with the express purpose of making new friends. I've been in Greenville six months, and I still hardly know anybody.

"The GLC is better than the Junior League because we actually *work* on our *selves*," Maylyn had bragged, tapping her towel around the edges of her fully made-up face after our class. "Keekee's husband is on the board at Clemson, so they're practically town royalty."

I smiled, gulping air like a fish out of water. I was a hot mess in no makeup, my blonde hair frizzed out around my temples, my cheeks pink, and my face shining with sweat. I wasn't sure I was ready to meet town royalty, but I was tired of eating ramen and watching reruns of *The Closer* with my dog every night.

Now I'm standing in the nicest room I've ever seen, introducing myself to a very select group of twin-set-and-pearls-wearing ladies with perfectly coiffed hair, surrounded by little flowery cups of tea.

Two arched, built-in bookcases are on either side of the fireplace. They hold books with titles like *Get Out of Your Own Way* and *Somehow I Manage,* and mixed throughout are little trinkets and pewter-framed pictures of Keekee's smiling family.

In one, a little girl in a smocked blue-and-white seersucker dress with a bow as big as her head sits beside a boy in a white short-sleeved shirt and matching seersucker shorts. In another the kids are joined by Keekee and her Ken-doll looking husband. He even has a sweater tied around his neck like one of those Ralph Lauren models.

This entire house could be a Ralph Lauren pop-up.

"We're so glad to have you, Birgitte." Keekee's voice is low and superior-sounding. She's dressed in a pale pink cardigan and pearls like she's a queen, and her dark bob looks like it wouldn't move in a strong wind.

"Everybody just calls me Britt." I exhale a laugh, glancing down.

I'm like one of those girls on that *Bridgerton* show on Netflix, standing in front of the queen, hoping for her approval. Maylynn's eyebrows are lifted and furrowed in a compassionate arch, and she presses her lips into a smile like she's so proud of me, her little find.

Glancing down at my thin, pastel dress, I shove my long blonde bangs behind my ears as I take a deep breath and answer the introductory question. "I guess my biggest fear is drowning."

I leave off the part about how I'm sure it's clearly related to my escape-artist father's tragic death by drowning when I was only ten years-old.

"Drowning." Keekee nods, and the other women follow her lead, nodding as they glance from me to her. "A valid fear."

Encouraged, I exhale, allowing all my anxieties to flow out on a tidal wave of words. "Like the other night, I had this dream I was driving a car with flat tires in a terrible rain storm. So I drove to a gas station to get air for the tires, but I didn't realize there was an enormous pool of water in the center of the pumps, and when I hit it, the water just rushed up the sides of the car. Well, I panicked and tried to keep just a-pumping the gas pedal so it wouldn't stall out before I got to the other side. Well, the engine started sputtering, so I opened the door to try and push it to the other side, Fred Flintstone-style…" I turn to the side, holding my hands on an invisible steering wheel in front of me, and I stomp to demonstrate how I was trying to push the car through the water. "But when I opened the door, all that water just flooded into the vehicle, and I was being sucked down deeper and deeper because the bottom of the car had disappeared and I was actually in a black ocean. Until I woke up in a panic, covered in sweat."

I shrug, helplessly slapping my hands down to my sides. "Analyze that," I laugh, nodding as I glance around the room.

It's so quiet, I hear a car door slam from across the street. All eyes in the room are fixed on me, and Maylynn's compassionate pride has turned to confused horror.

"Well, I'll be." Is all Keekee says. "It seems *someone* forgot the rule about not driving through standing water. Mary Pat? Would you like to go next?"

Heat prickles up the back of my neck, and the other attendees blink down to their teacups as if they're afraid my rejection might be contagious if they look at me.

I am clearly not the diamond of this season's *Bridgerton* court.

Mary Pat hops up quickly, stepping beside me in front of the fireplace. She bounces on the toes of her white canvas tennis shoes, effectively scooting me to the wings as she shares her biggest fear.

"My biggest fear is embarrassing Nelson when his parents visit." Mary Pat rolls her eyes and laughs as she tilts her pixie head side to side. "I know, I'm such an *airhead*, but I'm always afraid I'll put too much cilantro in the guacamole or I'll forget to empty the bathroom trash can. His mother is so strict about cleaning."

"Tell me about it." One of the ladies across from us joins the chat. "Bill's mother actually checks behind the children's ears when she hugs them. Like they're not bathed!"

All the ladies squeal and launch into stories of their monsters-in-law. My entire body is on fire with humiliation. I don't have a mother-in-law or kids, and I tuck my chin as I return to my seat beside Maylynn, who shifts away from me to talk to her neighbor.

The rest of the meeting, no one speaks to me, and I spend the hour nibbling a tiny sandwich with no crust and listening to the women discuss getting grass stains out of their children's "play clothes" or what to do when you accidentally shrink your husband's wool sweaters.

When the meeting finally ends, Maylynn stands and walks over to a cluster of ladies across the room, and I make my way to the front door alone. Keekee, the perfect hostess, catches me before I can escape.

"It was so *interesting* to meet you, Birgitte." Her tone makes me feel like an exotic insect she discovered in her yard. "You have such a unique perspective."

I'm pretty sure that's not a compliment. "You have a very nice house."

She tilts her head, smiling as she blinks slowly, as if to say, *I know*, and holds the door in a way that makes me think she might push me out with it.

It's the last straw. My mamma didn't raise me to be treated like dirt—even if my family is a bit… *different*.

"You have an *interesting* perspective as well." I lift my chin. "Thanks for the sandwich. It was the best part of the meeting, and even it was pretty bland."

Her jaw drops, and I walk out to my ancient Ford pickup. The door makes a loud popping noise when I open it, but I keep my head high, climbing inside and slamming it shut. I pull the visor down, and the keys drop into my lap.

My best friend Cass, who can literally fix anything, wired my old truck with a Bluetooth system, and I quickly type my address into the app on my phone.

It actually takes a map to escape this Stepford-wives subdivision. "Every third house is the same," I mutter. "I wouldn't be surprised if they actually were automatons."

Once I've got the route, I turn on my favorite Shania Twain playlist, and blast "That Don't Impress Me Much," as I pass two-story brick homes situated on cul-de-sac after cul-de-sac.

I'm singing at the top of my lungs and finally on the road to my place when my phone starts to ring. With a glance, I see it's my mom.

"Hi, Mom!"

"Are you sitting down?" My mother's voice is low and urgent—like every time she calls me.

"I'm driving, so I'd better be!"

"Oh, I'll call you back. I don't want you distracted driving."

"It's okay, Mom, I've got both hands on the wheel. What's the matter?"

"You need to come home now."

If I had a dollar for every time she called and said that, it would pay my gas bill for a year.

"What happened now?" I turn onto the street where I live, feeling a lot more homesick after that meeting than I have the last several times she's called with an emergency.

"That's the problem. We don't know. Last night, someone got into Terra Belle's Pickle Patch and absolutely wrecked her cukes. They left tire marks everywhere, and half her harvest is ruined."

"Have you called the sheriff?" The very thought of Aiden Stone stepping onto a crime scene, his fatigue green uniform pants hugging his ass, sends a shiver down my spine.

"I can only assume you're so focused on driving you've forgotten who you're talking to." My mother's tone switches from cloak-and-dagger to sarcasm in an instant. "It's the only reason you would *ever* suggest I speak to Aiden Stone."

I'd speak to him…

Aiden Stone is the hottest man alive—*People* magazine just hasn't found him yet. He's six-foot-two inches of pure muscle, with a square jaw and a take-no-prisoners gaze. Add to all of that, he's a former Marine, with dreamy blue eyes and brown hair that's somehow silky and wavy at the same time.

The last time I saw him, my last night in Eureka, he actually walked outside where I was standing and talked to me. *I know.* Until that moment, I'm pretty sure he'd never even looked at me. Not only am I seven years younger than him, he's also a member of the Stone family… which means he's *not* a fan of the Baileys. His straight-laced forebears have battled my hippie family for years.

Still, he asked me about my plans. I told him I wanted to start a new life, find my own path, get out of the shadow of my family. He said he understood, but I'm not sure he does. He's in Eureka carrying on his family's legacy of law enforcement.

The one time he softened was talking about his son Owen. My insides swooned as his blue eyes warmed telling me how Owen loves zebras and learning about animals. I think I stepped closer, wishing I could trace my finger along the cleft in his chin and bury my nose in the warm cedar scent of his clothes. Then he looked down at me, and the heat in his gaze stole my breath. I nearly fainted.

"Aiden Stone is not a believer."

"Maybe not, but it's his job to investigate crimes."

"Which is why we need you to come home. You've spent enough time in Greenville, and we need you here."

"Who's we?"

"Your grandmother and me. We need you here because you're part psychic."

Shaking my head, I exhale softly. "I'm not psychic, Mom."

"Still, you have fifty percent of my genes. Your intuition is very keen, and the spiritual vibration in Eureka is disturbed. I hate to say this out loud…" Her voice lowers to just above a whisper. "It reminds me of the last time I saw your father alive."

My throat knots, and as much as I push back on my mother's psychic abilities, she does have a knack for knowing things. She also has never believed my father's death was an accident.

I pull into the parking lot of my apartment building and look up at the small space I've tried to make my home for the last six months. It feels about as foreign as when I arrived.

Striking out on my own has not turned out the way I thought it would when I left my tiny hometown on the Carolina coast between Hilton Head and Kiawah Island. I haven't made a big splash in the big city, but I have learned a lot.

"I'll talk to my boss at the station and see if I can take a leave of absence."

"Thank you, Britt." Her voice is a heavy exhale of relief. "I knew you wouldn't let us down. The only thing you regret when you die is the time you don't spend with family and friends."

"Good lord, Ma, nobody's dying."

"Not yet, at least."

I roll my eyes at her dramatics. "Well, I'm coming, but things are going to be different this time. For starters, I'm getting my own place—"

"What?" she cries. "Why would you waste money like that when your room at home is waiting just the way you left it?"

"And I'm not helping with your tarot readings when you double-book yourself. Those days are over."

"I wouldn't dream of asking you to help me." Her tone is

wounded, but don't be fooled. She would *so* ask me. "I have someone helping me with the readings now, so you don't have to worry."

"Who's helping you?" Slamming the door of my truck, I trot up the stairs to my apartment.

Edward greets me at the door by sticking his cold, wet nose into the palm of my hand. I drop to my knees, giving his neck and ears a good, firm scrubbing. He licks my face in response.

"Cassidy started working with me shortly after you left. She has a real gift for spiritual things."

"*Cass* is helping you predict the future?" It's official. My bestie has done everything in Eureka.

"I've told you a hundred times, I don't predict the future."

"Oh, I know you don't, but I'm not sure your paying customers do."

"I give them counsel. I'm a guide, and Cassidy is actually quite good. She's very sensitive and empathetic."

"Sounds like I need to get home, *stat*. Next you'll tell me Jinx is running for mayor."

"You shouldn't call Piper that. Names are powerful. They connect us to our spiritual identity, and I'm sure she doesn't want to connect with bad omens."

"Piper named herself Jinx. I think it's her way of reclaiming her power."

"I don't like it."

"You don't have to like it."

She makes a harrumphing noise, and I pull my oversized suitcase out of my closet. I don't have much to pack, as I haven't really been here long enough to accumulate a lot of extra baggage.

"How soon do you think you'll be home?"

Glancing at the clock, I've got plenty of time to go to the station and speak to my supervisor. "If there's no problem, I could probably be home this weekend."

"That's wonderful! I'll tell your grandmother. You can stay here until you find your own place."

I have a better idea. "Is the loft above the Star Parlor still vacant?"

A bright little one-bedroom living space is located above my mother's tarot-reading studio. She used to rent it out after my dad died to make some extra money, but not enough people move to Eureka to maintain a short-term rental.

"It is, but nobody's lived there for a while. It needs to be cleaned and aired out and checked for pests."

"You do that today, and I'll let you know when I'm on the road."

"Okay," she pouts, but I'm not swayed.

If I'm going back to Eureka, things are going to be different. I have a life and a career, and as much as I love my family, I'm not interested in living their free-spirited, unreliable life.

I live in the real world. I'm not making my decisions based on magic anymore.

Chapter 3

Aiden

WHO WATCHES OVER YOU? THE SIGN IS HAND-LETTERED NEATLY IN canary-blue on a narrow strip of white wood. It's nailed to the utility pole outside the courthouse, and I cross my arms, silently reading and re-reading the message.

"Is it a protest sign?" Doug stands beside me scratching the gray hairs on the back of his neck. "Are they implying we're not watching the town?"

We're both in short sleeves, and he's wearing his hat to shield the top of his balding head from the sun. Even though it's March, it never gets very cold in Eureka, and the sun is almost always shining.

"I don't think it's about us."

"You want me to take it down?"

My hands are on my hips, and I shake my head. "Leave it."

I have no idea who's doing this, but they're essentially positive messages. They started a little over three months ago with a single word, *Happiness,* painted in dark pink lettering on a thin strip of white board. They resemble the pickets from a fence.

I haven't been able to figure out any reason for them, no pattern or connection to particular dates. It's like someone has a dream or gets an idea on a random day, and up goes a sign. Naturally, Edna is reading supernatural meanings into them.

We left *Happiness* up, and after a few weeks, it disappeared and another one took its place in a different location. I forget what it said, but the last one read, *You are rare,* in dark purple lettering.

It was hung near the only restaurant in Eureka, El Rio owned by Herve Garcia, and I had to wonder if it was a joke. For starters, Herve is one of the first to integrate Eureka, but he also makes a steak taco that will haunt your dreams at night— cooked rare.

"It's Sunday, so maybe it's a reference to God?" Doug is still puzzling, but the sound of Shania Twain singing about feeling like a woman coming from behind us distracts me from this latest missive.

The music is getting louder fast, and I look up just in time to see a beat-up orange Ford truck barreling around the corner with no sign of stopping.

In a blink, I register three things: The truck is headed straight for us, the driver's eyes are wide, and Doug isn't looking or moving.

"Doug!" Grabbing my deputy around the waist, I tackle him to the ground behind his SUV, and with a crunch of metal, the truck plows into the utility pole.

Shit. I'm on my feet at once, expecting the worst. I pause briefly to be sure Doug's okay. He's shaking his head, but he's not hurt. Then I hustle around to check on the runaway truck.

The driver's door opens with a loud pop, and a young woman in a white T-shirt, denim cutoffs, and cowboy boots stumbles out shaking her hands and walking in circles.

"Oh my God, oh my God, oh my God…" she chants, and a big dog barks from inside the cab. "Edward!"

She dives into the vehicle again, climbing across the seat and unfastening the buckle that holds the hound in place.

My eyes narrow as I approach the vehicle. "Miss...?"

She backs out of the cab so fast she slams right into my chest. A little "Oof!" poofs from her lips, and the dog jumps out beside her, barking and trotting back and forth beside the truck as if to inspect the damage.

I catch her before she loses her footing, and when she looks up at me, my stomach tightens. Britt Bailey's bright green eyes meet mine, and her full pink lips part. It's been six months since I've seen her, but her scent, the fresh flowers...

"Aiden Stone!" Her voice is a dazed whisper. "Did you save me?"

I release her at once, placing my hands on her upper arms and moving her arms-length away from me.

"Are you hurt?" My tone is gruff, and I lean closer to inspect her pupils.

They're not dilated, and I step away again, giving her small, curvy body a cursory glance. Everything seems miraculously fine—if I believed in miracles.

She shakes her blonde head. "I think I'm okay."

Anger and frustration war in my chest, and my tone is stern. "You could've killed somebody just now."

"The brakes went out! I was pumping them as hard as I could and trying to downshift..."

Hesitating, I make sure she's not going to collapse before leaving her beside the open door and walking to the front of the truck.

A good-sized dent is on the right fender, and a loud *Bang!* makes me jump back. The new sign drops onto the hood, facing up like a portent. *Who watches over you?*

"Lord have mercy, Britt? Is that you?" Doug scuffles around the back of the truck to where she's standing. "You nearly flattened me like a pancake."

"Doug! I'm so sorry!" She rises on her toes to hug him, and

I tear my eyes away from the edge of her cutoffs rising dangerously high on her perky ass.

"What happened?" Doug continues, and the two of them walk to where I'm standing at the front of her orange death mobile.

"My brakes went out," she starts, then she gasps, clutching her hands. "Oh, no! My truck!"

"When's the last time you had this thing inspected?" Doug leans down to look inside the tires.

Her nose wrinkles. "Is that a thing?"

I shake my head. "Looks like you're due for an upgrade."

"No! I can't part with my truck! It belonged to my dad."

"Now, now." Doug pats her shoulder. "Nobody's making you get rid of your dad's truck."

He's treating her like she's made of glass, and I exhale a growl of frustration. She's just arrived in town, and the mayhem has already begun.

"I couldn't believe it when I hit the brakes, and it didn't stop. I thought that only happened in movies." She shakes her hands again. "I'm still kind-of… freaked out a little."

"You've had a shock. Come inside and have a glass of water." Doug takes her arm. "We'll call and see if Bud can tow it to his garage and give it a good once-over."

"All my stuff is in the back—"

"Aiden'll take care of it. Won't you, Aiden?" Doug's paternal tone is starting to annoy me.

"Sure. I'm not doing anything." I shake my head, lifting an enormous suitcase out of the truck bed.

Turning, I catch Britt's eyes fluttering from my shoulders down to my arms, and her cheeks flush pink.

"I guess that's what you call starting off with a bang?" She gives me a cautious smile that hits me in the chest in a way I don't like.

"It's all good." Doug nods to the sign on her hood. "Someone was watching over you."

It takes all my strength not to lose it entirely. That's just the sort of shit Edna needs to hear.

"I'll meet you inside," I grumble, rolling her suitcase into the courthouse while Edward trots along beside me.

Glancing down, I can tell he's part bloodhound from his long ears and droopy cheeks. He's black and tan, and he looks like a good dog. I give his head a pat.

Town offices are technically closed on Sundays, but I always come in to be sure everything's calm. Holly Newton, our dispatcher, must've called Doug about the sign, because he normally goes to church. I pretty much let all that God stuff go the way of fairy tales and magic when my wife died. Finding that stack of love letters further solidified my position on the matter.

"I didn't intend to come to the office today." Britt's voice carries through the empty space. "I'd have dressed differently."

"I didn't even know you were joining the team." Doug's shoulders bounce with his laugh. "I guess it's classified information."

Returning to the main office, I level my gaze on them. "Edna thought we could use some extra hands with all that's been happening lately. She was supposed to let me know your ETA."

Britt gives me another cautious smile. "They made it sound like an emergency, so I put in a request for leave."

"In that case, you can start tomorrow, eight a.m." My tone is clipped. "After that, you and Doug can sort out your days off. I'm here every day, but if nothing's happening, I don't expect you to work more than five days a week."

"I like my Sundays off." Doug shrugs. "Otherwise, I'm flexible."

"What if you take Sunday off, and I'll take Saturday?" Her tone brightens.

They do a little high-five, and I clear my throat. "Just work the other day out a few weeks in advance, so I know what to expect."

"Yes, sir, Sheriff." Doug salutes, clearly feeling his oats with a pretty young woman in the office. He's never so chipper.

"And Britt." I nod briefly at her torso. "You're one of us now. You'll need to think about how you appear in public."

Her face flames bright red, and she blinks quickly, which I'm picking up is something she does when she's nervous or flustered.

Still, a touch of defiance is in her reply. "I know the proper dress code for my job."

"Good." She's not made of glass, and I'm the boss. "I wasn't sure what to think about your choices. The last time we spoke, you said you were never coming back to Eureka."

Her shoulders straighten, and she puts her hands on her hips. "As I'm sure you know, Sheriff Stone, I was *asked* to come back to Eureka because your department couldn't handle the workload. I'll stay until my help is no longer needed."

My smile tightens, and I cross my arms. "Are you making a comment about the quality of my team?"

She smiles sweetly, but the sass hasn't left her tone. "Not at all. I'm here because the mayor, my grandmother, asked me for a favor, and I think as we get older, we realize the importance of family and making time for the people we love."

"So you came back for your family?" I'm not liking the sound of this. I'd thought she was the sane one.

"Of course. It's important to help our loved ones when they need us."

My brow lowers. "Depending on the outcome."

Silence descends on the room and Doug looks from Britt to me and back again. "Did anyone call Bud? We need to get that truck off the street before church lets out. We might even need to have the utility company check that pole."

"Thanks, Doug. I'll let you handle it. I've got to pick up Owen from Sunday school." I turn and start for the door. "Call me if you need anything. And, Miss Bailey?"

"Yes, Sheriff?" Our eyes strike like flint, and even if I don't like it, my stomach heats in response.

"I'll see you in the morning, dressed to work a crime scene."

"I'll be ready."

"Whose truck crashed into the light pole?" Owen is on his knees looking out the window of my truck at Bud's towing operation in progress.

His dark hair is brushed neatly, and he's dressed in a light-blue, short-sleeved shirt with a clip-on tie and khakis. Even if I don't attend, my mother taught me how to dress for church.

"It belongs to my new forensic photographer," I grumble under my breath.

Looks like Bud went to church this morning, which means a crowd of onlookers has gathered while he hitches the front of Britt's truck to his tower.

Owen drops onto his butt again, looking up at me with a frown. "What's a forensic photographer?"

"It's a person who takes pictures of crime scenes to try and help us figure out what happened or who did it."

"Like a private investigator?"

"Something like that, but with pictures." I'm driving us slowly to my mother's house for our weekly Sunday lunch.

"You said facts are the only things that matter."

"That's right."

"No magic." He looks down at his hands, and I can tell something's bothering him.

"What's on your mind, Froot Loop?"

"Dad!" he groans loudly. "I told you not to call me that anymore!"

"What? It was your favorite food for the first five years of your life."

"It's not cool."

I glance in the mirror, wondering when he started worrying about being cool. He used to laugh at his nickname.

"Sorry, I'll try to remember that."

Quiet falls in the cab and an old Shania Twain song comes on the country station about boots being under beds. I reach forward to turn it off. I've had enough of her voice for one day.

"Jesus walked on the water," Owen blurts, and my brow furrows. "Miss Magee said so in Sunday school today. There was a bad, bad storm, and the disciples were all afraid, and they looked out and Jesus was walking on the water to their boat. How could that have happened if there's no such thing as magic?"

Shifting in my seat, I give the accelerator a little nudge to get us to my mom's house quicker. I hadn't expected to have this conversation with him so soon—or ever.

"Well…" I start, wondering how the hell I'm going to answer him.

"I said you don't believe in magic, and Miss Magee said I should talk to you about it after church. Ryan said I'd better not."

"Don't you listen to Ryan." I'm quick to squash that notion. "If there's something you want to know, you can always come and ask me. We don't keep secrets from each other."

"Ryan said you'd get mad." My son squints up at me. "You look mad."

"I'm not mad. I just didn't expect to be talking about Jesus this morning."

"It's Sunday, Dad." He looks at me like *duh*. "Everybody's talking about Jesus."

I don't bother pointing out not *everybody* talks about Jesus on Sunday. We are in Eureka, after all.

Pulling into the driveway of my mom's large, white farmhouse. I look up at the wrap-around porch, the swing in the corner, and I wonder when my life got so complicated. I can remember sitting there, listening to the chain squeak as I talked to my dad about some problem, as we slowly rocked back and forth with the slightly briny, humid breeze wrapping around us.

Damn, I miss that old man.

Green, spiky palmettos line the space between the porch and the ground, and rising above it all is a giant live oak tree so old its black limbs reach almost to the ground. All my brothers and I had to take pictures with our dates before homecoming and prom and whatever else my mother deemed photo-worthy in front of that tree.

My brother Alex's Tesla is already in the drive, and with Owen's question hanging in the air, I grimace at the sight of my youngest brother Adam's Jetta.

Adam's as big a believer as the Baileys. I'd hoped being a pilot in the Navy would have worked some of that out of him, but it didn't. In fact, I think it made him worse—flying helped him see the world from God's perspective, he said.

If I don't wrap this up, I'm sure he'll be glad to provide some outlandish answer to my son's question.

"Here's the thing, Owen." I shift in my seat. "The stories in the Bible are more about helping us understand how to live our lives better. You're not supposed to try and sort out how everything in them happened word for word."

"How is Jesus walking on the water supposed to help us live our lives better?"

Fuck. I'm trying to remember that damn story from when I was in Sunday school. "Remind me what happens."

"You don't remember the Bible story?" His blue eyes cut up to me, very disappointed.

"It's been a while, and you just heard it. Refresh me."

"There was a big storm, and all Jesus's friends were in a boat. So Jesus walked out on the water to where they were. Peter saw him and wanted to walk on water too, so Jesus said, 'Do it!' But Peter got scared when he stepped on the water, and he started to go under. So Jesus caught him and told him he didn't have enough faith."

"Got it." I jump in ready to salvage this. "So it's a story about faith. Jesus told Peter he could do something, but Peter got scared when it looked impossible. It's a metaphor. If you believe you can do hard things, you've got to have faith, even when it's scary."

Damn, that's pretty good, even if I did say it.

"So it *was* magic?" Owen narrows his eyes. "Peter *could* walk on water because Jesus said he could? Like a magician?"

"Jesus wasn't a magician." My mom will really let me have it if Owen whips that one out over Sunday dinner. "The story is about Peter. He wanted to do something he thought was impossible, but even when Jesus said he could do it, he still got scared. He just had to have faith. Have you learned about metaphors in school yet?"

"I'm in second grade, Dad. We got a worksheet about it. Custard is happiness in a bowl."

"Or Froot Loops." I reach over and scrub his head, and he pushes my hand.

"No more Froot Loops."

"Yeah, no more Froot Loops." I exhale. "The metaphor is walking on water. That's impossible, right?"

"Yeah…"

"What's something you think is impossible?"

"Making a basket from the free-throw line," he groans loudly.

Mental note.

"Okay, if you believe you can do it and you work hard, you can. Have faith, and don't be afraid when it gets scary. Right?"

His little brow furrows as he thinks, and my chest tightens. I remember the first time he tried sweet potatoes, and his brow furrowed just that way—only he was five years younger. Damn time is moving so fast.

"Okay!" He nods, and I smile.

"Look, there's your Gram. Let's get inside and have some fried chicken."

His eyes light, and he grabs the door handle. "Race you to the house!"

I watch him run at top speed to where my mother is holding the glass door open and shaking her head as she smiles. She raised three boys, so she's used to the tornado of a seven-year-old.

I hesitate before stepping out of my truck, thinking about how much I sounded like Adam just then explaining that Bible story, and while I do believe in working hard and not backing down when things get tough, it's also important to keep in mind there's no invisible force that's going to stop you from drowning when you're in over your head.

Or stop your otherwise healthy dad from dying of a heart attack at fifty-five.

Or keep your cheating wife from being hit by a car.

My jaw tightens when I remember myself at twenty-eight, praying with the minister before we got married, standing in the front of that church, making promises in front of God and everybody. *Believing.*

Britt Bailey drifts through my mind. She's twenty-eight. Her pretty green eyes are all full of faith and hope, and she doesn't let me push her around, which was an unwelcome turn-on. She's got a sassy mouth, shapely legs, and a cute ass. The image of her standing by that truck in short shorts and cowboy boots jumps to the front of my brain, and I immediately push it out of my head.

I got over believing in romance and dreams a long time ago. All I care about now are cold, hard facts.

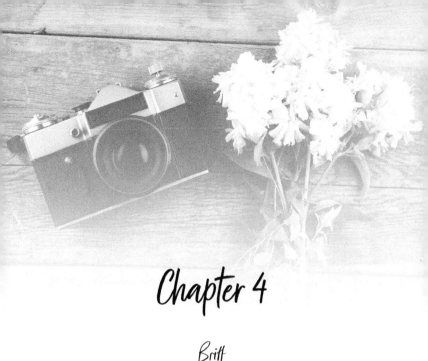

Chapter 4

Britt

"YOU NEED TO THINK ABOUT HOW YOU APPEAR IN PUBLIC." My voice is exaggeratedly deep and nasally as I mimic Aiden's words.

His annoying, superior words. Then I exhale a *Jerk* as I take a pile of shirts out of my suitcase and sort them into my new dresser.

Edward sits straight as a judge, all long ears and droopy jowls, on the couch in the living room watching me. True to her word, my mother had the loft above her Star Parlor cleaned and de-pested and even somewhat furnished in less than twenty-four hours.

"She must've really wanted us to come back, Ed." I take a fistfull of hangers and carry them to the small closet beside the queen-sized bed.

A line of windows is above it, and I open them to allow a cool breeze to circulate.

"Britt Bailey! Is that you?" The familiar voice makes me

scream, which makes Edward bark, and I run across the room to grab my best friend Cass around the neck in a hug.

"I'm home!" I cry as we jump up and down. "And I'm never leaving again!"

"Well, thank God for that." Piper bustles in behind her, her auburn hair tied back in a ponytail. In her arms are two giant boxes.

Cass releases me to run back into the hall and retrieve two more big boxes, which she carries into my small kitchen.

"What in the world are you carrying?" I watch as Piper opens the first box.

"Your mom said you needed plates and spoons and kitchen items and bathroom items." She takes out a stack of plates and carries them to the cabinet. "We just grabbed all the things nobody was using to get you started. Mom's got more shit in her 'end of the world' cellar. She'll never miss these."

Piper's mom is a doomsday prepper, which drives Piper nuts.

"You're the best." My heart is so full, and I'm so happy to be back with my people. "And if the world is ending, I'll be sure to pack them all up and head straight for your mom's cellar."

"We'll have a party," Piper deadpans.

"I brought wine glasses!" Cass shoves her long, dark hair behind her shoulders as she opens her box and pulls out newspaper and bubble wrap before emerging with three large crystal stems.

"Just put them on the table, and I'll pour us all a glass of wine."

"I can't believe you're here." Piper unpacks a smaller box of flatware then pulls out a frying pan. "I thought you were never coming back to Eureka."

If one more person says that… "I'm learning you should never say never out loud in front of anyone." My sarcasm is thick.

Cass puts her arm around my shoulders protectively. "Clearly Britt learned everything she needed to know in six months, and she brought it all home for our benefit."

I give her arm a squeeze. "Actually, Mom called and said y'all are having a crime wave, and I had to get back here and help out before Eureka went to hell in a handbasket."

Cass puckers her lips, nodding. "We're basically St. Louis, but without all the good music and barbecue."

"I wouldn't go as far as St. Louis." Piper holds her glass to the light before extending it to me for a pour. "Based on the numbers, we're more in the Mobile, Alabama, range."

I unscrew the cap on a bottle of Barefoot Pinot Grigio and divide the bottle into thirds among us. "How's the newspaper racket, Jinx?"

"It's going great, and I'm barely staying afloat." She frowns before taking a large sip of white wine. "Leave it to me to pick a dying medium and fall in love with it."

Cass carries her glass to the couch to sit beside Edward. "You know, Jinx, at some point, all this 'born under a bad sign' talk becomes a self-fulfilling prophecy. You should start a meditation practice, say affirmations." She leans forward talking in her doggy-voice to Edward. "Don't you agree, Jacob?"

"Don't start with all your newfound mystical guidance." Jinx follows her into the living room and sits on the other side of my dog. "I've been practicing positive thinking for years. And don't confuse the Notorious D.O.G. He's not a Jacob."

"He's definitely not an Edward. Edward was a vampire."

"Stop confusing my dog. He's named after Shania Twain not *Twilight*, and why didn't you tell me you were doing tarot readings with my mom, Cass?" I level my eyes on her.

"No negative talk!" She holds up her finger. "Your mom says I'm very good at tarot. I'm an empath."

She lifts her chin with so much exaggerated pride, I can't help but shoot it down. "My mom would tell Aiden Stone he was an empath if it would get her free help."

"Rude!" Cass pushes my arm, but I sip more wine, giggling at the thought of my mother calling Aiden Stone an empath.

"Speaking of Aiden Stone!" Jinx hops onto her knees, almost

spilling her drink. "I got a hot tip you almost hit him with your truck this morning. Give me all the details."

"Oh, God!" Exhaling a groan, I sit on the floor, leaning my back against the sofa. "You are not going to write it up in the paper. I'm completely humiliated, and on my first day back in town. I wasn't even supposed to see him until tomorrow!"

"Traffic accidents are catnip for news readers." Jinx's eyebrow arches. "My octogenarian subscribers will have my hide if I don't give them all the scoop. Now spill."

"There's nothing to spill. The brakes went out while I was driving into town."

Cass's eyes widen. "Like the minute you entered town? That could have significant spiritual connotations."

"I don't know *when* it happened. All I know is I went to slow down, and nothing happened. It's a good thing I'd been coasting for a while already."

"The grandparents will blame it on your obsession with Shania Twain. You were probably blasting that fake country music and not watching the road."

"I was watching the road all the way until I hit the light pole. It's just a good thing Edward and I were wearing our seatbelts."

"Where's your truck now?" Cass sips her wine.

"Bud towed it to his garage. I'm not sure I can drive it."

"It's a good thing you can walk to work." Jinx crosses her legs on the sofa, scrubbing her fingers along Edward's neck. "I'll try to downplay the reckless endangerment angle since you're the newest member of law enforcement."

"Jinx! I will murder you if you print that."

"The Eureka crime wave intensifies with the newest arrival at the courthouse." She waves her hands as if printing in the air, and I hit her with a pillow, which makes her laugh. "Don't make me spill my wine! I'm just teasing. I'll pass the buck to Greenville. Big city mechanics think they know everything, but they can't even check the brakes during a routine service inspection. When was your last service?"

Chewing my lip, I look down. "I've been really busy."

Jinx shakes her head and drinks more wine. "You're just writing the story for me."

"Blah blah blah, Jinx won't throw you under the bus." Cass hops onto her knees on the couch, shaking my shoulder. "I want to hear about Greenville! Did you meet any hot guys? Did you hook up with anybody? You were so quiet the whole time you were gone."

"Sadly, the answer is no. And no. I was quiet because nothing happened, and then when it did, I was completely humiliated."

"What does that mean?" Her brow lowers.

I proceed to tell them the story of the Greenville Ladies Club and how that all went down. I'm pretty sure I'm not exaggerating what I said or the response I received, and as I talk, Cass's brown eyes grow even wider while Piper's blue ones narrow.

"What a bunch of pampered—" Piper starts.

"I can tell you what happened," Cass interrupts. "You were being your adorable Cancer self in a room full of Capricorns and Libras!"

"I don't even know what that means." I take a bigger gulp of wine, trying to drown the residual humiliation of that luncheon.

"You're in the right place now. I happen to know Aiden Stone is a Taurus, and you know Taurus and Cancer are fire in the bedroom."

My stomach flips, and I hold up both hands. "No—don't even start with all that. I'm in astrology recovery."

Some people get addicted to substances. I got to where I wouldn't make friends with certain people. I started questioning every relationship... I wouldn't even leave the house if my horoscope made a bad prediction. It was a sickness, and I had to stop cold turkey.

"That's because you're just a cute little crab hiding in that shell and trying to clip anyone who reaches out to you." She makes little snipping-claw motions with her fingers like she's about to pinch me, and I shove her with my foot.

"I lived my life that way too long." I study my empty wine glass. "I'm turning over a new leaf—just the facts, ma'am. No astrology. No magic. No tarot cards predicting the future."

"Your mom says we don't predict the future. We give advice based on intuition and asking the right questions."

Piper hops off the couch, bending down to hug Cass, then scrubbing the top of my head. "Time to put a comma in this. I've got to get home before Mamma has Ryan stockpiling tuna."

It's our classic sign-off. Our visits never end with a period. We simply insert a comma until next time.

"Ryan's probably grown a foot since I saw him last." I put my arm around Jinx's shoulder. Her seven-year-old son is the cutest thing. Cass and I were in the room when he was born. "Thanks for coming over and bringing me all this stuff!"

"Do you need groceries?" Cass opens my refrigerator, which holds a block of cheese, a dozen eggs, and a bottle of wine.

"I'll be okay until tomorrow." I pat her on the back.

We all group-hug at the door, and Piper slides my long bangs off my cheeks. "I'm so glad you're back, BB. I know you wanted to make a big splash in the big city, but I bet you can make an even bigger splash in this small pond. We won't let you drown."

My eyes heat at her words, and I tuck my head, pulling them closer for another hug. "I'm not sure what I was looking for when I left, but I've got my people right here."

"I'll swing by Bud's and make sure he doesn't try to screw you on those repairs." Cass lifts her chin.

"Would Bud try to screw me?"

Her nose wrinkles, and she starts to laugh. "I doubt it. I just like to mess with him. He's so old, he still can't believe a girl knows anything about mechanics." She puts her hand on her chest dramatically, exclaiming, "A *girl*!"

Another group squeeze, and they head out, waving and calling back to Edward with all their variations of his name.

I close the door, feeling both full and quiet at the same time. Dropping onto the couch, I scrub Edward's head, which he lowers onto my lap.

"I've got the best friends," I muse, tracing my fingers along the many lines in his hound-dog head. "You're going with me to work tomorrow, so you'd better be ready."

He's not worried about our first day on the job. It's his nature to sniff out clues and find bad guys.

I, on the other hand, have a little more to do proving myself in this town where I'm the daughter of a tarot-reader and an escape artist and the granddaughter of a magician. While I love my family's unconventional lifestyle, I want to be taken seriously for my real-world skills.

My mind drifts to the last time I said those words out loud to anyone. I was standing on the back porch at my mom's house, buzzy from a few glasses of champagne, the excitement of striking out on my own, and Aiden Stone standing over me in the silvery moonlight.

Aiden Stone, the star of all my teenage fantasies, was actually talking to me. It was a first.

I'd been swooning over him since I was a teenager, and he'd pick up his younger brother Adam from school. He was all broad shoulders and stormy blue eyes, then he left to do a tour with the Marines and came back even hotter than when he left.

His face had acquired an edge, a sharpening around the jaw, which now has a brush of whiskers that made me shiver wondering how it would feel against my soft skin.

Was it only six months ago we'd stood together, chatting in the moonlight? I'd been captivated by the fullness of his lips, the light in his eyes, the fresh cedar scent hanging around him. He was so big and strong and solid and *sexy*.

"When I left Eureka, headed to San Diego, I thought I might never come back." He lifted the drink, and my eyes traced the flex of his muscles—so hot. *"But when my four years were up, Ma asked*

me to come home. Alex was on active duty, and Adam was off flying planes. Dad was gone…"

He looked down, and I swooned a little closer. I'd had just enough champagne to give me courage, and the low vibration of his voice resonated in my insides, heating every part of my body.

"Now you have Owen, and you're the sheriff. Looks like it all worked out for you." I smiled, lifting my chin and imagining him lowering his lips to mine.

"I wouldn't say that, but Owen makes up for it." His blue eyes moved from the trees to me, drifting from my parted lips to my eyes and along the edges of my hair like a hot caress. "Adam said you're going to be a forensic photographer. That can be a pretty rough field."

"I don't mind." I exhaled a laugh. "I've always liked working on puzzles and finding clues. When I was little, I collected rocks that had unusual markings, and I took pictures of animal tracks back there in the woods. I liked to pretend I was Veronica Mars or Brenda Johnson."

"The Closer?" He chuckled.

Heat bloomed from my stomach to my chest, and I did my best not to fidget or blink too fast. "I thought if I got a serious job, people would take me seriously and not think of me as… you know." I shrugged. "One of the town clowns."

"I would never call you a clown." We were so close to touching, and he was looking at me for the first time with something like interest. I almost forgot to breathe. "You're a smart girl. I bet you'll do well."

"You do?" I focused on blinking slowly, meeting his intense blue gaze, slipping my tongue out to wet my bottom lip.

His lips parted, and his eyes flickered to my mouth. In my mind I chanted, Kiss me, kiss me, kiss me, and if there was any inherited magic at all in my entire body from any member of my family, it was about to happen.

His eyes met mine once more, and he seemed to be on the verge of saying something life-changing, something that might make me stay in Eureka…

Until Adam burst through the back door breaking the spell.

"Hey, bro, here you are. Time to hit the road. Everybody's heading *out."* Adam stepped forward, pulling me into a hug and away from his devastatingly sexy brother. *"I'm going to miss you, Birgitte!"*

I pushed him with my elbow. "Nobody calls me that."

"Ow!" Adam cried. It's possible I pushed him a little too hard out of frustration. "Sorry, Britt."

"I wondered where you were hiding!" Piper was right behind him and Cass was on her heels.

Our special moment was officially smothered in an avalanche of my friends wishing me luck and telling me goodbye. I'd left the next day with a longing in my chest, wondering what might have happened if we'd have gotten two more minutes…

I never expected to be back so soon. Or that I'd nearly run him down with my truck. Or that he'd be my boss—or that he'd glare at me with such annoyance as he lifted my heavy suitcase, his body still as muscular and tempting as ever.

All I can do now is be true to my words by being seriously good at my job. I said I would distinguish myself from my family, and whether it's in Greenville or Eureka, I'll show him I can.

Chapter 5

Aiden

"**W**ELL, I'D BETTER GET GOING." I PACK ALL MY DAD'S TOOLS in the red metal box and replace it in the garage.

Sunday lunch at my mother's turned into trimming limbs off a Bradford pear tree in her garden, fixing a gutter that had come loose from the side of her house, and changing the filter on her HVAC.

"You never did tell me what was on your mind when you got here." Mom crosses her arms, leaning against the door to the garage as I wash my hands. "I can always tell when something's on my boys' minds."

"Is that so?" I pick up a towel to dry my hands, thinking about Owen's questions about Jesus and magic.

"Call it a mother's intuition."

"I see where Adam gets it from." Hanging the towel on a hook, I walk over to where she's standing and signal to Owen on the tire swing. "Time to go."

"You know, you could enlist your brothers' help with some of these chores."

It's true. Between her house and mine, I feel like I never stop repairing shit, but today I had my own reasons for doing it all myself.

Adam had hung around for a little while before saying the waves were perfect today, and took off to go surfing. I'd practically escorted him to his car. If Owen had started his twenty questions about Jesus, my youngest brother would have been all too happy to engage, challenging me on my "lack of faith"—his words—and wanting to know how I explain love or the wind or a million other things I don't care about explaining.

Alex, on the other hand, is possibly the one person in our family who works more than I do. He also brings in some major cash running my late maternal grandfather's distillery Alex renamed Stone Cold.

When Alex left the Marines, he thought it was time to expand the generations-old business—a relic that had actually put my mother's family at odds with my dad's all the way back to Prohibition. Ma's side was the bootleggers; Dad's was law enforcement.

Through the years, the distillery had been more or less a hobby handed down to whichever relative was interested, but my brother saw an opportunity and ran with it. Now he takes home sixty percent of the profits and divides the remainder with twenty to Ma, and ten between Adam and me.

It was a manageable career until two years ago when a reviewer claimed our Stone Cold original single barrel was the best small-batch bourbon since Blanton's. After that, money hasn't been much of an issue for any of us.

I still serve as sheriff twenty-four seven, seven days a week, because I actually like doing the job. I care about Eureka, and it helps me feel close to my dad's memory. Alex never gets a day off, and while he never complains, I can't tell if the family hobby hasn't turned into a burden for him.

"A mother's intuition is stronger than any force of nature."

Mom puts her arm around my waist, and her head comes right to my chest.

She's small, but she's a force of nature herself, keeping three boys in line after my dad died.

"Dad doesn't believe in the force, Gram." Owen skips up behind us, putting his small hand in hers as we walk to my truck. "He doesn't believe in anything."

"What the hell, Owen?" I snap.

"Don't swear at my grandson!" Mom pinches my waist hard enough to make me flinch.

"*Hell* isn't a swear word."

"It is, and it's not like you to speak to Owen that way." Her forehead wrinkles, and the guilt trip is real.

"Sorry, Froot Loop."

"Dad!" Owen cries, then stomps away. "I'm getting in the truck."

He hugs his grandmother's waist and climbs in the cab, slamming the door.

I exhale a growl, and my mom crosses her arms. Hesitating, I look down at her.

"What's that all about?" Concern lines her eyes.

"He doesn't want to be called Froot Loop anymore."

"I'm surprised he ever did."

That hurts. "It used to make him laugh. It was something we had after Annemarie…" I can't even go there.

Compassion fills my mother's blue eyes. "Aiden." She reaches up and puts her palm against my chest. "You can't raise a son and hold onto bitterness. You have to learn to forgive what happened and let go of the past. It's what I had to do after your father died."

Taking her hand in mine, I lower it. "I know, Ma. But I'm not the same guy I was then. I never will be."

"Even so, Owen needs to believe in magic and dreams. It's what young people live for."

"He can have his dreams. I'm just not going to tell him

things that aren't true and that will ultimately break his heart. The only magic is what we make ourselves."

Her lips press into a disapproving line.

Shaking my head, I start for the truck. "I've got an early morning, and now I've got Britt Bailey to deal with. Like I didn't have enough on my plate with this spike in vandalism."

"Don't go away angry." She catches my arm.

Turning back, I give her a brief hug. "I'm not angry, Ma. I'm just tired. Been dealing with the Baileys all day."

"You know, Andrew used to spar with Edna, but at the end of the day, they respected each other. They both loved this town, and they wanted the best for it. In their own ways."

"Edna's a kook, and Gwen's worse. I only hope Britt hasn't turned out as flaky as them."

"I remember Britt from your brother's group of friends. She always seemed like a bright young woman. Adam spoke highly of her."

"I'm sure he did." I lean down and kiss the top of her head. "Night, Ma."

"Take care of yourself, Aiden. I want you to be happy."

On the short drive back to our place, I apologize for snapping. I also apologize for forgetting about the nickname. Owen says it's no big deal, and by the time we pull into our driveway, he's asleep.

I carry him inside, helping him brush his teeth before leading him to his bed, giving him a hug, and tucking his blanket all around him like a cannoli. Hesitating, I study his sleeping profile highlighted by the moon shining through his window. The echoes of childhood still flicker around his eyes, and he's so peaceful, just like I always want him to be. It tugs at my chest.

In my own room, I shower and change into sleep pants and a tank. Standing in front of my large, empty bed, I think about my mom's words. *I want you to be happy.*

I'm happy here with my son and my work, but I know from

watching my mother, the day will come when Owen will leave to pursue his own life. What then?

There have been times I've wished for someone to share my life with. A real partner to be with me, comfort me, play with me. Then I think about my own experience with trust, love, and having the shit kicked out of me.

What I'm doing here is easy. It's predictable and safe. I've got enough dangerous shit to deal with in my professional life. It's better to keep things as they are and not let people try to get in my head and tell me what I ought to do.

I know what I ought to do, and it's take care of Owen and keep the town running. It's not magic. It's hard work, and I'm doing just fine.

"My guess is these tracks were made with some kind of lightweight all-terrain vehicle. One with wide tires." Britt is on her knees examining the path cut through Terra Belle's cucumber vines. "Three-wheelers were outlawed in the eighties, but some are still out there, especially in small, rural pockets."

She gets close with the digital camera and takes several photos from different angles. She places small, numbered cards all over the field, and she places another one beside the tracks.

When she's done, she lifts a long strand of damaged fruit and carries it to where I'm standing out of her way. "See these tracks? The square treads are typical of an old-school ATV. Our getaway vehicle was a three-wheeler."

My eyebrows lift. "That's a very specific clue."

Her cheeks flush a pretty pink, and her full lips fight against a smile. "That's why I'm here."

She's impossible to ignore, taking command of the scene, confidently organizing everything we've found into sections and numbers.

Instead of Daisy Dukes and cowboy boots, today she's

wearing a long sleeved, zip-up canvas bodysuit in fatigue green. Her blonde hair is cinched up in a tight bun, and she has big, clear goggles over her eyes. Plastic gloves are on her hands as she carefully turns the vines and takes pictures.

Since we got here, I've been pretty much standing aside watching as she meticulously sifts through every bit of evidence and takes pictures from all possible angles. I can't get over how focused she is on this tedious work, and I have to admit, she's good at it.

She's also fucking magnetic as shit, working the crime scene like a seasoned professional. My eyes are drawn to her every move like I'm watching one of those crime shows.

I watch as she slowly walks to the far edge of the field, eyes fixed on the ground. Then she stops short, dropping to a knee. "Sheriff!"

My breath hitches at her shout, and I pick my way to where she's kneeling. "You found something?"

"Look!" She stands, holding a beat-up brown work boot. "Does this belong to one of your men?"

My brow arches. "Doug is my only man." *Besides you,* I don't say. "I'm pretty sure he didn't leave a boot here over the weekend."

"We need to run this past Terra, make sure it's not hers or a friend's." She carries it with two gloved fingers to her dog, holding it out for him to sniff. "I'm going to put a card here to mark the spot where I found it."

Nodding, I step aside as Edward puts his nose to the ground and follows a trail through the crime scene.

She follows him back to the spot where she found the boot and holds up a hand, frantically waving me over again. "Come here, quick!"

I do my best to avoid stepping on any of her cards as I pick my way to where she's calf-deep in cucumber vines.

"What is it?" I'm not sure why I'm whispering.

"Lean down here, and look at this!" She's whispering as

well, but she's excited. She drops to a squat, and I bend closer, catching the bug of her enthusiasm. "What do you think made these markings?"

While I'm squinting at a series of linear channels pressed into the soft soil, she pulls out her camera and takes several more pictures.

"A hoe, maybe? Or a shovel?" I can't think of what else would make such deep, narrow indentions.

"They begin right past where I found the boot, like he stepped out of it in the middle of walking."

Straightening, I study her green eyes shrouded by science-class-looking goggles. "What are you saying, Britt?"

"I think whoever did this was wearing that boot, and when it came off, he had to keep going on his prosthetic foot."

My eyebrows shoot up, and I take a knee, getting closer to study the markings again. Sure enough, looking at them from this angle with that in mind, it's got to be.

"Fuck me," I mutter. "The perp has a prosthetic leg. How did we miss that before?"

"You're not required to get as close as I am, and something like this is easy to miss in a farm where equipment is used for harvesting."

I'm not going to lie. I'm impressed as hell. "So now we have a potential suspect with a fake leg who owns a three-wheeler. I can't imagine too many people will fit that profile."

"You might be surprised how many are lurking in these older communities." She pulls the goggles off her face and wipes a hand across her upper lip. "It's getting hot out here."

"It's the humidity, and you're in all that." I motion to her getup. "We could take a break and come back this afternoon."

"When it's even hotter?" Her nose wrinkles as she shakes her head. "No thanks. I'm almost finished, then I think we need to talk to some of the old-timers. They're usually the best place to start if you're looking for an unusual character."

"Old-timers." I almost laugh at her word choice. "I'm probably an old-timer to you."

"You definitely are not." She squints one eye in almost a wink.

Damn, she's pretty, even in all that canvas with her hair on top of her head, and a red goggle-ring around her eyes. I know what she's hiding under that getup. She's small and smart and fucking sexy.

"I'm seven years older than you." I say it as much to remind myself as her.

"Oh, I'm going way farther back than seven years." She quickly packs up her things. "I'm going to start with my grandmother."

Chapter 6

Britt

"HELLO, DARLING." MY MOTHER WALTZES THROUGH THE SITTING area of her Star Parlor. "To what do I owe this visit? And what on Earth are you wearing?"

I glance down at my green, canvas jumpsuit, a drab contrast to her red velvet pants with leopard inlays down the sides. Her curly, caramel-brown hair hangs in a cloud of spirals around her cheeks, and she's tied a scarf over the crown of her head, with the ends hanging over her shoulder.

Her white top is scoop-necked and sleeveless, and she has a filmy shawl around her bare arms, which end in gold bangles. Rings are on most of her fingers.

It's her standard tarot-reader getup, although to me, she looks like she escaped from the cast of the Broadway musical *Hair*.

"We're both in our work clothes," I tease. "I'm actually here because Gran wasn't in her office."

I walk over to the small, round table covered in a paisley-patterned, silk scarf. A gold-foil tarot deck is halved in the center, and I slide my finger over the card facing up. It's the Knight of Swords, which means you're highly driven and ambitious. He's in the upright position, which means a change is coming.

I can't help wondering if she put him in that position for my benefit, also *dang*, I know way too much about this stuff.

"That's not a very complimentary way to frame a visit." She's pouting, and I look up, trying to think of what I said to hurt her feelings. "You have a ring around your face."

"What?" I turn to the mirror behind me, and sure enough, an unflattering red line in the shape of my work goggles is on my forehead and cheeks.

Heat climbs up my neck when I realize I was walking around like this in the field just now with Aiden. Aiden, who looked like a Greek god in his short-sleeved khaki shirt that hugged his broad chest and biceps, and those dark uniform pants that squeezed his ass and toned thighs. I was sweaty from the sun and my long sleeves and pants, but looking at him made my insides slippery as well.

Now, realizing I looked like Dr. Benson Honeydew with a red line around my face is a bucket of ice water dumped over my head.

"Can't be helped now." I exhale heavily, walking over to where my mother stands and giving her a quick hug. "Sorry, I am glad to see you, and thanks for getting the apartment ready for me."

"You can always come back and stay in your room if you get too lonely." I smile, but don't take the bait on that one.

When she sees I'm not going to respond, she drops with a flourish onto the gold velvet sofa near the fireplace. "How can I help my beautiful daughter?"

"You heard about what happened to Terra Belle's pickle patch? Sheriff Stone thinks teenagers tried to recreate those crop circles from that movie *Signs*, but I dug a little deeper. I think it's something else entirely."

"I'm not surprised. Aiden Stone has zero intuition." Her

hazel eyes roll as she shakes her head. "This is exactly why I wanted you to come home. The crime in Eureka is out of control."

"Right." I walk over to sit beside her, taking out my 35 mm digital camera and angling it so we can both see the images. "These pictures are of the tire tracks left by the getaway vehicle. It's clear from the treads it was a three-wheeler."

"A three-wheeler?" She places her hand on the camera and leans closer. "I thought those had been illegal for a long time."

"They have, which narrows our search a lot. We're looking for someone who's had one since 1989."

"That's more than thirty years ago! Would it still run?"

"I guess if you maintain it properly." I don't point out I'm still driving Dad's old truck, which is about thirty years old. "See these markings in the soil? Whoever drove off on that three-wheeler also has a prosthetic leg. So I'm guessing we're looking for a male in his mid to late sixties, maybe a veteran…"

My mother's shoulders stiffen, and she stands, going to the small table and scooping up the tarot deck. She begins shuffling, her eyes fixed on the cards, and my lips twist into a frown.

"Mom?" She doesn't stop shuffling. "Ma, I'm not here for a reading. I want to know if you can think of any males that age living in or around Eureka with a prosthetic leg and a three-wheeler."

She shuffles the deck one more time, then sets it down in front of her. "I don't understand you, Birgitte. You're one of the most gifted tarot readers I've ever worked with, yet you want to walk away from your talents. You'd rather look at dead bodies than listen to what they're trying to tell you."

More heat rises around my collar, but I take a beat, glancing down at my camera. "I don't actually look at that many dead bodies. It's mostly robberies or car accidents or vandalism, and in my opinion, reading the clues at crime scenes is better than reading cards. I'm helping people get justice."

"I did not raise you to be such a nonbeliever."

"You raised me to use my head, and right now, I'm trying to do my job." I stand, going to the table where she's doing her best not to look at me. "It's a pretty straightforward question. Do you know anyone who fits that description?"

"I'd like to consult the cards first." Her hazel eyes cut up to mine, and for a moment, we're locked in a silent battle of wills. "Do you have a problem with that?"

Frustration twists in my chest. I don't know why she has to turn every conversation into a battle. Inhaling slowly, I relax my eyebrows and exhale slowly. There's no point fighting. I can talk to Gran about this, and it's possible I might need to have my mom's help down the road.

"No problem at all." I force a smile and lean forward to kiss her cheek. "It's good to see you, Ma. Let me know if you learn anything."

"You're not going to stay for the reading?"

"Nah, I've seen enough of these things to know how it goes." I pull my bag over my shoulder and start for the door. "You know where to find me."

Without another word, I'm on the street, walking back to the courthouse. I was dead serious when I decided to make a clean break from magic. It wasn't so long ago I couldn't make a decision without consulting my horoscope or doing a reading.

Just now when she called me a gifted reader, the bloom of pride in my chest reminded me I still have work to do. I'm like an alcoholic who got too close to a drink, because with all my determination and knowing I'm doing the right thing, a small part of me wonders if maybe I might be wrong.

I'm going against the way I was raised. How do I know my decisions are better than my mother's and my grandmother's? All I can do is trust my gut.

Pushing through the glass door of the courthouse, I glance at the clock to see it's almost five, quitting time. Holly is sitting at her desk wearing her dispatcher's headset, and Doug is wandering around the front of the room like a bear looking for a donut.

"Hey, Britt!" He drifts to where I'm placing my bag under my desk and plugging my camera into my laptop. "I heard you had a break in the case today!"

"I don't know if it's a break, but we found some pretty specific evidence." I study his lined face and realize Doug is getting pretty close to retirement age. "Hey, Doug, you don't happen to know of anyone living in or around Eureka with a prosthetic leg, do you?"

"Ha!" His shoulders shake with his silent laugh. "Ho, well, I guess it makes sense of you to ask me, but no. I can't think of anyone who fits that description."

"Hi, Doug! Hi, Holly." A young boy's voice rings clear as a bell. "Got any donuts for me?"

Doug's face lights, and he turns in the direction of the kid. "Hey, there, Owen! Your dad's out taking care of a little business, but he'll be back soon."

Owen Stone is not quite the spitting image of Aiden. His hair is darker, but he has the same intense blue eyes. He walks up to where I'm standing, and even though he's a little boy, I can tell he'll be a heartbreaker one day just like his dad.

"Hi, Miss Bailey!" He skips up to where I'm sitting beside my desk. "Dad said you were the mayor's granddaughter. Is that true?"

"Please call me Britt." I smile, sitting straighter as he skips around like an antsy little kid. "The mayor is in fact my grandmother."

"Do you know how to do magic, too?"

Tilting my head to the side, I wrinkle my nose at him. "You know magic isn't real, right? It's all illusion and distraction and sleight of hand. The real magic is being able to divert people's attention while you do something they don't expect."

His blue eyes widen as I speak. "Show me!"

I snort a little laugh. "I don't know any magic, sorry." His face falls, and I fumble for something to cheer him up. "I know a couple of card tricks. They're like magic."

"Okay!" He jumps, and I stand, catching his hand and leading him to the break room.

"I think I saw a pack of cards back here." We pass through the desks, and I hear him skipping behind me.

His voice is loud. "You're friends with my friend Ryan's mom!"

"I am." We enter the break room, and I walk over to lift the lid on a small box and take out a deck of playing cards. "I was there when Ryan was born."

"Really?" His eyes are wide.

"Yeah, now check this out."

I spend a lot of time elaborately shuffling the small deck, cutting the cards, moving them back and forth. "The preparation I'm doing right now is part of the trick. It makes me look very skilled."

Owen's wide eyes never leave my hands, and he nods, fascinated. "I don't know how to shuffle cards."

"You need to learn if you're going to do card tricks." Holding the deck in front of him, I circle my hands around and take two cards off the top—but it appears I've only taken one. Bending them slightly, I show Owen the bottom card. "Remember this card."

"It's the three of diamonds."

"Good." I split the deck and return the card I've palmed to the top, then I split them again, using my thumb to take the top card away and fold them together. "Now… Is this your card?"

The three of diamonds pops up, and Owen's eyes bug. "It is!"

He's nearly shouting, and I almost start to laugh… *almost.* Years of training have taught me never to break character in the middle of a trick.

"You did magic! You are like Mrs. Edna!"

"Not really." I smile. "Come here, and I'll show you what I did."

It only takes a few minutes for me to teach the simple trick to him, cutting the cards, lifting two in your fingers, and bending them. It's a little more difficult for him, since his hands are small, but he's a fast learner. After a few tries, he's doing it like a pro.

"You just need to work on shuffling. The presentation is as much a part of the act as the trick itself."

"I try, but I kind of throw the cards everywhere."

"You just need to work up the muscles in your fingers." Stepping back, I hold out my hands and announce, "Now the Magnificent Owen will demonstrate his skills!"

He's all ready to take the cards from me when a sharp, male voice interrupts us.

"What's going on back here?" My heart jumps, and I turn to see Aiden standing over us.

He's hot as ever in that uniform, but his gray-blue eyes are blazing. If it were possible for steam to rise out of his collar, it would.

"Hi, Sheriff!" My tone is light, but the waver in my voice gives away my nerves. "Where have you been?"

"I rode out to the Jones place. What are you doing with my son?"

"Britt taught me a magic trick, Dad! It's so cool. She's better at it than I am, though." He tugs the sleeve of my jumpsuit. "Do it for him, Britt. Show dad the magic trick!"

I hesitate, chewing my bottom lip. "It wasn't really a *magic* trick…"

"I thought you wanted to separate yourself from all that." His tone is controlled anger, and I do my best not to fidget.

"It wasn't like that. Owen just asked if I knew any magic, and I didn't want to let him down."

"You're here to deal with facts. Not tricks. Not tarot. Not magic. We work in the real world, Miss Bailey, and if that's going to be too difficult for you to remember, you need to let me know right now."

A knot twists in my throat, and the anger burning in his eyes has me on the verge of tears, which is *so* not happening.

I blink away from his intense gaze. "I'm sorry. I didn't realize I was overstepping."

"Don't drag my son into your family's nonsense." His tone is painfully sharp, and I nod quickly, backing away.

"I had no intention of dragging your son anywhere. I was only being friendly. I won't make that mistake again." I take a step back and crash into a chair, turning to catch it quickly before it hits the floor. "I'll just head home now since it's after five, and I need to check on Edward."

Before the first tear dares to fall, I'm hustling out the door and through the outer offices. Doug says something to me, but I don't stop. Hurrying across the street, I keep my chin down, watching the movement of my shoes and dodging pedestrians until I make it to the neon purple sign for the Star Parlor.

I duck around to the stairwell and quickly run up to my apartment. Edward is sleeping on the couch when I enter, and I go straight to my bathroom, gripping the sides of the sink and doing my best to catch my breath.

I didn't do anything wrong. It was just a silly card trick. There's no magic in card tricks.

Turning on the water, I scoop a handful and drink it. Then I dampen my fingers and press them against my hot cheeks.

I've never had anyone glare at me with so much anger, like the grudges of twenty years were all descending on me as the scapegoat.

My chest hurts, and I'm not sure if I'm upset he was so mad or if I'm upset it's clear I'll never be more than my name to Aiden Stone.

As much as I want to distinguish myself, in his eyes, I'll always be Britt Brewer Bailey. What I think is innocent or harmless is irrelevant, and as much as I'd like to avoid the things he hates, I have no idea where the landmines are hidden.

Chapter 7

Aiden

THE ROOM IS SO SILENT AFTER BRITT LEAVES, I CAN HEAR THE PEOPLE talking on the street outside. Owen stands in front of me, still holding the deck of playing cards. His blue eyes, identical to mine, are narrowed.

"You were mean, Dad." The excitement in his voice when I first arrived has turned to reproach, and I feel like a shit.

I can still see the fear in her eyes. I can still see her running away from me like a rabbit from a wolf. I can't argue with my son. I *was* mean, and I hate it.

"I don't like magic." My voice is quiet, almost like I'm explaining my ridiculous overreaction to both of us.

"I know." His tone is little-boy impatience. "You tell me that at least twenty times a day."

"I don't think it's that much." Rubbing my hand over the tightness at the back of my neck, I wonder how things went so off the rails.

When we left the field today, I was impressed as hell by all she'd accomplished in only a few hours. She made my puny investigation look like child's play, and I hated that I was going to have to eat crow and tell Edna she was right. Britt is a great addition to our team.

She's very professional with her work. She carefully documented every leaf, every misplaced stone, every stray cut in the soil. She sussed out a very promising lead, and I won't be surprised if we have a suspect in custody by the end of the week.

Then I came back and blew it all up over a silly card trick.

"You have to go and tell her you're sorry." Owen puts his hand in mine, and pulls me towards the door. "It's what you tell me when I do something wrong."

My throat tightens. "I'm not sure she wants to talk to me right now. I was pretty harsh."

"Yes, you were." He presses his lips together, nodding. "You yelled at her worse than you yelled at me that time I left the milk out on the counter all night."

"That was wasteful."

"I know, and she only taught me a card trick."

God, I feel so fucking stupid. I feel like I threw all my dirty underwear on the front lawn for everyone to see. Want to see me lose my shit? Teach my son a card trick. *Jesus.*

"Maybe I'll just talk to her about it tomorrow. Let her cool down first."

"When I jerked Maya's ponytail for saying Zander wasn't a real zebra, you said I had to apologize that day. You said if I didn't, she'd think I meant it, and it would damage our friendship."

I look down at this smart little guy I'm raising. "You remember everything I say to you?"

"Everything."

"Well, come on, then." I exhale heavily.

We enter the main office area, where Doug is packing up his laptop.

"Hiya, Aiden, do you know what's up with Britt? She ran out of here so fast… looked like she was about to cry. Was it something about the case?"

A knot is in my throat, and I glance down, meeting Owen's disappointed eyes. "We just ah… had a little misunderstanding. I'm taking care of it."

Dropping to one knee, I put my hand on Owen's waist. "I have an idea. Would you be okay with going to Grandma's for dinner tonight?"

"Yeah!" he shouts. "She gives me chocolate cake for dessert."

"Perfect." Standing, I catch Doug at the door. "Hey, man, would you mind dropping Owen by my mother's place on your way home?"

"Sure thing." He holds out a hand to Owen. "Let's go, champ."

Owen scoops up his backpack and slings it over both shoulders. As he passes me, he gives my hand a squeeze. "Don't worry, Dad. Apologizing is hard, but Britt's really nice. You got this."

I shake my head. "Thanks. When I get home, I want you to show me that card trick, okay?"

"Okay!" He skips out after Doug, and I glance at the clock.

It's just after five. If I hurry, I can run home, take a shower, and change into civilian clothes, hopefully before she has time to eat anything. I scoop up my phone and text my mom what's going on, then I jog out to my waiting truck.

The Star Parlor sign glows purple in the twilight as I park on the street in front of her apartment. It's like a warning sign: *Dangerous territory, turn back.* But my son is right. I have to apologize for overreacting and being a dick at work.

I'm technically Britt's boss, and the way I acted wasn't just rude, it was unprofessional. This dinner is a nice gesture, nothing more. It's not an idea borne out of the persistent interest humming in my veins… like I've crossed a desert and found the first glimmering pool of water waiting on the other side.

Fuck that.

It's an olive branch.

I open the glass outer door and climb the wooden stairs to her apartment above Gwen's studio. Hesitating, I hear the soft strains of music coming from inside. More Shania Twain. It sounds like "Any Man of Mine."

Glancing down at my jeans and navy tee, it's time to do this. I lift my fist, ready to knock when the door swings open, and a piercing scream throws me into a defensive crouch.

"What's the fuck?" I shout at the same time Britt yells, "What are you doing?"

Taking a step back, I lean against the wall, placing my hand on my clenched stomach. "Dammit, Britt, you scared the shit out of me."

"I scared you?" Her voice is loud, and she's standing there in plaid boxer shorts and a tank top with no bra. "What are you doing lurking outside my door?"

I avert my eyes from her nipples piercing the thin cotton, looking down at her smooth, muscular legs and red toenails. This is not how I expected this to go.

"I'm sorry." Clearing my throat, I lift my eyes to hers and push off the wall, stepping closer to where she's standing in the doorway. "I came over to apologize for the way I acted this afternoon."

Thankfully, she crosses her arms over her breasts. Her hair is piled on her head in one of those buns I don't understand. It's a big mess on her head, but it's cute in a way that slides easily into sexy.

She lifts her chin, and I drag my eyes from her sex hair to the traces of dampness around her lashes. *Fuck, did I make her cry?* It's like a punch to the gut, and I scrub a hand over my mouth.

"Damn, Britt, I acted like an ass, and I thought maybe you might let me take you to dinner to make it up to you."

Her chin pulls back, and she blinks several times, looking away from me. In her bare feet and hardly any clothes, she's so small and vulnerable. It's like I kicked a kitten.

"I guess that would be okay." She's quiet, glancing down at her outfit. "I need to change and touch up my face and hair."

"Of course, whatever you need to do." I take a step back. "I was going to suggest we go to El Rio if you like Mexican food."

"Luckily, I do." Her arms are still tight over her bare breasts, which I can't seem to get out of my brain. "El Rio is the only restaurant in town."

"Should I wait?" I look around the small landing in front of her door.

I happen to know the apartment inside is a studio with a small bathroom. No privacy there.

"Why don't you go ahead, and I'll meet you in ten minutes. It's close enough to walk."

I look down the stairs, thinking I don't want her to walk alone or enter the restaurant alone. "Text me when you're ready, and I can meet you halfway."

Her nose wrinkles like she's thinking of a humorous comeback. Instead, she simply says, "It's okay. I've been walking around Eureka a long time."

"I'll walk slow."

"See you in ten." She shakes her head and turns to go back into her apartment.

Just before she closes the door, I catch another glimpse of her cute little ass, and my fingers curl. Yep, I'm officially that guy. I want to claim every part of her body.

Clearing my throat, I descend the stairs slowly, thinking about being her boss, being seven years older than her, being the asshole who just bit her head off for being sweet to my son. It's enough to get my thinking straight.

Olive branch.

Nothing more.

El Rio is a typical Mexican restaurant with polished wood tables in the center of the dining room and round, vinyl booths arranged around the walls. The colors are vibrant and festive, key lime, lemon yellow, orange, and red.

Spanish-language music is playing, and the crowd is small for a Monday—a few guys hanging at the bar watching football and a few people eating. The hostess said we could seat ourselves once Britt arrived, and I've been standing at the bar long enough to have a beer when I glance up to see her in the doorway.

She's dressed in blue jeans and that same white tank top, only with a bra this time, and her hair is down, hanging long around her shoulders. Her green eyes meet mine, and when she smiles, for a second, my brain kind of blanks.

Of course, I get it under control by the time she closes the space between us.

"I hope I didn't take too long. I just threw on the first thing I could find." Her face is so fresh with just a touch of something glossy on her full, pink lips.

"You were perfect." My reply makes her brow furrow, and I rephrase quickly. "I mean, your timing was perfect, and you look great."

Holding out my hand, I gesture to the room. "We can seat ourselves when we're ready. Would you like a beer? Or a margarita?"

"Oh…" Her eyes light, and she presses her lips in a mischievous grin. "Would it be bad to have a margarita on a Monday?"

"Nope. It's Margarita Monday." I turn to the bartender and order her drink and another beer for me.

While we wait, I turn to her again, ready to face the music. "So I kind of overreacted this afternoon."

"Did you? I must've missed it. What happened?"

Exhaling a chuckle, I drop my chin. "I was a dick, and I'm sorry. If it makes you feel any better, Owen was very disappointed in me. He suggested I head over right away and apologize."

Her smile turns sassy. "You added the changing clothes and inviting me to dinner parts all by yourself?"

Damn, her mouth. "It seemed like more of the adult approach."

"I see. Well, Owen is a sweet boy. Where is he anyway?"

"Having dinner with my mom, which made him very happy. Apparently, she serves chocolate cake with dinner."

"My kind of place!" She laughs, lightening the entire mood.

My arm is propped on the bar, so close I could extend a finger and trace it along her skin.

I don't.

The bartender slides our drinks across to us, and I ask him to add them to our tab. Then we walk over to a booth near a window.

A busboy quickly places a basket of chips and two little ramekins of salsa, and a waitress stands behind him, waiting to hand us our menus.

"I know what I want unless you need a minute?" I glance at Britt.

"I'm ready!" She holds up her hands.

We both order the steak soft tacos with a side of street corn, and the waitress cuts her eyes at us before making a note.

"We didn't even plan that!" Britt laughs, taking another sip of her margarita.

I'm relieved she doesn't seem to be holding a grudge about what happened earlier, and my two beers have loosened me up a bit.

"It's time I said it." I hold up the beer, ready to clink her glass. "I think you're going to be a great addition to the team."

She's just put a chip laden with salsa in her mouth, and she covers her smile with her hand, ducking as she lifts her margarita and taps it to my beer. "You do?"

"Hell, yeah. Your first day on the job, and you've already cracked the case."

We both take a sip of our drinks.

"I'm not sure I've cracked it, but to be fair, our perpetrator was very sloppy."

"Or he wasn't expecting anybody to look that close."

Our food comes out, and I scoop up a steak taco while Britt digs into the street corn. We both let out noises of delight.

"Herve makes the best street corn." She groans between bites, making me grin.

"For me, it's the steak tacos. Rare."

Nodding, she quickly picks one up and takes a bite, letting out a muffled, "So good," from behind her hand.

For a few minutes, we stuff our faces, until she sits back with a sigh. "So much better than scrambled eggs and cheese."

"Was that your dinner for tonight?"

"I haven't had a chance to shop! I'll get groceries tomorrow."

"Okay." I nod, grinning and noticing her empty glass. "Do you want another?"

"I'd better not."

"You sure?"

She sits up a little straighter. "Maybe I could just have a Corona?"

I order us each a beer, and she tilts her head after the waitress leaves, giving me a smile that tightens my stomach. "What?"

"Thank you for this, the dinner and the compliment—what you said about me being part of the team. It really means a lot to me." She hesitates. "And I promise not to teach Owen any more card tricks. I really had no idea you wouldn't like it."

That part makes me groan. "I'm not a monster. I'm just not a fan of magic and… all that."

I don't really want to read off the laundry list of her family's behavior while we're getting along so well.

She nods. "I understand."

"You do?" My brow arches.

The waitress places two beers in front of us, and she lifts hers, taking a short sip. "I actually, really do. My mom is still obsessed with finding Dad's killer—through any spiritual means necessary."

"Gwen still believes your dad was murdered?" It's more a musing question, based on what I remember of how hard my dad investigated the case.

The conclusion was indisputable. It was simply a terrible accident, caused by a fault in the machinery.

Britt nods, taking another sip. "According to her, there's no way Dad should've drowned in that box. She was convinced it was tampered with." A sad smile curls her lips. "Because there's no magic. It's all distraction and manipulation and making you look that way while something else happens over here."

The resistance in my chest is all but gone at this point. "You surprise me, Miss Bailey."

"I aim to please, Sheriff Stone."

She has no idea.

With an exhale, she traces her finger along the bottle. "I watched my mother throw herself into astrology and tea leaves and tarot—anything that would reveal his killer."

"I get that. She was hurting." I can't believe I'm relating to Gwen.

"She wasn't the only one hurting, but my pain didn't appear on her star chart."

Ouch. I reach across and place my hand on hers. "I'm sorry."

I imagine pulling her into my arms, sliding my hand down her soft hair, and comforting her.

"I was right there with her, suffering right beside her." She traces the tip of her finger along mine. "Tarot and magic were the only ways I could be close to my one remaining parent. Until I realized it wasn't helping anything. None of it would make her see me." She sits straighter in the booth, moving her hands to her lap with an exhaled laugh. "I'm sorry—that was a major downer. Let's change the subject!"

"My wife cheated on me." The words tumble out like more dirty laundry.

Britt inhales a short breath, then her hand is on top of mine. "I'm so sorry. Was it before…"

"A few months after her funeral, I was cleaning out her stuff, and I found a box of love letters between her and this guy, Clive Stevens."

"Oh my God!" Her eyes widen. "The guy from the library?"

"Yeah, that guy. Who knew?"

"Not me… You must've been devastated."

"It wasn't a great moment for me." I hesitate, thinking. "I've only told one other person about that."

"Your mom?"

"No, actually." I pick at the label coming loose from my bottle. "I told Adam. We were having some argument about faith."

I don't feel like going down that road again, but somehow she seems to understand.

She gives my hand a squeeze, and her voice is sure. "I won't betray your confidence."

Shifting in my seat, it's my turn to exhale a laugh. "You wanted to change the subject. What about our case? Did you learn anything from your mom today?"

The waitress returns, and I motion for the check.

"She wanted to read the cards." Britt rolls her eyes, shaking her head. "I swear, the woman makes me crazy."

The lightness in her tone makes me grin. "Parents are like that, I guess."

"What about you? What did you learn from the Jones boys?"

"They weren't home. I briefly talked to their dad." I polish off my beer. "I expect they were up to no good somewhere else that night, but I was planning to go back tomorrow and ask about the three-wheeler and our guy with the prosthetic leg."

"I'd like to go with you if that's okay? Maybe take Edward?"

"Sure." I pay the bill, and we slide out of the booth.

The warmth went away with the sun, and it's a cool spring night. Britt crosses her arms, and I wish I had a coat to put over her shoulders. I'd like to put my arm around them.

When we get to the tarot sign, I hesitate outside her door. "I can walk you up?"

She looks up at me, and the streetlights shine in her pretty green eyes. "You want to be sure I climb the stairs safely?"

"Accidents happen all the time."

"I guess you're right." She exhales a laugh, wrinkling her nose.

I follow her up the steps slowly, my eyes drifting to the curve of her ass in those jeans, and I remember the curve of her ass in those Daisy Dukes.

"What will you do tonight?" We're outside her door, but I don't want to let her go.

"Watch a rerun of *The Closer* until I get sleepy and go to bed."

Her back is to the door, and my hand is on the door frame above her head. A yellow light is above us, and the landing is shadowy and intimate. It reminds me of the night before she left, when we were outside in the moonlight, talking about our dreams.

"What will you do?" She's quiet.

Her pink tongue touches her bottom lip, and electricity hums around us. I'm standing too close to her, and I can't help myself. Her fresh scent of flowers and the ocean surrounds me. My eyes trace her skin, her soft cheek, her full lips, and I just want to touch her, slowly tracing my fingers down her shoulders…

"Aiden?" My eyes drift from her lips to her green eyes, so warm and inviting. "You didn't answer me."

"Sorry, I was thinking…"

Her dark lashes flutter to my chest, and her slim hand rests lightly on my shirt. "What were you thinking?" Her eyes lift to my mouth.

"I won't sleep tonight if I don't taste your lips."

"You won't?" Her fingers trace the fabric of my shirt, and I imagine her pulling it higher, her mouth on my body.

"No." It's a hoarse whisper.

Her chin rises and mine lowers, bringing our lips dangerously close.

"Lack of sleep is the number one cause of accidents." Her eyes meet mine, the tips of her white teeth pressing against her bottom lip. "And Owen needs his Daddy."

Fuck, don't say Daddy. "Is this okay?"

Lowering my face, I brush my lips across hers, and I fucking swear it sparks. My heart beats in every part of my body, specifically the parts below my belt.

"Mmm," she hums. "Yes."

"This?" I do it again, only this time, I use a little more pressure before pulling her lips with mine.

My chest burns with hunger, and her fingers curl, clutching my shirt.

"Yes..." It's a throaty whisper that makes my dick hard.

"Or this?" I repeat the movement, this time nipping her bottom lip before sealing our mouths together, warm and soft.

Her lips part, and my tongue sweeps inside, tasting her, spicy sweetness. Her fingers rise to my chin, and we repeat the process, growing hungrier with every little taste, with the increasing pressure.

My hands go under her ass, and I lift her, pressing her back against the door, and she whimpers as our tongues curl together. Her legs are around my waist, and she rocks her hips in a way that massages my cock through my jeans.

Fuck me. My hands go to her waist, slipping under her tank and moving higher, over her soft skin to her bra. I want to shove the garment up. I want to lift and knead her breasts. I want to roll her tight nipples between my fingers. I want to devour her flesh and make her moan. I want my teeth against her skin as she begs for more.

One of her hands fumbles to my waist, pulling my shirt higher and tracing her fingers across my tightened abs. Her back arches, and her skin touches mine.

"Fuck," I groan. My dick is an iron rod in my pants. My lips are at her ear, and I pull the soft shell with my teeth. "I want to be inside you."

"Oh, God," she moans.

I want to fuck her so badly. I want her body riding mine, and I want her bent over the couch as I ram into her from behind. I want to taste every part of her, spend all night claiming her. How long has it been?

How long... It's been since Annemarie, since I was betrayed, since I realized I'm a grown-assed man who doesn't believe in lust at first sight. Not to mention love. I'm the sheriff. I have a son who needs me to be an example.

I'm her fucking boss.

With a groan, I lift my chin to break this contact. I lower Britt to her feet and grip the doorjamb so hard my knuckles ache as I struggle to find control.

"I'd better go." It's a rough statement of fact from a man hanging by a thread.

Opening my eyes, I look down at her. Her cheeks are beautifully flushed. Her green eyes are wide and dilated, and her lips are pink and swollen from our kisses.

Her hair is messy from my fingers threading in it, and her shirt is shoved to the side, revealing the top of her bra. My eyes linger on her breasts rising and falling with every rapid pant. It's hypnotic.

I still want her.

"Yeah, I've got to go." I push myself away from her.

Her hand covers her lips, and she nods, blinking down. "Goodnight, Aiden. Thank you so much for dinner."

I want to touch her one more time, but I'm afraid if I do, I'll push her through the door and finish what we've started.

"Goodnight." I force myself to jog down the stairs.

I force myself not to look back as I push through the glass door, and I force myself to walk in the cool night to the courthouse, where I get in my truck and drive the short distance to my house.

When I get there, I text my mother to ask if Owen can spend the night. She sends me a picture of him asleep in my old bed, peaceful and happy.

A quick thank-you, and I toss my phone on the bed. I've got to hit the shower and take care of this need surging through my veins.

Chapter 8

Britt

MY ENTIRE BODY IS ON FIRE. MY HEART BEATS SO FAST, IT ACHES, and I can still feel the echoes of his fingers on my skin, my arms. I can feel his hands sliding along my waist, rising higher as his lips touch mine, savoring, tempting, then taking.

I just made out with Aiden Stone in the hallway.

Sheriff Aiden Stone just devoured me like his last meal—and it was so fucking hot.

Edward lifts his head off the sofa when I enter, and I give him a pat as I pass. He lowers it again, and I go straight to my bed, turning and falling backwards onto it. Aiden Stone touched my bare skin… He kissed my lips.

I want to be inside you.

Staring at the ceiling, I'm literally vibrating with need. My eyes cut to the top drawer of my nightstand, and I lean forward quickly, taking out the small bullet vibrator. Then I drop back again, flicking it on and sliding my hand inside my jeans.

Closing my eyes, I relive every moment of what just happened. The dim yellow light, casting his perfect face in warm shadows. His broad shoulders stretching his shirt as he leaned on his hand over my head. I leaned back against the door, lifting my chin and doing my very best to project all the *kiss me* vibes I could summon.

Then he did.

He kissed me, and that kiss…

The floor disappeared.

The entire world disappeared.

All that existed was him and me and his unexpectedly soft lips brushing mine, pulling mine, nipping mine. I couldn't breathe. I could only hold on to his shirt so I didn't fall.

Until he lifted me off my feet, and I could feel how much he wanted me. His cock was so hard and long in his jeans, grinding against my clit through mine. I could've come right then. My fingers curled in his hair, and his beard scuffed my chin, my cheeks, my lips.

I imagine his beard scuffing my inner thighs, and my core tightens. Orgasm spikes in my veins as I imagine riding his face between my legs, large hands squeezing my ass, rising higher to cover my ribs, higher to my breasts. Another flash of orgasm makes me whimper, and the muscles in my core begin to spasm.

I traced my fingers over the hard planes of his abs… *so sexy*. Our eyes met briefly, and the storm in his raged furiously. His strong body held mine firmly against the wall, and I had to arch forward. I wanted his skin touching mine.

Then he said those words.

I let go as I imagine him not stopping us before it goes too far. I imagine giving in to these feelings. I imagine the two of us entwined, touching, tasting, letting the heat consume us. I picture his hands holding mine hostage above my head, the weight of his body pinning me against the door as he thrusts that massive cock faster, harder, while my head falls back.

His lips are on my nipples, pulling, sucking, and I moan so loudly. My back arches, and the orgasm shudders through my stomach and thighs. His hoarse groan fills my mind, and we're coming together in a mixture of salt and cedar and sweat.

"Oh, God…" I roll onto my side as the powerful aftershocks tremor through me.

Flipping off the vibe, I pull my knees to my chest. My eyes are still closed, and I hold onto the image of him leaning close, powerful and gorgeous…

And *impossible*.

We work together. He's practically my boss.

I won't sleep tonight if I don't taste your lips…

My stomach tingles, and a smile steals across my face. So much hunger was in his words, in his eyes, in his tone. How could I say no?

I wonder if he's asleep right now. I wonder if he's thinking of me.

"Britt and I are heading over to talk to the Jones boys." Aiden's standing by Doug's desk looking at his phone. "Holly, would you mind if we stop by your place on the way and let Edward sniff around your chicken coop?"

Holly gives a thumbs-up, holding her hand over one ear of her headset.

I'm waiting by my desk with Edward, and Aiden hasn't said more than ten words to me since I got here—*good morning,* and *are you going with me today?* (My reply, "Good morning, and yes.")

Let's go will make ten.

"You ready?" He turns, and his gray blue eyes meet mine like a shock.

"Ten," I almost sigh.

"What?" His brow furrows, and I wave it away.

"Yes! Edward and I are ready."

Today, I'm in jeans and a long-sleeved navy tee. It has *K9 Unit* on the pocket, but Edward was never officially part of the K9 unit—those dogs have special training, and he only has a good nose. But he's as good as any K9 unit to me.

"Come on, Mr. Ed." I scratch his ears, and we follow Aiden to the back door, through the break room.

Chewing on my lip, I watch his ass flex in those dark brown pants, and all the feelings from last night are simmering under my skin. From his behavior today, I guess we're going to act like it never happened, which I suppose is the right approach. We're professionals, and I want to be taken seriously.

Serious law-enforcement professionals do not make out with the sheriff in the stairwell outside their apartments.

Pulling my hair into a ponytail at the base of my neck, I put a pair of aviator sunglasses over my eyes and switch my brain into work mode. Objective: Find the man with the missing leg.

"Which episode of *The Closer* did you watch?" Aiden breaks the silence in his truck, but his eyes don't leave the road.

For a second, I'm confused. Is he joking? "I didn't watch anything last night. I was a little preoccupied by all the things that happened yesterday."

He glances at me, and my chest squeezes. I bite the inside of my cheek to make it stop.

"Anyway," he continues, "Holly had several of her chickens stolen a few days before Terra's farm was demolished. Figured it couldn't hurt to let you check the place out, see if Edward picks up a scent."

"It's a great idea. I can't imagine this guy's motives, unless he was making chicken salad and needed pickle relish."

Aiden exhales a laugh, and it breaks the tension between us. I'm glad, and a little proud I made him laugh after everything.

"Owen asked me a similar question. It's hard to know why people do things these days."

"Could be the next social media trend."

"That's all we need." He turns the truck into the driveaway of a small house close to town.

Most of the neighborhoods around Eureka are clustered

close to Main Street, where the courthouse is located, where I live above Mom's Star Parlor, where El Rio is located, and where most of the thrift stores and the one small grocery store are nearby on Beach Street, which is across the courthouse square.

Edward hops out of the bed of the truck, and Aiden leads us up the drive to the backyard, where a cute little henhouse is located behind a small fence made of chicken wire.

Slipping plastic gloves over my hands, I take the old boot out of a large plastic bag and hold it down for Edward to get a good sniff. At once, his nose is to the ground, and he's running all around the yard, sniffing up close to the coop, going around a tall pine tree near the back fence.

I follow him, studying the soft ground around the chicken house, dropping to my knee and checking for prints or any sign of metal indentions. I don't see anything.

"You said it's been a week since the burglary?"

"A week today."

Nodding, I walk to the fence at the back of the property and rise on my tiptoes to try and look over it. I'm too short.

"Is there an alley behind these houses?" I glance back at Aiden, and he's watching me as intently as he did when we were at Terra's.

"I think there is." He goes to a door in the chain-link fence leading to the wooden barrier.

I follow him to a mostly grassy alley behind the fences. It's large enough for walking or biking, but not big enough for a car or truck. Edward is right with me, furiously sniffing every blade of grass.

"He should be able to pick up week-old clues." My heart jumps to my throat when Edward barks loudly at a corner of the gate. "Jesus, Ed, you nearly gave me a heart attack."

I walk over to where he's running up and down and drop to my knee again. The plastic gloves are still on my hands, and sure enough, just off the path in the soft mud near the fence, I spot two things.

Whipping out my camera and a card, I drop a number one and two and take several shots of what I've found.

"What is it?" Aiden is beside me, leaning close enough that I can smell his sexy, clean scent.

"Just what we need." I hold the longer grasses to the side so he can see the boot print right next to a partial indentation of square-nubbed tire treads. "Same ATV tires, and I'm guessing this print will match our boot."

"Amazing." His voice is quiet admiration, and I can't help a smile splitting my cheeks.

"Edward's my not-so-secret weapon." I stand, and we're face to face for the first time all day. My voice is softer. "I probably wouldn't have found that without his nose."

Our eyes meet, and so much energy is in Aiden's gaze, my stomach tightens. We've been in this position before, and I know where it can lead and how incredible it is. My bottom lip slips between my teeth, but he blinks and turns away.

"Good work." He puts his hands on his waist and goes through the gate. "We'd better head over to the Jones' unless you need to do more here?"

I remember to breathe and glance at my dog, who's standing beside me waiting for his next orders. "I think Edward's found everything we need."

Back in the truck, we're headed to the outskirts of town. The radio is playing the local country music station softly. Willie Nelson is singing about his heroes always being cowboys.

"I don't want you to take this the wrong way." Aiden glances at me, and my throat tightens.

Please don't take everything back, I pray silently.

"Okay?" I pull my bottom lip between my teeth again.

His eyes go to my mouth then back to the road quickly, and he clears his throat. "Let me do all the talking with these guys. It's not that I don't think you're capable. Clearly, you're very good at your job. It's more, these guys can be real shits, and I'd rather you listen and observe. Watch for anything you think we should follow up on."

Exhaling softly, I nod. "I can do that."

He turns onto a narrow road cutting through tall pine trees. Palmettos growing in sand line the shoulders on both sides of the road, which means this land isn't good for farming or pretty much anything. I'm not sure if we're even still in Eureka.

"Here we go."

The dirt road ends at a double-wide trailer with an attached, screened-in front porch. Junk is scattered around the yard—old paint buckets, a broken laundry basket, and a tire with a little flower bed planted in the middle. The one bright spot.

Three lawn chairs are arranged around a fire pit, and it looks like somebody had a party here last night from the number of beer cans scattered around them.

An ancient El Camino is on cinder blocks off to one side, and a motorcycle is parked beside it. Behind the two is a covered area where a truck is stored along with something large under a tarp. My spidey senses are on high alert, and I wonder if it might be an old three-wheeler. It's the exact place I'd expect to find one.

"How old is Thad?" I ask quietly as we approach the front door.

"Mid-to-late sixties." Aiden lifts his hand and knocks sharply.

"Does he have both his legs?"

An older man in a dirty white T-shirt and jeans opens the door. "You're back?"

"Morning, Thad, I was hoping to catch Bull and Raif at home."

My eyes fly down to his bare feet—of which he has two. I exhale the breath I was holding. Like solving the case would be that easy. Edward is sniffing all around the property, but so far, he hasn't barked or seemed to find any scents he recognizes.

The old man's eyes narrow on me. "Who's this?"

Aiden answers quickly. "Britt Bailey is working with us now. She's Edna's granddaughter."

"I remember you, little girl." He scratches the white scruff on his chin. "That your dog?"

I don't say a word, and Aiden cuts in again. "He's with me. Are the boys home? We won't take much of your time."

He leans into the house and yells their names, and I take a step back, going to where Edward is sniffing around the El Camino.

The slow thud of feet on the elevated porch precedes the appearance of two men I vaguely remember.

Bull and Raif Jones are older than Aiden, which means they were way out of school before I started—if they even finished. They never spent much time in town, and I think Bull is a welder. I vaguely recall Raif going out with the fishing crews.

"What's up, Aiden?" Raif shakes his hand, but Bull stomps down the steps, walking straight to where I'm following Edward and itching to look under that canvas tarp.

"What are you doing over here?" My heart jumps, and I look up to see Bull Jones scowling down at me.

Bull is as tall as Aiden, with dark hair and menacing eyes. A tattoo is on his neck, and his bottom lip is sliced with a silver scar.

I'm not sure I can get away without speaking, but Aiden walks to where we're standing, with Raif right behind him. Raif has lighter hair and isn't as tall as his brother. He's also way less scary, with only one visible tattoo on his forearm and no apparent scars.

"There's been a series of burglaries and vandalism happening around town—" Aiden starts, and Bull's quick to step to him.

"So here you are, rounding up the usual suspects." He's practically nose-to-nose with Aiden, and my throat clenches.

Aiden doesn't back down, meeting Bull's menacing glare with a pretty menacing glare of his own. Despite my nerves, I confess, it's pretty hot to think he could take this guy if he wanted to fight.

Aiden says one word. "No."

Seconds tick past with the two men locked in a staring

contest, until Raif steps forward, catching his brother's arm. "If you're not here to arrest us, what do you want?"

Bull allows his brother to pull him away, but he's still seething.

Aiden's glare doesn't break, and his voice is commanding. "We discovered evidence pointing to someone with a prosthesis on his right leg."

"What's that mean? Prosthesis?"

"It means he's got a fake leg," Raif answers his brother quietly.

The exchange seems to make Bull angrier. "You can keep on looking, Sheriff. We've got all our body parts around here. Two good legs to walk on, and one to give you the ride of your life, little lady."

My brows shoot up, and a low growl comes from Aiden's throat. "You'll treat my officers with respect."

"Oh, don't listen to him." Raif steps between the two men, giving me a smile that's faint but sweet. "He's got a twisted sense of humor."

I kind of feel sorry for Raif trapped in this place, but I follow Aiden's request and keep my mouth shut.

"Our suspect was also driving a three-wheel ATV."

Raif turns his back to Bull, looking up at Aiden. "Those have been illegal as long as I've been alive."

"Doesn't mean they're not still around." Aiden glances between the brothers. "Do you know anybody who fits that description?"

"Nope," Bull answers fast, and I figure he wouldn't tell us even if he did.

"I've come across a lot of folks with a lot of challenges, but nothing like that." Raif shrugs, and I'm more inclined to believe him.

"If you do come across anyone like that, give us a call." Aiden hands Raif a card.

"Will do, Sheriff." He takes it, and Aiden hesitates a moment, looking around the area.

Edward is finished sniffing, and he's back to standing beside me. My hand is on his head, and even though I'm dying to look under that tarp, I wait to follow Aiden's lead. We don't have a search warrant, and at least two of the men here are on the defense.

"All right, then." Aiden takes a step towards the truck. "I appreciate your help."

"You said your name was Britt Bailey?" Bull's black eyes are on me, and I immediately look to Aiden.

"She's Edna's granddaughter." Aiden answers his question.

"She can't speak for herself?"

"If you've got something to say, you can say it to me."

"I've got something to say." Bull crosses his arms, his voice a taunt. "You've stepped in a big pile of shit bringing another Bailey on the force, Sheriff. I wouldn't be surprised if the next thing you know, you're out on your ass. Those people are not your friends."

Aiden's jaw tightens. "And you are?"

"I'll tell you what you should be asking," Bull continues. "Why does Edna Brewer want only her family in charge in Eureka? What secrets are they hiding?"

A knot is in my throat, and my fingers start to tremble. The muscle in Aiden's jaw moves, and I can tell he's pissed. What I don't know is if he's pissed at Bull or if he's pissed at me and my family. Would he believe what this guy is saying? I have no interest in taking Aiden's job, and I definitely don't want him out on his ass.

Aiden's tone is calm. "Anything else you need to get off your chest?"

"Nope."

"Then we're headed back to the courthouse."

"You'd better watch your back, Sheriff." Bull's eyes are

on me now, and my stomach is queasy. I thought he said he was done. "There's things nobody knows about that family. Buncha redneck carnies acting like they've gone straight."

His words are as bad as a kick in the gut, and the anxiety in my chest twists harder. I remember why I left, and I wonder why I thought it was a good idea to come back. I'll never be free of my family's reputation, and I'm afraid to look at Aiden.

I'm afraid he agrees.

Aiden lowers the tailgate, helping Edward jump into the truck bed, and his voice gives nothing away. "Let's go, Britt."

Chapter 9

Aiden

BRITT SITS SILENTLY IN THE PASSENGER SEAT ACROSS FROM ME. Her eyes are on her camera, but she's not scrolling through photos. She seems upset, and I'm pretty sure it's my fault.

After last night, I've done my best to be professional and give her space—even in the alley behind Holly's house. We got too close, and all I could think about was how soft her lips were against mine. How easy it would be to take another hit. How no one was in that alley to see what we did.

Just now at the Jones place, it took all my strength not to pop Bull Jones in the face for his crack about her family being shit. Like that asshole has any room to talk. Britt's family is reckless and probably unhinged, but they're not habitual offenders living on the outskirts of town in what amounts to a junkyard.

We drive a little farther, and when her mood doesn't change, I shift uncomfortably in my seat. I have to make this right.

"I'm sorry if I've made things uncomfortable between us. Last night, I mean."

Confusion lines her brow. "I really enjoyed last night."

I'm probably too happy to hear that. I look back at the road, but when I glance at her again, she still seems worried. "Is something else bothering you?"

Her lips press together before she answers. "I was just thinking about what Bull said about my family and your job. I hope you don't think he's right. I'm not here to undermine you or get you fired."

She looks up at me again, and her green eyes are so open, my stomach tightens.

Still, I won't lie to her.

"I've had my issues with Edna, and I'm sure you know your mother and I don't see eye to eye." She nods slowly, and I continue. "But I'm not worried about my position or anything Bull Jones said. I meant what I said last night. I think you're doing a good job, and you deserve to be judged on your own merit."

The smallest hint of a smile touches her lips. "That means a lot to me."

We're back at the courthouse, and I pull into my reserved space. "That being said, we need to keep our eye on those boys."

She smiles, wrinkling her nose in that way I'm starting to find irresistible. "They are pretty suspicious."

Edward hops out of the back, and we walk to the large, white-brick building. When we reach the door, she pauses. "Except for Raif. I think he's trying."

My gut doesn't agree. "I think when push comes to shove, he'll be loyal to his family. His kind always is."

Her smile melts a little, but she doesn't argue. She pats Edward's head. "I'll take him home and try talking to my mom again. If I find out anything, I'll let you know."

I hesitate, watching her go. Her usual lightness hasn't fully returned, but at least we cleared the air.

"Where do we stand on this vandalism?" Edna sits at her desk across from me, and we're having our biweekly check-in, which has turned into a weekly check-in since the incidents started.

"Britt turned up some pretty good evidence, so we have a solid lead." Her eyebrows rise, and I'm ready to go on the record. "She's a good addition to the team. You were right."

A smile breaks across Edna's face. "That wasn't so hard, was it?"

"Don't push it."

She leans back in her chair still grinning. "My granddaughter has always made us proud. She's smart as a whip... if a bit more of a perfectionist than I'd like."

I don't say what I'm thinking, which is that Britt's perfectionism is what distinguishes her from the rest of the kooks in her family.

Instead, I maintain the peace. "She picked the right field for it."

"Yes," Edna sighs, sitting forward. "However, it can be a burden to be so focused on the details in life. I'd like to see her a little more balanced, getting out more, having fun. Perhaps she might date. Your brother Adam was always a good friend. Is he seeing anyone?"

A stab of anger hits me at the suggestion. "Adam's a bit of a free spirit."

"Hmm..." Edna smiles. "I like that, and friendship is a solid foundation for a relationship. Maybe you could reintroduce them."

"No." It comes out as a sharp retort, which I quickly try to smooth over. "Britt's old enough to manage her own social life."

"Of course." Edna exhales a light laugh. "Listen to me talking like a grandmother. My apologies, Sheriff."

"It's okay." The collar of my shirt feels too tight, and I have an unreasonable urge to punch my hippie brother in the junk, which is ridiculous.

She lifts a sheet of paper off her desk. "Speaking of social lives, the Founder's Day festival is ten days away. Is it possible we might have this burglary case wrapped up by then? Or is that wishful thinking?"

Shaking off my irritation, I refocus my mind on business. "Perhaps you can help us. We're looking for a male, mid-sixties, prosthetic leg, driving a three-wheel ATV. Know anyone in or around Eureka who fits that description?"

Edna's hazel eyes rise from her phone to mine. "A prosthetic leg?"

"On the right side, at least missing a foot, possibly more." Glancing down at my phone, I see a note from Doug reporting no leads, which frustrates me.

"That is very specific."

"It's all your granddaughter's work. You'd think with that much information, we'd be able to put our finger on the perpetrator—and you'd be wrong."

"Why is that?" Edna watches me with a curious expression.

"Three-wheel ATVs were outlawed thirty years ago, so sales records are all but gone. None of the clinics we've checked have records of an amputee, so we're having to count on the memory of citizens who might know or remember someone who fits the description."

"How's it going?"

"So far, nothing's turned up."

Edna exhales with a nod and stands, crossing her arms. "He can't hide forever." Her voice is quiet, and she walks to the window, looking out.

My eyebrow arches. "Do *you* know anyone who fits that description?"

"Not for certain." She turns, arms still crossed, facing me. "Why would anyone destroy a pickle farm? Did he seem to be searching for something or someone in particular?"

"Not that we can tell. So far, it's just random acts of vandalism and minor burglary."

Edna presses her lips into a straight line. "Thanks for keeping me in the loop, Aiden."

"That's my job." I push out of the chair, but before I go, I pause, resting my hand on my gun holster. "It's hard to imagine someone that distinct going unnoticed. My thought is he's from out of town, or he's a Eureka native who's come back for some reason."

"Your instincts are good." Picking up her bag, she starts for the door. "I was thinking something very similar."

The change in her demeanor has me suspicious. "You sure there's nothing you need to share with me?"

"If there is, you'll be the first to know." Her heels click on the linoleum as she strides through the door. "I'm glad my granddaughter is working out. Perhaps you can help me get her to stay."

I'm not sure what to make of those parting words, but I'm certain she doesn't mean them in the way Bull Jones thinks she does. I'm not going anywhere, and Britt staying in Eureka doesn't sound half as bad as it did before she arrived.

Doug glances up from his desk when I return to the main area. "Still no luck tracking down three-wheel ATVs, Sheriff."

"Any amputees?"

"I checked the clinic near Hilton Head, and they have no records of anyone being fitted with a prosthetic in the last five years."

"Five years?" My brow furrows.

"It's as long as they keep records of that sort of thing."

I'm distracted by my conversation with Edna. "Are you planning to go to the Founder's Day festival next weekend?"

Doug smiles broadly. "Wouldn't miss it. I'm the star of the

library's annual dunking booth, so come on by and show your support."

Nodding, I have an idea. "I think all of us should attend as a group. Show the town we're a unified force committed to their safety."

"Aw, I'm sure the town knows that. Even with all that's happening, folks say they know we're on the case."

"I'll talk to Britt and make sure she's going as well. Maybe I should show her around, since she's been gone a while."

"Trust me, Sheriff, Britt's familiar with Founder's Day. She dunked me on her first throw last year." He chuckles.

"I see her name is on the schedule for Saturday."

"We switched so I could attend the festival."

"Right." I nod, thinking. "She should take the afternoon off and socialize."

"Socializing does lead to tighter bonds." Doug gives me a side-eye. "As a team, of course."

"Of course." I pick up my keys.

Nothing wrong with escorting her to the event. It's part of my job to help her learn the ropes and mesh with the group. Even Doug can see that.

The more I think about it, the better I like my plan as I head out to pick up Owen.

Chapter 10

Britt

EDWARD'S FED, WATERED, AND CURLED UP ON THE SOFA WHEN I trot downstairs to the Star Parlor to chat with my mom. Pausing at the frosted-glass door, I lean close and listen. I don't want to walk in during the middle of a session.

Hearing nothing, I knock lightly as I open the door and take a step inside. "Hey, Mom?" I call. "You around?"

A shuffle of Birkenstocks, and Cass appears in the parlor dressed in a flowing wrap skirt and a white tank top with a beaded shawl tied around her shoulders. Deep red lipstick compliments her olive skin, and her dark-brown hair is behind her ears, exposing large gold hoop earrings.

"Hey, Britt!" She hops over and gives me a hug, surrounding me in the faint scent of patchouli.

"Somebody's following the dress-code," I deadpan.

"Are you here for a reading?" Her eyes widen, and she skips over to the tarot table. "I am *dying* to see what the cards have to say about you and Mr. Taurus."

"How do you know Aiden's star sign?"

"I made his birthday cake one year, back when I was still doing cakes."

"You stopped doing cakes?" I'm sad to hear that. Cass is an amazing baker.

"It took over my life and my house! I'm trying to simplify, live life on my own terms, with purpose."

She has definitely been hanging out with my mom. "What else are you doing that I don't know about?"

"Tarot is the only new thing. I'm still grooming pets, and I'd like to get back into preschool ballet. Those little tutus and squishy arms make me so happy!"

"I'm almost out of that body lotion you made for me. Can I get some more? Ocean Gardenia?"

Her lip curls, and she shakes her head. "I'm not doing that anymore either. Too many raw ingredients, too messy."

"Cass!" I flop on the gold velvet sofa. "I really like that scent."

"Maybe I can make one more especially for you." She pokes my arm with her finger. "And I'll put a special love potion in it for Aiden. Mmm... those Stone brothers are so hot, although you two are kind of like the Sharks and the Jets."

My brow arches. "From *West Side Story*?" Cass loves all things Broadway.

She nods, shuffling the cards. "Aiden is way too law-abiding for our kind."

"Then it's a good thing we're not together." She doesn't need to know about *The Kiss*, which apparently he regrets now, based on what he said in the truck. "We work together. He's technically my boss. That's all."

"You never know what the future holds." Her eyebrows waggle as she holds out the cards. "Let's see what they say!"

"No." Holding up my hands, I stand and move away from the temptation. "I've made a clean break from all that. I'm done with living my life by a deck of cards."

"You know, I really don't understand you. You've got magic

in your blood, and you don't even want it. I'm over here wishing I had half your genes."

"Trust me, there is no magic. It's all fake." My voice shifts. "The moment you forget it, the second you start believing it's real, it leaves you alone at the bottom of the ocean, trapped in a cold, dark box."

"Oh, Britt." Cass's face crinkles. "Do you still have dreams of drowning?"

Exhaling a sigh, I remember Greenville. "Not as much as I used to."

Setting the cards on the table, she walks to where I stand, lifting my hands in hers. "What happened to your dad was a horrible tragedy, but it was a risk he was willing to take. Escapology is a craft, not a spiritual path."

"My mother went down that spiritual path, and it took her further and further away from me when I needed her the most. It's an obsession, and I'm done with all of it."

"Okay." Her voice is quiet. "I can show you my skills some other time. I'm getting pretty good at your mom's technique, though!"

"Where is she, anyway? She was supposed to be finding information on a suspect in our case."

My bestie's wide eyes return. "You've got a suspect! Who is it?" Catching my hands, she drags me to the velvet sofa again. "Tell me everything."

I briefly fill her in on what we know so far. "It's hard to believe we can't find anyone who fits that description."

"But now you know what you're looking for when it happens again."

"If we had some idea of what to expect. All these incidents are so random." I glance out the window. "And what in the world do those wooden signs mean? Are they supposed to be clues? Warnings? Explanations?"

"Wait..." She sits straighter. "You think the prosthetic guy did the signs, too?"

"We don't have a direct link, but he stole Holly's chickens and he tore up Terra's pickle farm."

"But those are real crimes, theft and destruction of property…"

"The signs are real crimes."

"They're positive messages! *Happiness, You are Rare*… How is that a crime?"

"Trespassing, criminal mischief, vandalism. Ignoring small crimes opens the door for larger ones to follow."

Cass's lips turn down. "I guess we'll have to agree to disagree on this one. I think they're uplifting. Someone was watching over you when your brakes went out."

"To be honest, I'm way less worried about the signs than the perpetrator." Pushing off my knees, I stand, walking to the door. "You have no idea where my mom went?"

"I heard her say something about Kiawah."

"What would she be doing there?" Cass shrugs, and I decide to let it go for now. "I need to get groceries, and I don't know why Bud hasn't called me about my truck. I'll have to find a way to get over there."

"I told you I took care of it!" She hops up smiling. "Your insurance information was in the glove box, and I went over everything with Bud yesterday. He's going to replace your front fender with one I found at the junkyard, and he's giving your brake line a thorough inspection. I'll follow up with him at the end of the week."

I shake my head. "That should be your job. I can't believe your knack for auto mechanics. What do I owe you for your time?"

"Stop it." She playfully slaps my arm. "You've been up to your ears in official police business, keeping us safe from creepy men with missing feet. It's the least I could do."

"Don't tell anybody what I told you about the suspect. We don't want him going into hiding."

She makes a motion of zipping her lips. "I won't breathe a word."

"Good luck with your readings."

Her shoulders drop, and she follows me to the door. "It's pretty slow. I'm probably going to have to find another gig soon. I'm not making any money here."

"If you won't be my mechanic, I'll pay you to keep me stocked in Ocean Gardenia."

She waves me away. "No, you won't. I'll figure something out."

We air kiss, and I jog up the stairs to grab my bags. The little Safeway across the square has enough of the staples to keep me going until my truck is ready. Hopefully, I'll have it back by the weekend, so I can do some real shopping.

By the time I get back, it's almost dinner, and I have to take Edward for a walk. Quickly unpacking the staples I bought, I grab the leash and my phone and head out before the sun goes down.

Edward has always been efficient about his bathroom habits, but Cass's words have been on my mind since we talked. I take him past the locations of the signs and let him sniff all around them, watching to see if he recognizes anything.

While he's doing his sniffing, I study the messages painted neatly on a white board, and I try to imagine if a man with no foot or leg, we don't know which, would be able to climb a ladder and balance well enough to nail them where they're located.

"Maybe it is two different people," I say to my dog.

Edward hops over and slides his head under my hand. I give him a good scratching. "Come on, Mr. Ed. Time for dinner."

Standing alone in my kitchen, I'm reading the frozen pizza box when my phone buzzes with a text. Absently, I pick it up, expecting it to be Cass or Jinx.

My heart stutters when I read the words from an unknown number. *I hope you're not having scrambled eggs and cheese for dinner.*

Hesitating, my fingers tremble slightly as I tap out a reply. *Aiden? How did you get my number?*

I asked Doug to pull it from HR. Please tell me you got groceries today.

Tingles prickle in my belly, and I quickly reply. *I just got back from the store.*

What's for dinner?

Squinting at the frozen pizza box, I confess. *Frozen pizza.*

Terrible.

Don't dinner-shame me. As if I'm proud of frozen pizza. *What are you having?*

It takes a few seconds, then a picture of a grill with four hamburgers appears on my phone. They're rare and mouthwatering, and my stomach growls. *That looks delicious.*

Come have a burger with Owen and me.

My heart jumps, and I want to say yes so much. *I can't have dinner with you every night, Sheriff.*

I expect some nights you'll have dinner with your family or friends.

I don't have my truck.

I'll pick you up in five.

Aiden! A grin splits my cheeks at his bossy butt. *I'm still in my work clothes.*

Be ready when I get there. I don't like leaving Owen home alone for long.

Dropping my phone, I run to the bedroom and whip off my jeans and long-sleeved shirt in record time. I dash into the small bathroom and switch on the water to take a lightning-fast shower.

In two minutes, I'm out and towel-dried, then I use the smallest amount of the special lotion Cass makes for me on my arms and chest and elbows. It smells like the beach mixed with the gardenia bush in my mother's backyard, and my eyes close at the heavenly scent.

I will pay her so much money to make more for me.

I just have time to pull on a sundress dotted with light pink flowers and a denim jacket, shove my feet into a pair of white canvas tennis shoes, and pull a brush through my hair, before I hear the sound of his truck through my open windows.

Stopping at the mirror, I slide light pink gloss over my lips and check my face. I managed to keep my eyeliner and mascara somewhat intact through my quick shower. Licking my fingertips, I gently scrub away the black flecks under my eyes.

I pause at the cabinet and give Edward a scoop of dog food. "Back later, Ed."

Grabbing my phone, I head out the door. I'm halfway down the stairs when I freeze in place, and my breath stutters. Aiden is on the other side of the glass door looking like a fucking male model in faded jeans and a white tee with an unbuttoned plaid shirt on top.

Opening the door, he steps inside and stops when he sees me on the stairs. For a heartbeat, we're frozen, taking each other in. The familiar heat rises around my neck, and we're in that place again, alone, with the energy building around us, growing in intensity.

We both speak at the same time.

"Sorry, I wasn't quite ready," I start.

"Did I give you enough time?" he asks.

We both exhale a laugh, and for as much time as we've spent together these last few days, I don't know what to say next. My fingers fidget, and I curl them lightly. It feels like he's picking me up for a date, and I'm sure my cheeks are pink.

Finally, he breaks the spell. "Are you ready? Owen's waiting for us."

"Yes!" The mention of Owen helps me remember how to move, and I hurry down the rest of the stairs, meeting him at the door.

He waits for me to reach him. The faint scent of cedar and soap meets my nose, and I glance up, meeting his gray-blue eyes.

The grumpy, bossy man who was all in Bull Jones's face this afternoon appears a bit lost.

"You're really pretty." His voice is quiet, and he lifts his hand to touch my sleeve. "I like this dress."

The air around us thickens, and my breath disappears. I wonder if he'll kiss me again. His gaze drifts to my lips, and I sway a little closer. I want him to kiss me…

He steps back, holding the door. "Owen."

One word is all it takes.

"Right." I force a smile. "Nobody wants a cold burger."

He follows me out, lightly touching my lower back as he holds the truck door for me. We should get to his house where his son is waiting to have his dinner, where I won't be alone in my stairwell beside the Star Parlor, where magical things seem to happen—which neither of us believes in anymore.

Chapter 11

Aiden

"**M**Y FRIEND RYAN'S MOM MAKES THIS FOR HER WORK." OWEN is on his knees at the picnic table turning the pages of the *Eureka Gazette*.

Britt's beside him holding a beer and looking way too pretty for burgers in my backyard. The two of them slowly peruse the thin local paper, as Owen holds Zander and tries to understand this nearly extinct form of mass communication.

"Piper wanted to be a journalist from the time we were in high school." Britt scans the pages containing mostly public notices, police reports, and a few local articles and photos sprinkled throughout.

Speaking of high school, when I saw her on the stairs tonight, I felt like I was going on my first date all over again. My eyes landed on hers, and she looked so fresh and pretty and she smelled so good, I momentarily lost the ability to form sentences.

Of course, it's not a date. I'm not in high school, and I recovered quickly.

"I don't get it." Owen wrinkles his nose. "Who wants to look at this when they can look at stuff on their phone?"

"Local news is actually pretty important to the community." Britt's tone is gentle, like one of Owen's teachers. "It lets you know about events that directly affect you. It keeps you informed about changes in city government, what's happening at the schools, who's getting married, who died… All that creates a bond in the community."

He squints at her like he doesn't believe her. "What does that mean?"

"Well…" She turns a page back. "See this story here about the high school bake sale? It has pictures of the students raising money and the nursing home residents happily receiving the donation. It has quotes from the teenagers and the residents. All that makes the town feel closer to each other. It establishes trust."

"What about this one?" He turns to the front page, where a photo of Britt's truck plowed into the phone pole is above the fold, under the headline "Courthouse Employee Arrives with a Bang."

Her lips twist, and I almost think she's going to laugh. "That one shows how the sheriff is very forgiving when the newest member of his team flies into town with no brakes, almost kills him and Doug, and then hits a phone pole."

"Someone was watching over you," I tease from where I'm taking the reheated burgers off the grill. "Do you want cheese on yours?"

"Yes, please." She hops up, walking to where I'm placing the burgers beside toasted buns on a large platter. "These smell amazing."

"Dad puts a secret ingredient in his burgers that makes you dream about them for weeks!" Owen skips in the middle of us, talking loudly. "Maybe I should tell Ms. Piper about that so she can put it in her paper!"

"Don't sell my secrets to the media!" I scrub the top of his head.

"I could sell it to her?" His eyebrows rise, and Britt shakes her head, carrying the platter to the table.

"Now you've done it. You've created a monster."

"You want another beer?" I open the outdoor refrigerator and grab one for myself.

"I'm good." She returns to her seat beside Owen, who is arranging plates, napkins, and silverware at our three places.

It's a crisp spring night, laced with the occasional singing of a frog from the nearby creek. Citronella lanterns and jar candles are positioned around the perimeter, and yellow lights are hidden in the rafters of the covered deck behind my house, where we're sitting.

Twinkle lights are wrapped around the beams, and the golden glow reflects off her smooth skin, her soft, blonde hair. She's fucking gorgeous.

"You have such a beautiful place here." Britt looks around the backyard as I set a bowl of potato salad and another bowl of chips in the center of the table. "Should I be asking for a raise?"

"Most of this is dividends from the family business." I take a seat across from her, twisting the top off a fresh beer, doing my best to keep my eyes from devouring her. "When Alex decided to expand the distillery, we all chipped in to get him started."

"That's right!" She smiles. "Stone Cold is really doing well now, isn't it?"

"My brother might say it's doing too well. I think he needs to hire more help."

Owen jumps forward, grabbing a big handful of chips. "Did you know zebras communicate nonverbally?"

"Easy on the chips, little man." I motion to his plate. "Eat your hamburger."

"Is that true?" Britt smiles as he wiggles on the bench beside her.

He takes a huge bite of hamburger, nodding. "If they're

happy to see you, their ears go forward." He drops the burger on his plate and demonstrates, cupping his hands on each side of his head. "But if a predator is around, they go flat against their heads."

"Sounds like my grandmother's cat." Britt takes a bite of burger and makes a little noise, covering her mouth with her hand. "Oh my gosh—this is delicious! You have to tell me the secret ingredient!"

"Nope!" Owen shakes his head. "I'm selling it to Ms. Piper!"

That makes me laugh. "My little mercenary. I don't know if it's much of a secret. I chop up some mushrooms, add a little soy sauce and black pepper, and mix it with the ground chuck."

"Soy sauce, of course!" Her eyes widen, and she nods. "It was so familiar, and it makes total sense."

"Do you know why zebras are black and white?" Owen has eaten half his burger and two fists full of chips. "It's to keep them cool in the hot sun because the white stripes reflect the heat. And it camouflages them in the tall grass!"

"I didn't know that." Britt's body is angled to face him, and I study her sweet smile.

Edna's words filter through my brain, and my jaw tightens at the thought of Adam touching her. His lips being where mine have been.

"Did you know zebras only have one toe?"

"One toe?" Britt's nose wrinkles.

"Yep! They walk around all day on their tiptoes!" Now he has Zander dancing on the table.

"Take a breath, Owen, and let Britt eat her dinner."

He twists his lips, making a face at me, but he makes a big show of taking another bite of hamburger. Britt's eyes flicker to mine, and her smile is a shot of dopamine right to my chest.

After a few minutes of chewing, Owen tilts his head to the side. "Dad said it was okay that you taught me a card trick. He said he overreacted." Her eyebrows rise, and she gives me another quick glance. I give her a little wink in response, and her cheeks flush.

Owen continues, undeterred. "I showed it to him when we got home, but I didn't do it right."

His little shoulders slump, and she pats his back. "Your hands are still growing. I'll teach you an easier one next time." Then taking a sip of beer, she smoothly changes the subject. "How did you learn so much about zebras?"

"I read a lot. My teacher, Mrs. Priddy, says readers are leaders."

"I remember Mrs. Priddy!" Britt's eyebrows rise. "Is she still teaching? She's got to be about to retire."

"I think she's getting close." I polish off the last of my burger, watching my son doing his best to impress our dinner guest.

"You're nice, like a teacher." He tilts his head up at her. "Do you like being a lady cop? Do you know how to shoot a gun?"

"I'm actually a forensic photographer, so the only thing I shoot is a camera." Her nose wrinkles with her smile.

"That's right! My dad said you take pictures at crime scenes." His voice drops, and he leans closer. "Do you ever take pictures of dead people?"

"Sometimes," Britt whispers back. "It's my job to be sure no piece of evidence is left undocumented."

Owen's eyes blink wider, and I'm pretty sure he's in love. "I want to do that when I grow up!"

A pretty smile curls her lips. "Maybe you can tag along and help me one day—if it's okay with your dad."

Owen jumps around in his seat, practically shouting. "Can I, Dad? I'll be real quiet, and I won't get in the way or anything!"

"You'll be real quiet?" I lift a finger to my ear, and Britt exhales a soft laugh. "Maybe one day when you don't have school. In the meantime, you need to head up and take a bath, get ready for bed…"

He jumps off the bench, hesitating a moment to hug Britt's shoulder. "I like you! Your job is cool!"

"If you think my job is cool, you should meet my dog." She smiles, hugging his small waist.

"You have a dog?" My son's eyes are wide, and I wince, remembering how many times he's asked for a puppy—that we have no time to care for.

"I do. His name is Edward, and he's part bloodhound, which means he has a super sniffer. I'll bring him to the courthouse one afternoon so you can meet him."

"Okay!" Owen is definitely in love.

"Bath time now." He takes off into the house, and I call after him. "Speaking of sniffing, I'm going to smell you, so you'd better use soap."

He yells a grumpy *okay* on his way up the stairs, and I turn back to see Britt smiling, her green eyes warm. "He reminds me of somebody."

"He's a lot like my brother Adam." *Whom I have no reason to be annoyed with.*

"I was thinking he's a lot like you. He's adorable." She almost seems shy saying it as she stands, collecting her plate and Owen's.

I stand, taking the plates she's holding. "Adorable?"

"For now, but I expect he'll grow out of it like you did."

"Ouch, not sure how to take that." I stack their plates on top of mine and take them into the house, doing my best to keep it light.

She puts the lid on the potato salad and carries it and the bowl of chips behind me. "I just mean, I'm sure you were adorable at his age, whereas now, you're something very different."

"And what's that?" I pause, leaning my hip against the counter.

A naughty glint is in her eyes. "You know what you are. Grumpy, broody, bossy."

"Is that so?"

"You know it is." Her easy flirtation sends blood racing below my belt, and I quickly rinse and put everything in the dishwasher while she packs up the rest of the condiments and puts them in the refrigerator.

"I thought I was being friendly." I'm holding the towel, drying my hands, and my eyes run over her petite frame, hungrily taking in her smooth legs, that short dress.

Her hands are behind her back, and she leans against the bar, sliding her pink tongue over her lip and sending my thoughts so far from friendly.

"As soon as I get my truck back, I'll have you and Owen over to my place for dinner."

At first I'm confused, then I realize. "You can't drive to the store."

"Correct." She leans forward slightly. "Which means I need you to give me a ride back to town."

"Let me get Owen in bed, and I'll see if Vanessa can walk over and sit with him a minute."

"Vanessa?"

"High school girl across the street. She helps me sometimes when Mom can't." I scoop up my phone, sending a quick text and hoping...

I get a quick reply saying she'll be here in ten minutes. "She'll be here in ten. Can I get you something while you wait? I have a bottle of Stone Cold Original." I walk over to the cabinet beside the fireplace.

"The best small-batch bourbon since Blanton's?" She turns, leaning on her elbows on the bar.

"You heard about that?"

"My best friend runs the town paper. I know all kinds of things about Eureka."

"I bet you do." Setting two tumblers on the bar, I pour us each a finger. "I'll tell you the secret about this guy. It's my grandfather's original recipe. Alex found it in a folder in the back of his desk."

She lifts the glass of amber liquid, tilting it side to side. "That's really special, like a family heirloom. You know there's a black market for this stuff?"

"Alex can't make enough to keep it on the shelves." I clink my glass against hers and take a small sip just as my son starts yelling he's done.

Placing the glass on the bar, I take a beat to watch her sip. Her eyebrows rise, and she nods. "I don't know a lot about bourbon, but this is nice. Smokey."

Our eyes meet, and the room seems smaller, the air closer. Watching her tonight talking to Owen, telling him about her job and listening to all his zebra facts, she seemed happy and entertained, not bored or impatient.

She's light and fun, and Edna's words about her being friends with Adam are in my head. They can be friends, but I'd prefer something a little different.

I'd prefer to think of lifting her onto that bar, stepping between her legs, and sliding my hands higher under her skirt...

"DAD!" Owen yells, and my eyebrows rise.

Britt snorts a laugh, and I'm hooked a little more. "Be right back."

Owen holds out both his arms for me to sniff for soap, but I skip the fake-out, sniffing the top of his shoulder instead. It smells fresh enough, and I give him the okay to exit the tub and dry off. When he's finally in his PJs with his hair towel-dried, I tuck him in the bed and sit beside him reading his favorite *National Geographic* book about zebras.

"Zebras live in small family groups in the African savannah, where they keep each other safe." A soft creak in the floorboards makes me look up to see Britt standing in the doorway with her arms crossed, a curious smile on her full lips. "Family groups usually consist of one male and several females and their babies."

"Several females?" Owen's voice is less loud, which tells me he's getting tired. "Why do they do that?"

"To have lots of baby zebras." Glancing down at my son,

Zander is tucked under his arm, and his eyes are fixed on the photographs of the stunning, striped creatures.

I finish a few pages and lean forward to kiss the top of his head. "I've got to run Britt home. Vanessa will be downstairs, and I'll be right back. Go to sleep."

"Okay." He curls deeper into his blankets while he holds the book, turning back to his favorite pictures. "Night, Miss Britt!"

"Goodnight, Owen," she whispers.

Our bodies are close when I stand, and I look down, not wanting to move away from her warmth, her captivating presence.

A little smile curls her lips, and she blinks up at me. "Time to go?"

No…

"Yeah." I place my hand on her shoulder, giving it a little squeeze before leading her down the stairs.

Chapter 12

Britt

GRUMPY AIDEN STONE SCRUNCHED INTO HIS SON'S SMALL BED reading about zebras is possibly the hottest thing I've ever seen. My stomach filled with warmth as I stood in the doorway, watching them.

I wanted to step forward and trace my fingers through the side of his hair like I did the night he kissed me. This entire evening, I've had to stop myself from touching him as if his skin beneath my fingertips is a drug, and I can't get enough. He's the dream I was never allowed to have… until I was.

Now we're almost at my little apartment in town, and I wonder what he'll do. Will he let me out at the curb or risk entering that stairwell with me again?

Our kiss was pretty incredible, but the crack in his voice as he whispered *I want to be inside you* are the words I live for. I imagine his hands gripping the back of my thighs, his rough touch gliding higher against my smooth skin, sliding between my legs, ripping my thong aside.

I blink away the erotic images, doing my best to calm my

hormones. "You're really great with Owen. He's a lucky little boy."

"He's a good kid." He glances at me, and his eyes seem to catch on my lips before returning to the road. "I wanted to mention, Founder's Day is next weekend. The big festival?"

That's a switch. "Yeah, I'll be on duty that day. Do you expect it to be crazy?"

"Not at all." He shakes his head. "The most that ever happens is somebody has too much Founder's Day punch, and their family or friends have to take them home."

That makes me laugh. "I wound up skinny dipping with a bunch of friends after drinking too much of it in high school. I'm pretty sure your brother was with us."

His brow lowers, and he clears his throat. "I think you should take the afternoon off and go to the festival with me." My eyebrows rise, and he quickly adds, "Doug and Holly will be there, and I think it's good for us to engage with the community as a team."

"I agree." We're at my building, and he puts the truck in park, killing the engine before hopping out and walking around to open my door.

Anticipation mixes with the nerves churning in my stomach. He takes my hand, and I thank him quietly as I step out of the cab. My hand is still in his, and he doesn't let go as we cross the short sidewalk.

We stop at the door. He doesn't open it, and the streetlight at the corner casts long shadows across his face. I look up, and I can't tell what he's thinking or what he might do. Still, I can feel the tension in his grip on my fingers.

My heart beats faster, and I slide my hand out of his. "Thanks again for dinner and for the ride home."

Opening the door, I enter the stairwell, and my stomach flutters when he enters behind me. The yellow light above my door is on, but before I can climb the stairs, he catches my arm, turning me to face him.

My lips part, but I'm not sure what to say. My eyes trace his, memorizing the fine lines at the corners, more noticeable right now as he frowns down at me like he's fighting some internal battle.

"I don't want you to date Adam." His voice is rough.

My brow furrows. "I never wanted to date Adam." He takes a step closer, pressing my back to the wall, and I take a chance. "I only ever wanted…"

But even with a shot of bourbon in me, I'm not sure I can say out loud that I've always wanted him. It's too much of a risk. He has too many reasons to say no and walk away, leaving my broken heart bleeding on the ground.

"What do you want?" He lifts a hand, tracing his thumb along the line of my jaw.

I swallow the knot in my throat. My heart beats so fast it hurts, and I lift my hand, placing it on his stomach, curling my fingers in the thin cotton of his white tee.

"Something I can't have." I want to pull the shirt higher, slide my fingers along his warm skin I crave.

His face lowers, and his nose follows the line of my hair beside my temple, inhaling softly. My eyes close as chills skate down my arms.

"Why can't you have it?" His voice is raspy.

My eyes are closed as fire pulses in my veins. "He doesn't know I exist."

Lifting my chin in his thumb and forefinger, he whispers, "Look at me." Carefully obeying his command, my body goes liquid when our eyes meet. "He knows."

His mouth seals to mine, and a whimper aches from my throat. I grip his shirt in my fingers to keep from sliding to the floor.

Our mouths open, and at the first touch of his tongue, my orgasm flares to life in my core. He cups my jaw in one hand, tilting my head so he can kiss me deeper. The other slides down my back, covering my ass before lifting my leg to his waist.

"Oh," I gasp, and his lips move to my ear.

"We shouldn't do this." He groans as his fingers trace higher to the line of my panties.

"I know." I pull his shirt higher, desperate for his skin.

"Fuck, Britt." His mouth is on mine again, and I'm off my feet, my back against the wall as my legs wrap around his waist.

The dress I'm wearing gives him full access to my body, and he takes it, sliding his hands to my ass, curling his fingers on my bare cheeks as he groans against my neck. Only a scrap of lace and faded denim stands in the way of our complete union.

"I want you so much." He pulls my lips with his, and my entire body is on fire. "I can't think of you with him."

I'm so confused. "With who?"

"Anyone." It's a possessive groan, and his mouth is on mine again as his hands move higher, lifting my dress on a path to my breasts.

Shoving my bra up, his hands cover them, lifting and kneading, teasing my taut nipples. I exhale a moan, dropping my head to the wall. We're desperate and wild, and I swear, if he doesn't fuck me right now…

"God, you feel so good." He's tugging at my dress, and as quickly as possible, I undo the tiny buttons on the front.

It bursts open, and his mouth immediately covers a hardened nipple. "Oh, God…" I gasp, plunging my fingers into his hair.

My hips rock against his pelvis, creating friction directly against my clit. He steps back, lowering me to my feet. Sweeping his hungry eyes over my body. I'm breathing fast, and he lowers to one knee, pressing his face into my dress against my belly.

"I want to taste you."

Heat races through me, and I nod. "Yes."

Lifting my dress, he places hungry kisses to the tops of my shivering thighs. His beard scratches my skin, and my head drops back with another groan. My fingers are in his hair, and I don't think I can stay on my feet.

I'm on fire, a column of molten need, and his mouth moves higher, his beard scuffing my hypersensitive inner thighs. My stomach twists. It's irresistible and incredible, and with the first swipe of his tongue over my clit, my entire body jerks.

"Oh, God…" I moan as his tongue moves faster, sliding up and around, over and over my clit.

I can't breathe. He grips my leg, placing it over his shoulder, and I'm out of my body, rising higher, faster, until I can't take any more. A loud moan escapes my throat as the orgasm explodes through my core, shimmering up my spine to the top of my scalp.

He gives me a few more passes, and I squeal, holding his head and moving him away from the overload of sensation. I feel his smile as he presses a kiss to my lower stomach then another to my hip as he rises slowly to his feet.

Gorgeous eyes devour me, and he threads his fingers in the side of my hair. "I'm not leaving this time."

Orgasm swirls through my bloodstream, and I reach for the button of his jeans. "I don't want you to leave."

He digs in his back pocket, removing his wallet. "It's a bad idea."

"The worst." I press my nose against the thin cotton of his shirt, inhaling his luscious scent as I push his jeans lower on his hips.

"So many reasons we shouldn't." A tear of foil meets my ears, and I'm so relieved he has a condom.

"So many." I turn to face the wall, ripping my wet thong down my legs.

"Fuck, Britt." He leans forward, and I feel his erection, long and heavy against my ass. "You're fucking perfect."

One large hand slides inside the front of my dress, squeezing and caressing my breast. The other fumbles between my legs, to my drenched core. I can't believe this is happening. My eyes squeeze shut, and in one powerful thrust, he's inside me.

"Oh, fuck," I gasp as he groans the same deeply beside my ear.

He starts to move, and my mind blanks. I'm rising on my toes with every gentle thrust, with every murmured swear as he takes his time, allowing my body to stretch to his size. I've never been so full. I've never been so on edge, my entire body electric.

He picks up speed, going deeper, and my orgasm simmers in my veins. His hand swiftly massages my clit, and I exhale a sharp whimper.

His lips press behind my ear. "You like that?"

Another fast thrust, and I'm on my tiptoes.

"Yes," I gasp, bending my knees to open my legs wider.

A harder thrust, and he's fucking me off my feet.

His hot voice is in my ear. "You're so wet for me. Do you want to come again?"

"Yes…" I'm begging for it now.

I just came in the most spectacular way, but his persistent strokes, his fat cock, his firm thrusts and dirty words have me at the breaking point.

"Say it." It's a low order.

"Make me come again."

"Say *please*."

"Please," I gasp, my fingers curling against the wall.

He groans, picking up speed, his fingers never leaving my clit. Little explosions of pleasure flood my core with every thrust, and my thighs are slick. The orgasm twists tighter, lifting me higher, so high, until I break again, with even more intensity than before.

My back arches, and my jaw drops as a feral sound leaves my body. The muscles in my legs shake violently, and he holds me, giving me two more hard thrusts before coming, pulsing deep with a series of punctuated groans and swears.

Our bodies are flush, and I can feel him tremble. I can feel his heart beating as hard as mine against my back. I'm completely wrapped in his strong arms, unable to move if I wanted.

I don't want to move. I never want to move again. I wonder if it's possible to stay this way, wrapped in the cocoon of his body forever. I'm pretty sure I've died and gone to heaven, or if this isn't heaven, it ought to be.

His arms relax, and he reaches down to dispose of the condom in the silver trash can beside the door. My breath slowly returns to normal, but he pulls me to his chest, wrapping his arms around me.

I'm surrounded by his scent and his strength, and when he speaks, he presses his lips to the top of my head. "I'd like to stay with you tonight, but I have to get home to Owen."

"I know." My hands are bent between our bodies, my palms flat against his chest.

Sliding them higher, I place my fingers on the sides of his neck, loving the feel of his strong arms around me as I come down from a place I've never been in my life.

"Come on." He takes my hand, leading me up the stairs to my door.

I'm glad he's holding me, because I'm still not completely sure-footed after that orgasm. *Those* orgasms. He waits while I unlock my door, and when I turn to him again, I don't want to let him go.

"Would you like to come inside?"

He's so tall, looking down at me. "Yes." He lifts his finger to trace my long bangs behind my ear. "But I have to get home. Vanessa has already stayed later than I said."

"Tomorrow's my day off. I was going to run some errands,

try talking to my mom again…" I'm not sure why I'm telling him my agenda, other than I don't want him to leave.

I hate that I won't see him all day.

"I'll be across the street if you need anything." He takes a step back, lifting my hand and kissing the top of my knuckles.

"Aiden?" He stops, and nerves squeeze my stomach. "I know what we did was a terrible idea…"

His brow furrows, waiting.

"But I really liked it."

A sly smile quirks his full lips, and he returns to me again. Placing his hand on my cheek, he leans down and slides his lips over mine once more before giving me a kiss, possessive and warm.

I'm completely melted, and he says soft and deep, "Me, too."

Chapter 13

Aiden

SHE'S ONLY BEEN HERE A WEEK, BUT BRITT'S ABSENCE FROM THE office has me restless and bored. The place is too quiet. We're not making enough progress on the case, and I keep lifting my phone to text her.

I don't.

It's her day off. She needs to take care of her own business—buy actual groceries, for Pete's sake, check on her truck, take it easy.

Adding to my restlessness is the fact I had the best night's sleep in years. Driving back to my house, her taste was on my tongue, her moans were in my ears. Closing my eyes as I settled into bed, I relived taking her body. She's petite, but her ass is round and soft. Her breasts are small, but they fill my hands, and her soft moans, her taste… I came so fucking hard with her.

A smile curled my lips, and I fell asleep with a deep sense of satisfaction in my stomach.

Today, I have to rationalize the big red line we crossed.

My jaw tightens as I sit in front of my computer, chewing

on a pen. For starters, I'm practically her boss. She's here on contract, so it's not as bad as if I were her actual superior, in charge of her promotions and raises. We're in a sort of gray zone, but it would be frowned upon if people knew.

If Edna found out…

Although, after our conversation in her office, I'm not sure what she'd say. I've found a tentative peace with Edna, so it's possible she wouldn't do anything crazy. Gwen on the other hand, would pitch a fit. I don't know what that would mean to Britt.

Our families don't have the greatest history, but Britt isn't like any of them. My thoughts drift to my grandmother's family versus my grandfather's. The bad blood between them went all the way back to Prohibition, but they were able to overcome it.

Which brings me to Owen.

I haven't wanted to date anyone while he's so young… That's not true. After the Annemarie shitshow, the last thing on my mind was letting another woman anywhere near me. Until this smart, sassy little lady waltzed in and turned my head. Exhaling a groan, I stand, rubbing my hand over the tightness in the back of my neck.

Owen's already in love with her, and I don't want him to be hurt if this turns out to be a short-lived, lust-fueled fling—which I'm not convinced it isn't. All this satisfaction could simply be getting laid for the first time in years.

I need to get out of my head. I exit my office to enter the main room, where Doug is leaning against the wall beside Holly's desk. Her headset is around her neck, and the two of them are discussing the festival next weekend.

"Hey, Sheriff!" Holly jumps up, attempting to disentangle her spiral curls from her device. "I might have something for you on the case!"

My ears perk up, and I walk over to where the two of them are standing. "Whatcha got?"

"Well…" She gives up on her headset and stands in place. "I was talking to my dad last night, and he told me about a clinic near Kiawah that worked specifically with Vietnam vets back in the day. He said it's closed now, but you might try poking around and see what comes up."

"Did he have a name or an address?" I've got my phone out, and it feels like the best lead we've had since Britt turned up all her clues.

"He said it was something easy like The Kiawah Clinic. He couldn't exactly remember, but he said it was by the discount casket place."

I can't help a grimace. "Discount caskets?"

"I know." She laughs. "It might not be in the best part of town. He said it was on a street with a funny name, like Manlove Street or Sangster Street."

"I've heard of Manlove Street." Doug perks up. "I don't know about discount caskets, but it's near the tracks. That's way before you get into Kiawah."

I look at the clock. It's about an hour and a half drive to Kiawah, but I'm not sure where I'm going or who I'm trying to find.

"I found it!" Doug calls out from his desk. "Kiawah Veteran's Care. Run by Dr. Sy Needleman."

I'm tapping on my phone as his fingers click on the keys. "He's dead," we both say at the same time, and my shoulders fall. "What now?"

An idea filters through my mind. We might not be able to access his records—not that we ever could without a search warrant, and we don't have enough evidence to get one. "If he is a veteran, we could possibly find him by his location and his injury. He would've received a purple heart if it was service related."

"On it!" Doug's fingers fly over the keys, and he accesses the government databases. "Shew, this is going to take a minute."

I look at his screen, filled with line after line of names. A dark realization passes over us all. A lot of young men died or were seriously injured in that war so long ago. It tore our nation apart and changed a lot of people's attitudes towards the military.

Thankfully, a lot of that bad blood had gone away when it came my time to serve. I was proud to be a Marine. Now I'm proud to be in law enforcement, even if we're struggling with a similar climate of suspicion.

I pick up my phone, sliding my finger over the screen. "Just see what you can find, Doug. I'm going to grab some lunch, but I'll be back."

I know it's her day off—and all the other things that kept me from texting earlier… Still, she'd want to know about this, and I want to see her face.

You awake? I tap out quickly.

Gray dots float and disappear, then they reappear and disappear. My chest tightens with every near-response, until finally, she answers, *Yes!*

I exhale a short laugh. *Took a long time for one word.*

This time I get a little more. *I'm trying to do better with not over-sharing.*

I don't like the sound of that. *You can over share with me.*

Again, the gray dots float and disappear, before, *What's up?*

So many responses float through my mind: *I want to see you; I can't stop thinking about last night; Maybe it's a terrible idea, but how bad can it be?*

Instead, I keep it neutral. *Need a ride to get groceries? I'll pick you up.*

Her reply is equally safe. *Sure, meet you out front.*

When I get to the Star Parlor, she's standing on the sidewalk looking adorable in another thin dress with some kind of blue design on it and a blue cardigan on top. I put the truck in park and hop out to let her in, but she's already got the door open.

"Hang on." I catch her arm, and standing on the step-side puts her face even with mine.

Heat flashes between us. Her body is so close; her lips are right there. Our eyes meet, and my impulse is to pull her to me and kiss her.

Instead, I take a half-step back. "I was going to help you."

"I didn't think…" She glances towards the building. "We're just getting groceries."

"Right." My hand is on the door, and once she's inside, I close it.

Get a grip, Aiden. I jog around to my side and get in, pulling away from the curb.

"That's not really a parking spot." She looks up at me almost as if she feels guilty. "I wasn't going to make you wait in the middle of the day."

"It's okay." I give her a little smile, and her eyes drop to her lap.

Her cheeks are a pretty pink color when I glance at her again, and she clasps her fingers together, which I know means she's flustered.

Reaching across, I put my hand on hers. She stills a moment before relaxing and turning her palm to mine. She places the other hand on top, and the tension in her body seems to ease. It triggers an unexpected urge to protect her.

I give her hand a squeeze and return mine to the steering wheel. "What did you do this morning that you didn't want to overshare?"

She exhales a little laugh. "Not much. Took Edward for a walk down to Bud's garage. He said my truck should be ready tomorrow afternoon. The dry weather helped with the paint job. I just don't know where I'll put it. I'll probably have to keep it at my mother's place, which still puts me out of a vehicle. Maybe I can borrow her bike, but that's just going to give her more ammo to try and make me move home, which I do not want to do."

"I see." My eyebrows rise, and she exhales a little sound, putting her hands on her cheeks.

"See what I mean? Too much information, Britt!"

"It's okay," I chuckle. "That's a lot to think about on your day off. You're supposed to be relaxing."

"I never get to do that." She looks out the window. "Something's always falling apart or on fire or disappearing."

"Not on your day off." I give her a glance before turning in at the grocery store. "We're getting groceries, and I'll help with your truck situation. I think my mom has a bike you can borrow."

Britt's eyes light. "She does? She wouldn't mind lending it to me?"

"I don't think she's ridden it in years. We might have to check the tires and make sure the chain is greased."

"I can do all of that!"

"I'll help you." My hand is on the door handle, and I touch her arm. "Don't move."

Walking around, I open her door, and her lips press into a smile. I reach up and help her out of the cab, and she says a quiet thank-you as her feet touch the ground. My hands are on her waist, and I really want to kiss her now.

"Hiya, Sheriff!" A cheerful voice breaks the moment. "I thought you were getting some lunch?" Holly pauses, carrying a box of Krispy Kreme donuts.

"Britt still doesn't have her truck, so I offered to give her a ride to the store."

"That's so nice. Hi, Britt!" She waves. "Had to get some donuts for the little man. Is Owen coming by after school today?"

"I expect he'll walk over."

"See you back at the office." She waves, continuing on to her car.

Britt crosses her arms over her stomach as we walk, and we're quiet, almost like we got caught doing something wrong.

"They're everywhere," she whispers, and I start to laugh.

"We're just getting groceries," I repeat her words back to her as I grab a cart and head into the produce section.

I hang back beside the buggy as she picks through the apples, grabs a couple of oranges, and a banana. "I always buy too much fruit, and I never eat it."

"Don't forget your buns." I hold a package of specialty bread at the level of her butt.

"Stop it." She swats it away, with a little laugh. "Hmm, how about this for size?"

She holds up a large zucchini and cuts her eyes from it to my crotch.

"I'm not threatened."

"You shouldn't be." A little arch of her eyebrow makes my dick twitch.

"We'd better get moving. I only have an hour."

She puts a bag of lettuce in the front, leaning closer to my ear. "But you're the boss."

Her breast lightly glides over my arm, and my grip tightens on the handle. "I think you have enough for now."

"I need soft drinks!" She skips over to grab a box of ginger ale.

I'm already in line to check out. "You can get the rest at the grocery in town."

"I did get eggs and coffee yesterday." Her lips twist as she inspects the items on the belt. "I've got frozen pizza. I don't drink milk…"

"No milk?"

"Lactose intolerant."

My brow lifts, and she places her phone on the keypad. We carry the bags out and return the cart to the bin. Inside the truck, I'm making good time back to her place.

I park on the curb, giving her a nod. "It'll be okay while we unload."

I'm ready to get inside and get under that dress. I've been a breath away from a hard-on ever since her sexy flirting at the grocery store.

Following her up the stairs, bags of groceries in hand, I watch the hem of her skirt dancing along the backs of her thighs, the sway of her ass beneath the fabric. I'm enough below her that I can almost see the place her legs come together, and the heat in my blood rises.

She unlocks the door, and I'm right behind her, pushing into the room and catching her around the waist. The door slams shut, and she turns in my arms, dropping the groceries on the floor and reaching for my face as our mouths crash together.

A little moan comes from her throat to my mouth as I lift her onto the counter in the middle of her kitchen. Her sweater is off, and she's peeling the dress off her shoulders while I unbutton the top three buttons of my uniform shirt and pull it over my head.

"Oh, God," she gasps, pulling my undershirt higher and pressing her lips to the top of my pecs. "So gorgeous."

My dick is an iron rod, and I need it inside her now. *Condom.* I dig in my front pocket for the extra rubber I shoved in there this morning. I figured it was good to be prepared for what I'd been dreaming about all night.

The top of her dress is at her waist, and I reach around to unfasten her bra. It falls to the floor, and I finally get my first look at her body in the light of day.

"You're so beautiful." I cup her small breasts in my hand, sliding my thumbs over her hardened nipples before leaning down to pull one between my lips, teasing it with my teeth.

"Oh!" She exhales a little noise, and her thighs tighten on my hips.

She tugs on my undershirt, and I pause to whip it over my head.

"To the bed," she gasps, and I eagerly comply, lifting her off the counter and carrying her with her legs around my waist to her queen-sized bed in the corner.

I drop her onto her back and quickly unfasten my pants. My blood is so hot, my fingers fumble with the zipper.

She sits up, covering my hands with hers to help, and with a swift yank, my pants are around my hips. Before I can think, she licks her hand and grips my shaft, squeezing and sliding up and down.

"Fuck…" It feels so good, too good, until she guides the tip into her hot little mouth. "Britt…"

It's a hoarse groan, and my fingers are in her hair as she licks and slides her lips down the side of my cock. *Fuck me.* I lean back to watch, but I'm too close. I'm going to come all over her pretty face if I don't get that fucking condom on.

"Lean back." I rip the foil, quickly holding the end and rolling it down.

She leans back, and I place my fingers on her clit, massaging while I lean on my elbow, tracing my tongue around her nipple. Her back arches, and she places her hands on my shoulders, rolling us so I'm on my back with her straddling my waist.

Reaching between us, she grasps my cock, and in one swift movement, she glides me fully into her before grinding fast and hard.

"Britt," I groan.

She's a fucking goddess, holding my neck and rocking her hips as her inner core pulls my dick faster and tighter. Her breasts bounce, and long waves dance over her shoulders. I'm so close to coming. I squeeze my eyes shut and grip her plump ass, grinding her harder against my waist, doing my best to get her off.

"Oh, fuck," she gasps. "Fuck me harder."

Jesus, I'm going blind. I've never been so desperate and wild. She scrambles off me and onto all fours, and I'm on my knees. I ram my dick inside her again and reach around to massage her clit as I fuck her mercilessly from behind.

She moans loudly, and her pussy tightens around my cock. I can't take anymore, and my orgasm breaks free, pulsing and filling the condom.

My stomach squeezes, and I grit out, "Fuck, your juicy little cunt…"

Her body jerks, and she breaks and shudders, spasming around my dick as I finish coming, as I hold her to me.

We collapse forward on the bed, gasping and sweaty. I'm on my side, and I hold her back to my chest, sliding my hands from her waist to her soft breasts, massaging them gently as I slowly return to Earth.

Her hands cover mine on her tits, and she arches her back, sliding higher to kiss my mouth. My tongue meets hers briefly before I have to take a break to dispose of the condom.

"Hang on." I hop off the bed and step into her small bathroom to toss it in the trash and clean up quickly.

When I return to the room, she's lying on her stomach with her chin in her hand, smiling as her eyes drift from my face down my chest to my dick.

"You look at me like that, and I want to fuck you again."

Her nose wrinkles, and she exhales a laugh. "I like your dirty mouth."

"I like your mouth." Leaning forward, I brace my hands on the bed before kissing her slowly, pulling her lips with mine and running my tongue across the length of hers. "I've got to get back to work."

"Boo." She pokes her lips out in an adorable pout.

"I swear, girl, the things I would do to you."

Her eyes light, and she sits up on her feet. "Tell me."

"Jesus." I'm stepping into my pants, gazing at her naked in that bed, and I'm about ready to say *fuck it.*

The town will survive an afternoon without me.

I pick up my undershirt, but she's off the bed, running to where I stand and taking it from my hands, quickly dropping it over her head. "I'm keeping this."

It falls past her waist, but her taut nipples are visible through the thin fabric. It makes me wonder if everything she does is unbelievably sexy or if I'm completely whipped.

"If I didn't have to check in with Doug…" I catch her around the waist, pulling her body to mine. "I wouldn't."

I lean down as she rises onto her tiptoes, holding my shoulders. Our mouths meet halfway, and when our lips part, when our tongues collide, an explosion of heat filters through my chest. My arms tighten around her, and I inhale the scent at the side of her hair, fresh flowers and ocean air.

"Mm," she hums. "What are you doing with Doug?"

Stepping back, I pull my uniform shirt over my head, buttoning the three buttons and shoving the tail into my pants. "Holly's dad gave us a pretty good lead on a doctor in Kiawah. Doug's trying to see if he can connect any of his patients with our suspect."

Britt's back straightens, and she blinks towards her door. "Kiawah?"

"Yeah." I step into my boots and follow as she walks to the door to collect the discarded groceries. "I'll let you know if it pans out."

She puts the bags on the counter and her expression is focused as she takes out the produce and bread, soft drinks and other items we picked up on our short trip.

"Nothing's ruined, is it?" I look in the bag in front of me. "None of this is perishable."

Shaking her head, she gives me a tentative smile. "It's all good."

"Owen and I can help you with your truck tomorrow. Sound good?"

She nods, and I catch her around the waist before going to the door. "Sleeping together is still a bad idea." Leaning down, I kiss her mouth, pulling her lips with mine. "But I'm liking it more and more."

Her green eyes soften, and she stretches higher to kiss me back, tracing her fingers through the scruff on my cheeks. "Me too."

Chapter 14

Britt

"**A**RE YOU SITTING DOWN?" I ENTER THE STAR PARLOR AFTER taking a minute to clean up after my afternoon delight with Aiden.

"You're beaming." Mom levels her eyes on me. "You had sex."

"I did not!" I'm a trash liar. My cheeks go hot as a firecracker, and my eyes blink too fast, not to mention my fidgety fingers.

"You're almost thirty, Birgitte. You don't have to lie to me." She lifts her chin. "At least it looks like it was good sex. Who with?"

"That's not your business." I can't believe she knows this.

She steps closer, and my back is to the door. "You're sleeping with Aiden Stone."

My eyes widen, and even if I don't believe it, the woman's psychic interrogation skills are intense. It's how she makes her money, after all.

Sliding my hand around my back, I'm about to open the door when she places her palm flat against the wooden frame, holding it shut. Her face is close to mine, hazel eyes boring into my soul.

"I'm not talking to you about my sex life!" I shut my eyes, doing my best to push against her invasion.

"Fine." Her tone is miffed, and she steps away, lowering her hand. "You don't have to share your life with your mother. I'm only the one person in the world you can always trust."

Anger flashes in my chest, replacing my embarrassment. "Is that some kind of joke? When have you ever shared anything with me? I chased you all over the spiritual world trying to be close to you until I finally gave up, and now you want me to trust you?"

"I have always been right here for you. You're the one who left the fold, went to that college and learned to be a detective."

"I'm not a detective." Pausing, I take a breath, *exhale…* "I didn't come here to argue with you, Mom. I need you to talk to me about what's going on in town."

Her brow furrows, and she walks over to her small tarot-reading table. "What else is going on in town besides you having an affair with your boss?"

"Gran is actually more of my boss than Aiden, and it's not an affair. He's single, I'm single. We're just…" I'm not going there with her. "We got a lead on the man I was telling you about. The one with the prosthetic leg? It seems he might be living somewhere in or around Kiawah."

"Is that so?" Her voice rises, and she scoops the gold cards off the table and begins to shuffle.

It's the first time I realize where I get my fidgeting hands. She hides it by shuffling the deck. I hide it by twisting my fingers together. Strangely, seeing her thrown off balance softens my feelings towards her.

"I came down here looking for you the other day, and Cass said you were running an errand near Kiawah." Her shoulders stiffen, and I continue. "When I was here the last time, you wanted to consult the cards about the case. Did you learn anything?"

It's a tentative question. I don't really think the cards tell her anything. I think they're a front she hides behind. At the same time, I have no idea what her connection might be to our suspect or his behaviors. Mom adores Terra's pickles, and I happen to know she's afraid of chickens.

"Are you really coming in here, trying to pretend like you're on my side after you've forsaken the supernatural and started sleeping with the enemy? Do you even remember how hard his father fought to keep your grandmother from becoming mayor?"

"That was years ago. Andrew Stone is dead, and Aiden seems to have made peace with Gran."

"A leopard doesn't change his spots. The Stones are not your friends."

She sounds just like Bull Jones, and an angry comeback is right on my lips.

Instead, I take a breath and bring down the heat. "We're all on the same side, Mom. We all want to keep Eureka safe. It's the reason you said Gran wanted me to come back, to help Aiden solve this case."

I want to tell her Aiden's not her enemy, but she's right. Our families have fought for years, and I'm pretty sure Aiden doesn't trust her any more than she trusts him. Which doesn't bode well for our budding... *relationship?*

My chest tightens, and it's probably best not to name it. Not yet. Not when it's still so new and fragile.

"Your grandmother would do anything to get you back to Eureka for good." She places the cards on the table. "She'd probably even look the other way if she knew what you were doing with him."

She's trying to distract me, but I won't let her. "You'd tell me if you knew something, wouldn't you? You care as much about Eureka as we all do, right?"

"I care about my family more than anything."

Reaching out, I take her hand in mine. "Why did you go to Kiawah?"

Sliding her hand out of mine, she takes a seat at the card table, placing three cards face down in front of her. I know this spread well, but I don't know which direction she's going with it.

"I went to Kiawah to visit an old friend." She turns up the first card. "The Tower."

My throat tightens when I see it. It's the card meaning danger, disruption, or chaos. "This reading is not for me."

"No, I'm looking at the situation, the action, and the outcome. The Tower tells us the situation is dangerous and chaotic, which can have many reasons." Her brow relaxes, and I know she's leaning into the intention of what's to come.

I've read the cards hundreds of times when I worked with her. I'm skilled at guiding their meanings to suit whatever the seeker desires, but my mom is too good. Even when I try to resist it, something in me wants to believe her interpretations. I've seen them come true, and as much as I don't want to be here listening, it's the only way I'll get her to talk to me.

She turns over the second card, and her brow arches. "The Ten of Swords."

I say the meaning with her, "Betrayal."

My mother doesn't move as she turns the last card. "The Knight of Swords."

It's the second time I've seen this card on her table since I've been home, and my scalp prickles. When I saw it in the upright position, it meant a change was coming, but like this, inverted…

My voice is quiet. "Death?"

She immediately scoops the cards together and puts them back in the deck and starts to shuffle. Her fingers tremble, and my heart beats faster. Chaos, betrayal, and death? The mantra on repeat in my mind is *I don't believe… I don't believe…* But the truth is maybe I do just a little.

"Before your father died, he was plagued by dreams." Her eyes are on the gold cards moving quickly through her ringed fingers. "He was never a spiritualist, but he had premonitions. He even canceled one of his shows following a very bad dream. The second time, it was too late, too many tickets had been sold, so he talked himself out of the warning his unconscious mind was trying to send him."

A desert is in my mouth, but I manage to ask. "What did he dream?"

"It was always the same." She lifts her eyes to mine. "He dreamed of drowning."

My breath stills, and I take a step away. "That reading wasn't for me."

"I told you it wasn't." She looks down, and I exhale. "You want to turn your back on magic, but it's in you, Birgitte. You know this reading means something terrible is coming... for someone."

I cross my arms over my stomach, turning away from her table and her superstitions. Her mind games and manifestations. It only works if you accept it, if you believe it, if you allow it to happen. *I don't believe.*

Focusing my mind on the facts, I clench my jaw. "There is no magic. It's all tricks and sleight of hand and reading facial expressions and body language. Penn and Teller make good money explaining how it all works. They even make it funny."

"What happened to your father wasn't a trick, and it definitely wasn't funny. He was murdered."

"Who's in Kiawah?" I cross back to her, placing my hand on her table.

"A bunch of rich assholes."

I exhale a soft growl. "Who's *near* Kiawah?"

"I'm handling it." She stands, fixing her eyes on mine. "Don't speak of this to Aiden."

"I'm definitely speaking of this to Aiden. I have to do my job."

"You can do your job, but give me time first. I'm closer than I've ever been to finding your father's killer."

"Mom…" I groan, dropping my chin.

A cramp twists my stomach, and I want to tell her it's time to move on, to let Dad go. But as much as I want to, I'm not sure I can say the words out loud myself. I'm not sure if I can let Dad go, even if I know we have to. I still have nightmares.

Grasping my hands in hers, my mother's expression turns desperate. "Don't choose Aiden over your father. I'll give you what you want. I promise. But I have one more chance to prove what happened. The spirits are finally moving. Give me a little more time—for him."

All the conversations I've had with Aiden flood my mind. I'm not like my family. I don't believe in magic or spiritual revelations. I believe in the law and the truth we can see and touch with our hands.

This feels like a betrayal. "How long?"

"A week?"

Inhaling slowly, I don't like this at all. "One week, then I'm going to Aiden—and Gran."

She pulls me into a hug, and I'm surrounded by the scent of ginger and patchouli. "Thank you, Birgitte. You're making the right decision."

I'm not so sure about that.

Pulling away, I need to get out of here. I need to breathe fresh air and clear my head of her incense and obsessions and superstitions.

"I've got to pick up my truck from Bud's. Would it be okay if I park it at your house for the time being? There's not really a good place for it here."

"Of course." She smiles as she slides my long bangs behind my ears. "Maybe one day you'll stay for supper?"

"Maybe."

Her smiles, and her affectionate caresses trigger all the distrust in me. I love my mother, but I've never known her to act with entirely altruistic motives. Now she's asking me to trust her, and after a lifetime of knowing her, I'm not sure I can.

Chapter 15

Aiden

"**W**ELP, I DIDN'T FIND ANYTHING WRONG WITH THE BRAKE line." Bud holds an old-school clipboard as he goes down the list of what he did to Britt's truck. "Your friend Cassidy said replacing that bumper with scrap wasn't a problem?"

"Whatever Cass said is fine with me." Britt's arms are crossed, and her brow is furrowed.

I can't tell if she's giving Bud the stern treatment so he won't talk down to her or if she's really upset about something. We didn't see each other much today. I was out of the office meeting with state troopers about security at the upcoming Founder's Day event, and when I got back in time to drive her here, she seemed a little less sunny.

"Wait." Stepping forward, I try to lend my support. "You said nothing was wrong with her brake line?"

She turns on me quickly. "I wasn't lying to you. My brakes didn't work when I pressed the pedal."

Whoa, talk about backfires.

"I believe you." Holding up a hand, I look at Bud. "Maybe you need to check it again. I can't have a member of my team driving around in an unsafe vehicle."

"I checked all the lines for leaks, and I added brake fluid." Bud huffs, getting defensive. "When it comes to safety, bad brakes are just the tip of the iceberg with thing. This truck has no airbags, no shoulder restraints—"

"That's enough," Britt interrupts. "If you added brake fluid and checked the line, that's all you can do."

"I've got a cousin with a newer-model Ford he'd probably be willing to sell you cheap?" he offers.

"I appreciate it, but I'm not looking to part with my dad's truck." Her tone is short, and she takes the clipboard to sign the receipt. "Thank you, Bud."

I understand how she feels. I still have items I collected from my dad's personal belongings after he died. Things like his old sheriff's badge, a watch he always wore, a bottle of his favorite cologne.

Still, when she climbs into the cab of that truck after everything Bud just said, my hand shoots out to catch the door before she closes it. "You want me to drive it to your mom's for you?"

Her brow quirks. "I think I remember how to drive my truck."

I don't recognize this tense, protective surge in my gut. "Just don't go too fast. Owen and I'll be right behind you."

Her lips press into a line, and for the first time this afternoon, her demeanor softens. "Are you worried about me, Sheriff?"

Stepping closer, I clasp her arm, pulling her closer. "Yes."

A little smile breaks across her face, and she cuts her pretty eyes up at me. "I'll be careful."

Reluctantly I shut the door and walk back to my own vehicle. Owen's sitting in the second row with Zander galloping all over his lap. "Are we going to Gram's now?"

"Yeah, we just have to follow Britt to her mom's house. She's leaving her truck there."

"How come?"

"There's no place to park it at her apartment." *And that truck's a fucking death trap*, I don't say out loud. "She's going to borrow Gram's bike."

"I like to ride bikes!" He hops onto his knees behind me, his voice growing louder. "Maybe we can all ride bikes together!"

"Sit down and put on your seatbelt. You're spending the night with your grandmother, and Ryan and your cousin Pinky are coming over."

"Yay!" He jumps his zebra in the air. "I'm going to show them my new card trick!"

My eyes are glued to the orange pickup in front of us that's very obediently following all the rules of the road. "That'll be fun."

We finally reach her mother's house, which is close enough to town that she could probably walk. I wait as she pulls her vehicle to the side and tucks the key in the visor.

My brow furrows as I watch her slowly walking back to the truck. She's in simple jeans and a long-sleeved, white tee. Her blonde hair is in a ponytail on her shoulder, and a loose wave hangs just past her eyes on her cheek. I like to push it behind her ears when she's sitting on my lap looking up at me. She's so damn pretty, but she still seems troubled.

"Dad says you're riding Gram's bike!" Owen jumps onto his knees to greet her as soon as she climbs into the cab of my truck. "I have a bike, too! Maybe we can go for a ride one day!"

Her face relaxes into a smile, and she gives his hand a squeeze. "That sounds like fun! I haven't ridden a bike since I was... Heck, I don't even remember how long it's been."

"Do you still remember how?" Concern enters my son's voice. "I can teach you. I just learned last year, so I know all the steps."

"You never forget how to ride a bike." I reach back to touch his shoulder. "Sit down and put your seatbelt back on."

He obeys with a loud huff, but it's short-lived. Mom's house is only a few blocks from Gwen's, and we're there before he can finish doing what I asked. Alex's Tesla is also parked in the drive-way, and as soon as we stop, his four-year-old daughter Penelope bursts through the door to greet us, squealing all the way.

"Bubba!" she cries, jumping up and down at the edge of the sidewalk, waving her chubby arms over her head like a lit-tle pink cheerleader.

"Daaad!" Owen groans. "Make her stop calling me that."

"I'll try, but you still call her Pinky."

"That's because she's pink! Her hair is pink, her skin is pink…"

"I think Bubba is sweet." Britt bites back a grin as she looks from me to my son.

"I'm not her brother!" he growls as he opens the door and roughly climbs out of the truck, going straight to his little cousin. "It's *Owen*, not Bubba."

"Bubby!" Pinky throws her arms around his waist as if she'll try and lift him off his feet. He unhooks her hands and pulls her by one to the house, yelling for his uncle Alex.

"I don't think she cares if he calls her Pinky."

"She thinks Owen hung the moon." I open the door, reach-ing back to grab his overnight bag. "My son, on the other hand, is going through a no-nicknames phase."

Not even Froot Loop.

"It must be fun to have siblings." She climbs out, walking with me slowly to the house, where she waits as I place the bags inside the door.

"It has its moments."

My mother's beach cruiser is parked behind her car. Last night, I drove by and went over everything, polished the seat, oiled the chain, checked the tires. It's in pretty good condition, considering it hasn't been ridden in years.

"It's adorable!" Britt places her hands on the handlebars of the light-blue bike. "It even has a basket!"

"Not much use for running errands without a basket."

"And a bell?" She flicks her finger over the silver bell, and it emits the classic *ring-ring* sound, which makes her laugh. "Are you sure she trusts me with it?"

"I don't think my mom will ever ride this bike again."

"Did something bad happen?"

"Nah, I think she's scared she'll fall off. Doesn't want to break a hip."

"I guess that makes sense." Taking her bag off her shoulder, she places it in the basket. "I should get going. Let you visit with your family."

"Hang on." I catch her hand, pulling her closer to me. "You okay? It seems like something's on your mind."

Her palms are flat against my chest, and my arms are around her waist. "You don't think this is risky? Anyone might walk out and see us."

"I don't care." She's warm against my body, and I lean down to run my nose along the line of her hair. I really want to kiss her, then I really want to fuck her. "I've missed driving you around town, watching you in action, finding the bad guys."

A smile curls her lips, but her eyes remain downcast. "Have you turned up anything on the Kiawah lead?"

"Not yet." I exhale slowly, releasing her. "Without a name or an address, we might not ever. So many people are scattered throughout those marshlands in little nooks and crannies. It's all dead ends and one-way dirt roads, like trying to find a needle in a haystack."

"I hadn't thought of that." She walks over to the bike, and a friendly voice interrupts us.

"Hey, Britt!" My brother Alex walks out to the patio, and her eyes lift. "How you doing, girl? I haven't seen you in ages."

"Alex! Hey!" She steps over to give him a hug. "Last time I saw you was when you left for Pensacola. You're looking sharp."

"This is not my normal dress code." Alex glances down at his brown suit. "I had to meet with some buyers this afternoon, or I'd be in jeans and a Henley."

She dusts his shoulder. "It's very nice."

"Thank you." He does a little head nod. "I heard you've joined the force. Working with this old grump. How's that going?"

I'm ready to push back on the "old grump" description when Britt's light voice stops me.

"He's not that grumpy." She gives me a little wink. "And I'm not really on the force. I'm just helping with this new case."

"She's really good." I lean against my mother's car, crossing my arms. "Britt found our best lead so far."

"I don't know about that." Her cheeks flush, and she twists her fingers.

It makes me want to pull her to me again, cover her hands with mine, and make her feel safe.

My brother laughs. "If he says you're good, you must be a freaking genius. Aiden never gives compliments."

"Thanks for all the support." I swear, this guy.

Britt grins up at us. "Well, I'd better get going. I'm meeting up with the girls tonight for a little sleepover party."

"Tequila shots and tickle fights?" Alex teases, and she laughs, joining right in.

"Followed by jumping on the bed in our underwear."

"Sorry, what was the address again?" He arches an eyebrow.

"I'll never tell." She bats her eyes, and this flirty little exchange is pissing me off.

"Well, you girls have fun. Come by the distillery sometime, and I'll give you a tour." He points to me. "I'll see you in a few minutes?"

"I'll be there."

Alex heads to his car, driving away in the growing twilight, and I walk with Britt and the bike to the road. Again the fucking tightness is in my chest, and the thought of her riding to town alone in the dark has me on edge.

"I could drive you to town." I lightly steady her arm as she climbs on the bike.

"I'll be okay. You need to visit with your family."

"Maybe just shoot me a text when you get there? Drivers don't always watch out for bikes around here, especially not at night."

She lifts her chin, wrinkling her nose adorably. "How did I ever make it to twenty-eight without you?"

"I've been working in law enforcement too long."

Her hand covers mine on the handlebars, briefly giving it a squeeze. "I'll text you. Have fun tonight with your brothers."

"Have fun at your tickle panty party."

Another laugh and she pushes off, riding away in the dark. I stand at the edge of the driveway with my arms crossed, watching her go and wondering how it happened. How did I get to the point where I'm standing here, watching her ride away while mentally restraining myself from driving after her?

It's happening. The thing I don't believe in, the thing I rejected years ago, is sneaking its way into my chest again, and I can't seem to stop it.

Chapter 16

Britt

"**MY SIGNATURE SCENT!**" I THROW MY ARMS AROUND CASS'S shoulders as she enters my small apartment carrying a bag of her homemade lotions. "Thank you, thank you, thank you!"

"It's the least I could do." She pats my arm, placing the bag on the bar beside three shot glasses. "Don't want you to start vabbing."

It's the first time the three of us have been together for a slumber party since I left for Greenville, and I'm so excited... And maybe a little distracted by thoughts of Aiden.

And my mother's ominous tarot reading, which I'm still working to compartmentalize in my brain. I'm not letting her scare me anymore or doubt my judgment. Still, if she knows something that will help me solve this case, I have to tolerate her eccentric behavior for a few days.

"I just barfed a little in my mouth." Piper twists the top off a bottle of tequila and pours each of us a shot.

"Why? What the hell is vabbing?" I call over Shania Twain blasting from my Bluetooth speaker.

Piper puts the bottle on the bar, I take a quick picture of it with our three glasses and send it to Aiden with a text, **Tequila shots starting.**

He was so cute this afternoon. All six-foot-sexy of his grumpy self towering over me, wanting to drive my truck and then asking me to text him when I got home. It's something I've never had in my whole life—someone watching over me, wanting to keep me safe. I've always been on my own in that department, and I like this new situation.

I like Aiden Stone worrying about me.

"You haven't heard of the ickiest TikTok trend?" Cass's eyes widen dramatically, and she takes her shot glass, holding it high in the air. "To the Whoopass Girls, together again!"

We clink and do our shots fast, snatching up lime wedges and sucking the juice as we squeal. Edward sits up and barks at our noise, which makes us laugh.

"You're upsetting the Notorious D.O.G." Piper walks over to scratch his head and calm him down while Cass continues with her explanation.

"Vabbing is when you *dab* your finger in your *vag* then put the juices on your neck like cologne. To attract a man… or a woman, I guess."

I'm halfway to the refrigerator when I stop in my tracks. "That is *not* a thing."

"I don't know how common it is, but that's the definition."

"For starters, it doesn't make any sense." I take out a ginger ale and carry it to where Piper is standing by the bar. "Unless you have an infection or you're on your period, vaginal secretions have no odor."

"Don't be a scientist." Piper bumps my hip as she pours three more shots. "Just be grossed out like the rest of us."

"I mean, it's not that gross. It's your body's fluids. It's not dirty. I imagine the theory is it works like pheromones—"

"Please stop!" Cass closes her eyes, holding up her hand. "I will keep you in Ocean Gardenia for the rest of your life if you promise never to put pussy juice on your neck."

I snort a laugh, sipping my drink. "Is that all it takes to get my signature scent for life? Oh no! Don't look! I'm going for it!" Holding out my finger, I lower it towards my crotch.

Piper slaps my hand away and does another shot. "Again, I barf."

Cass leans over the bar, giving me wide eyes. "Joke all you want, Miss Afternoon Delight. I happen to know you don't need any vabbing to bag a man."

My eyes widen, and Piper slams her shot glass on the bar. "What the fuck? Britt's having sex? You've only been in town a week! Who are you having sex with?"

Heat shoots from my chest to my neck to my face. "I don't know what you're talking about!"

I scamper away from the bright lights of the kitchen to hide beside Edward on the couch.

Cass is hot on my heels, laughing. "Don't even try to deny it, Britt Bailey. You're a shit liar."

"You're making shit up! How do you even know what I'm doing? I've been working all week."

"You were working, all right. *Grinding*." She circles her hips like a hula dancer. "Your mother and I got an earful, and it was possibly the most embarrassing moment of my life." She's instantly serious, heading back to the kitchen. "I need my second shot."

"My mother heard us!" I squeal, jumping off the couch and following her to the kitchen. "I need *my* second shot."

Piper stands watching us both with wide eyes. "I need you at the paper, Cass."

"I might take you up on that." She does her second shot. "Two seconds into the banging and moaning, I made an excuse and got the hell out of the Star Parlor. I haven't decided if I'm ever going back."

Pressing both palms to my flaming cheeks, I walk back to where Edward sits on the couch watching us. "That's how she knew," I say to myself. "And I thought she was getting some kind of psychic message."

"Who is Britt having sex with?" Piper yells.

"Huh?" I turn, and Cass crosses her arms with a sly grin on her lips.

"Do you want to tell her or should I?" Reaching out, she grips Piper's shoulder. "Get ready to have your hair curled."

My eyes widen. "You are the worst! I can't believe you'd listen to what I'm doing up here."

"Excuse me for not being deaf!" Cass cries. "You were having loud sex in the middle of the afternoon with your windows wide open."

Snapping my gaze to the windows, I drop onto the couch in realization. "I didn't even think about the windows."

"Sounded like you had a one-track mind to me." Cass laughs, skipping over to sit beside me. "Don't freak out. I think it's good you're knocking boots with the sheriff. It increases the chances you'll stay!"

"The sheriff!" Piper cries. "You're sleeping with Aiden Stone? How is that even possible? He's completely closed. Not to mention since his wife died, he's a total grouch."

"He didn't sound like a grouch to me." Cass winks. "He sounded hot."

"This is all very cringe." I am literally dying. "Did everyone in town hear us?"

"I'm sure everyone on the sidewalk did." Cass notes, and I wail, dropping my head onto her lap. "If it makes you feel better, it was a relatively quiet afternoon. Well, except for, you know... *You two.*"

Another wail, and Cass laughs, wrapping her arms over my back.

Piper sits on my other side, rubbing my arm. "Be happy

you're getting some. It's been so long since I've had sex, I think my hymen grew back."

"You gave birth." Cass shoves her shoulder. "That hymen ain't ever coming back."

Piper puts her hand over her heart. "I'm just a girl standing in front of a boy asking him to give me an orgasm."

"I'm just a girl looking for a boy who knows how to give me an orgasm." Cass rolls her gray-blue eyes. "Seriously, men settled the West, they were pioneers, they charted new territories, created maps. You'd think they could find the clitorus."

Piper snorts into her beer. "From what I understand, Britt has no idea what you're talking about."

Sitting straighter, I wave my hands in a cutting motion. "Stop. That's so unfair. Yes, we're having great sex, but what about all the other shit just lurking in the background, waiting to come crashing down on my head?"

"Like what?" Piper frowns.

"Like my family? Like his family hating my family. Like my mom being completely impossible with all her premonitions and all her… shit." The secret I'm allowing my mother to keep presses against my temples, but I can't tell them. Not before I've told Aiden. "Like him kind of being my boss?"

Cass throws out her arms. "What would Shania do?"

"She'd say don't try to run!" Piper jumps off the couch. "She'd getcha good!"

We've all had at least two shots of tequila, and we're in total drunk-friend, problem-solving mode. I'm off the couch as well, grabbing my phone and pulling up my favorite song. The Bluetooth speaker in the kitchen starts blasting "I'm Gonna Getcha Good," and we all start dancing as we sing along at the top of our lungs.

Cass has the best voice. Piper and I find the notes with varying degrees of success. We're two bars in when Edward hops to his feet on the couch and nods his head as if he's in distress. We don't stop singing, and he begins howling as loud as our singing, which makes us laugh and sing more. It's a tradition, the minute we start singing this song, he starts howling.

"You're going to get a fine for violating the noise ordinance." Piper wipes her eyes and sits beside Edward, petting his head to calm his howling.

"I'm sure Aiden will be glad to hand-deliver it!" Cass continues dancing, and I join her.

The tension I've been struggling with melts away in the warmth of my friends, Shania Twain, and Edward's howls of protest.

My phone lights with a text, and I lift it to see a photo of three glasses of bourbon with the words, **Bourbon tasting. Have fun.**

Chewing my bottom lip, my chest warms at his simple order to have fun. Cass and Piper are beside me at once.

"Who knew grumpy Sheriff Stone could be so cute?" Piper coos.

"I did a reading for you," Cass says softly, threading her fingers in my hair.

"Cass, don't…"

"I know, I know. You don't believe in that stuff anymore, but I did one. I saw the two of you together, happy, with babies."

I'm too buzzed to argue with her. In this moment, I want to believe her sweet dreams and fairy tales. I want to think it could be true. I don't want to think about all the reasons why magic isn't real or it won't work.

I want to believe in how maybe, it just might.

Chapter 17

Aiden

"It's right up there with Pappy van Winkle." Adam holds the glass of scotch, tilting it side to side. "We're about to blow up again."

"I hope so." Alex returns the bottle of straight bourbon whiskey to the shelf. "I spent a lot of time on that flavor profile."

"Wheat instead of corn." My youngest brother nods. "Makes it sweeter."

"Sure you don't want to come help me?" Alex lifts his tumbler, clinking it against Adam's. "Bartenders are essentially pastors. They're just a lot more honest."

Alex pours me another finger, but my eyes are on my phone, studying the photo Britt just sent me of Edward with his head lifted. It looks like he's howling, which makes me smile.

"You're very relaxed." Adam walks over to where I'm standing, and I quickly tuck my phone in my pocket.

"What's that?" I lift the tumbler and take another sip.

"You're always right there with him on the hypocrisy behind

the pulpit. Now you're looking at your phone... Are you *smiling*?" His hazel eyes hold a playful challenge.

Adam has the same square jaw and dark brow as the rest of us, but his easy nature makes him approachable. The tips of his too-long, light brown hair are gold from all the time he spends surfing, and he likes to joke around and tussle.

Normally, I'd join Alex in pushing back on the spiritual nonsense. Adam turned God to after Dad died, and it's caused a friendly split in our approach to things ever since. Tonight, however, I'm feeling more generous. The tight, angry-at-the-world fist in my chest has relaxed.

"You got laid." Adam snaps his finger, pointing at me.

"What the fuck?" Alex sets the bottle down, and I straighten, taking a step back.

"I don't know what you're talking about."

Adam starts to laugh. "Fucking liar. Who is she?"

"You're going to make a shit pastor if you don't clean up that mouth." My tone is sharp.

I'm doing my best to put up distractions, but it's not working. They're closing in on me, and I'll have to confess or leave.

"It's Britt." Alex arches an eyebrow, and my jaw tightens. "Fuck me, of course! It's Britt Bailey. That's why you were hulking over her like a fucking ape at Mom's house."

"I wasn't hulking over her." Anger burns in my neck.

"Yeah, that. Right there." He circles his finger at my face. "I felt that fury when we were talking about the tickle fights and tequila shots."

"Whoa, how did I miss that conversation?" Adam laughs.

"You were ready to throw her over your shoulder and drag her back to your cave." Alex leans back, crossing his arms. "I figured I'd better go before you punched me in the nuts."

"I was not doing any of that." *I actually was.*

"You can't lie to me, bro. I'm not even giving you a hard time. Britt's a sweet little piece of—"

"Don't say it." My voice is a low warning, just above a growl, and he laughs.

"I rest my case."

"Fuck off." I lean my forearms on the bar, and he pours me another inch.

Alex has always been the smartest of my brothers, but discussing my personal life with these two is not on tonight's agenda.

"So you're sleeping with Britt. So what?" Adam steps up beside me. "You didn't think you'd be single for the rest of your life. You're only thirty five."

I lift the drink Alex poured and sip it. "I didn't think anything. I don't want to talk about it, because there's nothing to say."

"Oh, shit." Adam, exhales a laugh. "This is serious."

"Look, Aiden. Sharing is not your strong suit, but we're your brothers." Alex rests his elbows on the bar. "What's the problem?"

My brow lowers, and my chest tightens as I study them. Alex waits placidly, while Adam's eyes dance like he's just waiting to jump on the next thing I say. It's not encouraging, but with an exhale, I relent.

"Britt's a smart girl, and she seems responsible and serious, nothing like her family."

"What's wrong with that?" Adam prods.

"I've got Owen now. I'm not a free agent. I have to think about his feelings, and him getting attached to something that could be nothing. I haven't known Britt for long. Maybe she is just like her family, and I haven't seen it yet."

"The Owen part I understand." Alex pours himself a bit more.

"I think you can relax." Adam's tone is serious, which I appreciate. "I've known Britt for years. In high school, she was always the responsible one. I mean, she'd let her hair down occasionally, but she always had goals. She wanted to get out of here and make a name for herself apart from Edna and Gwen."

His words tighten my chest in a way I don't like—a way that makes me feel like I'm already too attached. "Exactly. She's only here temporarily. Edna asked her to come and help us with this case, and once it's over…"

I don't want to say *she'll be gone*, but Alex reads my mind.

"Who can say what she'll do?" His tone is easy. "All Britt's family and friends are here. If you give her a reason to stay, she might surprise you."

My meeting with Edna in her office comes to mind, and I think about how she asked me to help her get Britt to stay. Edna and me being on the same team is some kind of through-the-looking-glass level shit, and it increases my unease.

"I don't want her to change her plans for me." It feels like the safest thing to say, but it's a fucking lie and it twists in my gut.

"I understand why you'd say that," Alex straightens, corking the bottles and starting to clean up the bar. "But I wouldn't foreclose what could be a good thing because you're scared."

"I'm not scared." The bite in my tone contradicts my words. "Britt's young. She's never been married. She's got a lot of living ahead of her. If she has dreams and things she wants to accomplish, she should do them and not settle for being here…"

I stop short of saying *with me*.

"If I know Britt, she won't do anything she doesn't want to do." Adam clasps my shoulder. "Who's to say she can't fulfill her dreams right here in Eureka?"

Pressing my lips together, I polish off my drink wishing the alcohol would make me more comfortable with this conversation. Saying it all out loud makes all the reasons it's a bad idea too close and too real. I prefer keeping things between Britt and me as they are. Questions lead to decisions, and we're not there yet.

"At least you've made it over the hill with Owen." Alex collects our empty glasses and loads them in the stainless steel dishwasher. "Penelope's so little, every day I work late or leave before she's awake, it's like I lost another day with her I'll never get back."

"Hell, that's no pressure." Adam laughs.

"I think you've got it backwards," I add. "She's so little, any time you spend with her is huge. Owen actually knows when I'm working too much, and he tells me. That's some guilt right there."

"At least he's a boy. I have no idea if I'm giving P enough of whatever girl shit she needs." He comes out from behind the bar to where we're standing. "I need to hire a nanny."

"I bet Mom could help you with that." Adam slides his backpack onto his shoulder.

"Mom's got enough on her plate without having to raise more kids."

"I meant help you find a nanny." He elbows Alex in the ribs. "You are too stressed out, man. You need to come ride the waves with me tomorrow. Let your mind roam free."

We walk up the plank-wood floors between the giant barrels towards the exit. Alex refurbished the place so it's now a destination, complete with a tasting room and a gift shop.

I glance at the clock over the doors, almost midnight. We started off sampling the three new blends my brother is launching, then we wound up in this conversation, which has my chest tight and my mind distracted.

Alex makes some complaint about being too busy to take a day off, and my youngest brother grabs me around the neck. "You need to get laid like this guy."

He dodges my attempt to punch him in the side, laughing. "You're getting slow, old man."

"I'm saving my energy for other things." My mind is on Britt, and I wonder if she's still awake. "I'll see you two tomorrow."

We climb into our vehicles, and Adam's the first to leave followed shortly by Alex. I have my phone in my hand, and I send a quick text, *How's the party?*

Gray dots appear, and I wait on edge. I had just enough

bourbon to heat my blood, and even with all my reservations still hanging in the air, I'd really like to see her.

A dark picture appears followed by the text. *Lightweights.* I have to spread my fingers to make it larger so I can see Cass and Piper lying side by side in her bed with their eyes closed. *So much for Sleepless in Seattle.*

Exhaling a chuckle, I text back, *Want to go for a drive?*

Her answer is quick. *Yes… pick me up?*

Mine is even quicker. *OMW.*

Stone Cold distillery is on the outskirts of Eureka, but even on a Friday night, our small town is dead after eleven. I pull up in front of her building in less than ten minutes, and as soon as my truck stops, she steps out of the glass door. I don't have time to take off my seatbelt before she skips across the sidewalk to climb into my truck.

"How was your night with the guys?" She slams the door, turning to face me.

For a minute I can't speak. She's so pretty and playful, and my eyes slide from her bare legs to the thin, long-sleeved T-shirt she's wearing. Her hair is loose over her shoulders, and she looks like just what I need to release the tension in my lungs.

"It started out good."

She exhales a laugh. "What does that mean?"

I'm driving us back to my place, because I don't know where else we can go—and I only have one thing on my mind.

"They were asking a lot of questions I didn't want to answer." My voice is thick. "About you."

She lifts her hands, placing them on her cheeks. "They know, too?"

Arching a brow, I give her another glance. "Did we just have the same night?"

"Cass said she heard us in my apartment, and now I feel like the whole town's talking about it."

We're at my place, and I pull the truck into the carport, switching off the headlights. It's completely dark except for the moon and the stars and the street lamps out at the road. I un-fasten my seatbelt and reach across the console for her.

"Come here." I'm pleased with how quickly she unfastens her seatbelt and climbs across the seat to straddle my lap. "I've been in the office two days, and nobody's said a word to me. I think we're still okay."

My hands are on her waist, and I slide them higher to dis-cover she's not wearing a bra. My cock hardens at once, and my hunger roars to life. I cup and squeeze her tits, and she ex-hales a little noise as she clasps my neck, leaning forward to meet my lips.

Our mouths open and our tongues slide together. We're expensive whiskey and cheap tequila, two flavors I wouldn't expect to blend, yet they're delicious. Her hips rock against my erection, and I exhale a groan, wanting to get her out of the thin cotton shorts she's wearing so I can get inside her.

"We should be more careful." Her head is down as she quickly unfastens the buttons on my shirt.

"We should." I sit up fast, reaching down to slide the seat back so we can have more room.

My shirt is open, and she slides her nose along my chest, touching my skin with her tongue.

"Fuck." I exhale a groan, reaching down to unzip my pants to relieve the pressure on my cock. Shoving them lower on my hips, I realize I didn't grab a condom.

"Shit," I groan as her mouth moves higher to my neck.

"What's wrong?" She sits up, meeting my eyes.

I slide her long bangs behind her ears. "I don't have a condom."

Blinking down, her lip slides between her teeth. "It's okay with me. I'm all clear."

"I haven't been with anyone since my wife, and I was fine then."

Her nose wrinkles, and a naughty smile curls her lips. "I'm still on the pill."

"Thank fuck," I groan as she laughs. My hands are on her ass, and I scoop her closer to my chest. "Not that contraception is your responsibility."

"You're very evolved." She whips the thin shirt she's wearing over her head, and my brow collapses at the sight of her bare breasts.

"No, I'm not." I bury my face in her tits, biting and sucking.

Her head drops back, and she holds my jaw, rocking forward on my lap as I ravage her body. As always, we're desperate and wild, and she turns in the seat, lifting her back and shoving her shorts down to her ankles. I only have a moment to register before she's guiding my bare cock into her slippery core and leaning her head against my shoulder.

"Fuck, that's so good," I groan, and my hands are on her tits as she begins to rock.

Sliding one hand down her stomach, I find her clit, moving my fingers up and down rapidly as I kiss the side of her neck, higher into her hair behind her ear.

"Oh!" she moans, and her pussy tightens around my dick.

"Fuck me," I groan, losing my bearings in the shocks of pleasure tightening my pelvis.

She sits forward, and I slide my hands up her smooth back as she takes over massaging between her legs. Ragged little moans gasp from her throat as she rocks her hips faster, getting herself off as I watch her sweet little ass bouncing on my lap.

"You are so fucking gorgeous," I groan as my orgasm winds unbearably tight in my stomach.

"Yes," she hisses, "More."

"Your hot cunt is so fucking wet."

"Oh, God," she whimpers. "More…"

I'm about to explode. Leaning forward, my chest is against her back, and I thrust up with my hips as I cup her breasts and speak in her ear. "Ride me, baby girl. Make me come."

Her body starts to tremble, and I'm so far gone, I can't hold back. Squeezing my eyes, my voice is a hoarse groan as I order, "Come with me."

"Yes…" She hisses, her pussy tightening and breaking into spasms.

I'm right with her, wrapping my arms around her waist as we ride the waves, surrendering to the pleasure swirling around us like a hurricane. I lift my hips once more, resting my face against her back as she shudders, her clenching core drawing me deeper.

We breathe in time, slowly making our way down from that incredible high. The tightness in my chest is gone, and new thoughts filter through my mind, trying to take root.

What we have is different from what I had before. I can't put this in the same category. It's not something I can dismiss or ignore. My brother's words echo, *Who says she can't fulfill her dreams right here in Eureka?*

It's dangerous thinking, and I need to be stronger. I need to slow down. I have no idea how she feels or if she's even interested in something more serious. I'm older, and I have a son. She's here to help with this case. She's young and terrific at her work. She could go anywhere.

If I could just keep my hands off her. I trace my lips across the line of her hair, my arms still around her waist, holding her body next to mine. It feels so good.

I'm a junkie on the world's strongest drug, and even though I know what I need to do, I can't walk away.

Chapter 18

Britt

Sgt Durango's head is shaped like a lemon.

Sitting in front of my computer, I pinch my nose to keep from laughing at Aiden's text as I reply, *Now I'm craving candy.*

I'm craving you.

Heat flashes through my stomach, and I chew my lip as I glance around the office to see if anyone notices. *You're on duty, Sheriff!*

I know a utility closet no one visits.

A tickle is in my core, and I smile at Doug leaning against the wall beside Holly's desk eating a donut. She's going on about something her prized pig Myrtle did. Myrtle is as smart as a dog, Holly likes to remind us daily.

Gran is holding a pamphlet, her brow furrowed as she reads.

All week, the courthouse has been a frenzy of activity—and not the crime-solving type. I've never been on the organizational side of the Founder's Day festival, but I have a lot more appreciation for all the details and minutiae that goes into it, not to mention the work keeping all the participants safe.

Aiden's been in and out meeting with the president of the Lion's Club and the adjutant for the American Legion. This morning, he had a meeting with the Beaufort County Sheriff's Department. With our recent "crime wave," he wanted to have backup deputies on call.

Apparently the sergeant has a lemon head.

I bite back another grin, returning my eyes to my computer screen where I've been reading an essay on reflected, transmitted, and absorbed light at a crime scene and how they impact photography.

Scooping up my phone, I tap quickly, *I feel the need to break a law.*

His reply is swift. *Then I'd have to cuff and stuff you.*

Heat flashes through my core, and the image of me in handcuffs being *stuffed* from behind by Aiden tightens my nipples.

I can't resist pushing us further. *You might have to chase me. Then I can hold you down.*

I almost lose it, but my grandma glides up to my desk. Placing my phone aside, I get serious fast and hope my face isn't as flaming as my insides.

She places a pamphlet on my desk for the third-grade Little Sunbeam Pageant, and I look it over, shaking my head. "I'm glad they didn't have this when I was a kid. Eight is awfully young to find out you're not pretty enough to be a sunbeam."

"Birgitte Brewer Bailey, that is not what the Little Sunbeam Pageant is about." Gran gives me a scolding look. "It's about community service. We pick three different winners over six categories ranging from poise, talent, public speaking, and a town project. Appearance is only a small part of it."

Gran has also spent the week meeting with leaders from the different town groups. I had no idea there were so many social groups in Eureka. We have a beautification society, a conservation club, a women's foundation, and of course, the Little Sunbeam Pageant that raises money for the Little Sunbeam Park.

"Appearance is still a part of it, and that's a lot of

disappointed little girls." My phone buzzes, and I glance down to see another text from Aiden.

You're hotter than a sunbeam. Pressing my lips together, I glance around the room, but I don't see him. *Where is he?*

Gran narrows her eyes at me. "What are you reading?"

"Nothing." I lower my phone to my lap and quickly reply, *All this reading material has me overheated.*

A rustle from the hall, and I look up to see him walking in looking like sex on wheels and acting very serious and focused. Not at all like we've been sending naughty texts all morning.

He stops at Holly's desk with his back to me, and I study the way his biceps stretch the short sleeves of his brown uniform shirt. His dark brown pants hug his butt just right, and I wish I needed groceries or a burger or just a ride around town.

He lifts his phone and studies the screen. Then he glances over his shoulder, and when our eyes meet, his full lips curl into a smile. Heat flashes all the way to my core, and I bite my lip to keep from exhaling a swoon.

"Can I see you in my office for a minute?" Gran's voice startles me, and when I look up, I realize she's been watching me watching him.

"Sure!" I stand quickly, shoving my phone in my pocket and doing my best to act casual.

Doug has been working with his own groups, the library and the high school, on their assorted fundraisers. The library is repeating its very popular dunking booth, and when I pass his desk, Doug holds up a poster that reads *Dunk Deputy Doug.*

"3-D," he announces. "Get it?"

It's a little corny, but I point both fingers at him. "I don't need glasses to dunk you."

His laugh shakes his shoulders, and he nods. "Oh, I know it!"

"You need to work on your heckling game." Aiden's deep voice makes my stomach squeeze. "Get people riled up so they'll try harder to sink you."

He walks over to where we're standing, and Doug shakes

his head. "I don't have to do much to get people to want to sink me. They show up ready to go."

"Are you still planning to attend the festival with Owen and me?" Aiden looks down at me, and I want to reach out and slide my hand into his.

"I am." My voice is quiet, and I smile up at him. "Do you want to meet here at the courthouse?"

"Sure. I can pick you up after lunch?" We're speaking softly, and I don't realize we've drifted closer together until my hand brushes his. It's a little shock of bliss.

Doug clears his throat, and I step back, glancing at him. He's studying his 3-D flier intently with his lips pursed, and I'm pretty sure he's fighting a grin.

I motion to Gran's office. "I'd better see what she wants."

"Owen has lacrosse practice, so I'm headed out. They've been going all week."

"Okay." I want to say *I miss you*, but I settle for, "Tell him I said hey."

"He'll be here tomorrow afternoon."

"I'll bring Edward so they can finally meet."

We linger a bit longer, my fingers longing to touch his. Our eyes hold, and words hang unspoken in the air between us. My grandmother calls, and with a little sigh, I turn away.

Gran is sitting behind her desk when I enter. A black binder is open in front of her, and she's holding a pen, sliding it down the list.

"I know it's your first time working here, and you're only with us on a contract basis…" My throat tightens, and I'm pretty sure she's about to bring down the hammer on Aiden and me. "But I think it would be nice if you'd take one or two of these honorary positions, since Aiden, Doug, and I can't possibly cover them all."

Relief whooshes through my lungs, and I step closer. "I'm glad to help. What do you need?"

"The different groups always ask for one of us to serve as a judge or to present the ribbon for the best cow or pig or what-not." She turns the binder so I can see the requests. "I'm serving as a judge in the pageant, not that I expect you'd want to do that."

"I didn't mean to dump on the pageant. I just—"

"I know what you meant, dear. Take a look and see if any of these interest you." She points with her pen to a few in the middle. "These are the afternoon events. Presenting the livestock awards only takes about twenty minutes. Starting the fun run is simply blowing an air horn."

"What's this Doggy Dash?" I glance up at her. "That's new."

"Have you met Harold Waters?" I shake my head no, and she sits back in her chair. "Harold moved here from Chicago a few years back and opened the Popcorn Palace on Beach Road towards Hilton Head. He wants to try this 40-yard dash for dogs, benefitting the kennel club."

"He expects dogs to run in a straight line for forty yards?"

"I think it calls for teams. One person holds the dog, and the other has some lure to draw it to the finish line at the end of the track." She shrugs. "He thinks it'll be funny. I think it'll be utter chaos, which will also be funny. It's a fundraiser, so it doesn't really matter."

"I see Mom has her tarot reading tent." My lips twist into a frown, and the secret she lured me into keeping for her burns in my chest.

The only good part about Aiden being so busy this week is I haven't had to face him knowing I have this potential bit of evidence, and I'm sitting on it.

For my mom.

"She's always a huge money maker, and it all goes to the women's shelter in Charleston." Gran studies my face, misinterpreting my displeasure. "Your mother helps a lot of people with those readings. You helped a lot of people when you worked with her."

"I only did it because I wanted to be close to her." Taking

the pen, I quickly put my name beside the livestock awards and the fun run kickoff. "I wanted her to let me in, which I now know she'll never do."

I've always been a distraction in my mother's ongoing obsession with finding my dad's killer, a theory with no evidence or merit. Andrew Stone, Aiden's dad, was sheriff at the time, and he did a complete investigation at the scene. He ruled it a fault in Dad's equipment, which my mother never accepted. Aiden's dad then called in a detective from Charleston to try and convince her, but nothing was ever good enough. Dad was murdered, and it was up to her to expose who did it.

I was only ten, and I believed every word she said. I learned to read cards, thinking I could be her helper in finding the man who killed my dad. I dreamed I would find him, and she would be so proud of me, she'd hug me and smile. The deep lines of sorrow and obsession would relax around her eyes, between her brows. Then I got older, and I realized she was running from a truth she couldn't face. Then my nightmares started.

"Don't be too hard on your mother. Perhaps you've never experienced the kind of love she had for your father." Gran's muscadine eyes fix on me. "Or perhaps you're getting close to it. Either way, until you have it, you can't possibly understand losing it. Lars was everything to her."

"But after all this time…" I don't finish my sentence.

I was about to say after all this time, she needs to put my father's death behind her, accept the truth, and move on with her life. But neither my grandmother nor I will ever say those words to her.

Even after I broke ties and swore I wouldn't get sucked into it again, here I am, enabling her. Clearly, I'll give her whatever she asks to pursue her obsession.

"I need to take Edward for a walk." I put my grandmother's pen on the desk, frustration burning in my stomach. "I think I'll walk over and check on her while I'm at it."

"It's so good to have you home." She stands, rounding the desk and pulling me into a hug. "I've missed you so much."

"I've missed you too, Gran." I hug her before leaving.

Edward is waiting at the door when I enter my small apartment. I don't waste time, grabbing his leash and slipping tennis shoes on my feet. I'm frustrated and adrenalized, and I can't believe I came back after all this time and fell right into the same old pattern with my mother. I even stood by and watched while she did a reading—and I believed it.

"Ugh!" I growl, following behind my dog, whose nose is to the ground the whole way. "I actually believed it!"

Walking has a double benefit. I can burn off my irritation and get a little exercise at the same time. It takes about ten minutes to walk from town to the old neighborhood, to the house where I grew up.

My parents bought the farm-style home as newlyweds and slowly fixed it up, adding features. It's white with wood siding and a chimney on each side. Most of the houses in this neighborhood are similar, but in different colors.

Mom's is unique because it has an imposing front porch with reclaimed wooden beams and a tin roof. She was so proud when that addition was finished.

We've just gotten close, when Edward jerks the leash with a loud bark. My heart jumps with surprise. He's typically laid-back and docile, until he comes across a scent he's tracking.

"Easy, big guy!" My voice is calming, but he's pulling so hard, my arm feels like it'll pop out of the socket. "What are you smelling?"

I'm practically jogging, doing my best to hold him as he leads me straight through the yard and around the side to where the sweet olive bushes grow. As we get closer, I look up and see a window shattered, and my heart plunges.

"Mom?" I drop Edward's leash as I run for the door, my heart beating out of my chest. "Mom, are you okay?"

I charge up the back steps, bursting through the door, yelling her name as I go through room after room to the one where the window is located. Fear tightens my lungs as I take in the scene. In every room, books are on the floor, and a table is overturned in the hall.

Dashing into the broken-window room, it's even more of a wreck. The sofa is on its back, and a desk in the corner has been broken apart. Papers are on the floor, drawers are open and ransacked. Someone was searching for something, and they left in a hurry.

"Mom!" I shuffle to a stop when I see her on the floor with a hand broom and a dustpan, sweeping up the shards of glass. "Mom, are you okay?"

I rush to her, wanting to hug her, but she stands, walking past me as if nothing is wrong. "Hello, darling, I didn't know you were coming for a visit."

My eyes widen, and I grab her arms, turning her to face me. "What happened?"

"It's nothing." She laughs, waving her hands to loosen my hold, but a tremor is in her voice. "Just a broken window."

"It's more than a broken window!" My mother never has a tremor in her voice, and I'm on edge. "Who did this? Was it our suspect?"

Edward is sniffing all around outside the window, lifting his head, and *Rooo*-ing like he's found buried treasure—which means he's identified the scent we've been tracking, and we've only been tracking one scent.

Mom doesn't answer, so I catch her arm again, forcing her to look me in the eye. "He was here. The man with the prosthetic leg was here at your house."

"I don't know who was here, Birgitte. I just got home a few minutes ago, and I found all of this like it is. Your guess is as good as mine."

I don't believe her, and I don't have to guess. I have Edward.

"Were you going to report it?"

"To Aiden Stone?" She rolls her eyes like I'm the crazy one.

"I have a gun and my protection spells. I don't need the Stones here meddling in my business and lying about what they find."

"Gran and I are also here. You have us." She tries to walk away, but I stop her, making her listen to me. "I have to report this to Aiden now. It's gone too far. The man broke into your house. What if you'd been home? He might have hurt you."

Her eyes narrow with impatience. "He's not going to hurt me."

"Who is he, Mom? You can't say he won't hurt you if you don't know who he is."

"We agreed you would give me until Sunday. Then I'll put him right in your hands."

My throat knots, and I like this even less than before. "You're jeopardizing my position." *Not to mention my relationship.*

"It's for your dad, Birgitte. You can wait two more days for him." She lowers her eyes to mine, and I want to scream *No. No more days.*

Instead, I do something I feel in my bones I'm going to regret. If I inherited anything from my loony-tunes family, it's an impending sense of doom that always turns out to be true.

"On Sunday I'm telling Aiden everything."

Chapter 19

Aiden

"**H**E'S SNIFFING ME!" OWEN STANDS BESIDE THE TABLE IN THE breakroom with his eyes closed, laughing as Edward sniffs and licks his cheeks. "He's trying to learn my scent!"

"More like he's getting all the Krispy Kreme off your cheeks." I chuckle, walking over to where Britt is holding the leash while the two become besties.

"Did you know bloodhounds can track things for more than 130 miles?" Owen's voice is loud, which means he's excited, and he holds Zander for Edward to sniff vigorously. "He could find my buddy if I ever lose him!"

"It's true." Britt grins, watching the love fest.

I slide my finger along the soft skin of her upper arm, considering how easy it is for her to make my son happy. How easily she makes me happy.

She leans back subtly, placing her back against my chest, and I have to fight to keep from sliding my arms around her.

"He can track scents as old as two weeks," she adds.

"Does he protect you from bad guys?"

Her pretty face scrunches, and she shakes her head. "He's not the best guard dog in the world. He thinks everybody is a friend, so he's not very aggressive."

I don't like the sound of that.

"Can he run real fast?"

"He's not like a greyhound or a Doberman, but he'll do in a pinch." She glances up, meeting my gaze. "All done for the day?"

"Finally." This week is finally over, and we're finally in the same room for longer than five minutes.

Preparing for Founder's Day is always hectic, but with all the unsolved shit hanging over our heads and Owen starting lacrosse, this week was damn insane.

I want to cup her cheeks and kiss her. It feels like forever ago I had her on my lap in the cab of my pickup truck, a sight that fueled my fantasies more than once this week. Not to mention the dirty texting that had my dick so hard I had to take a minute before I entered the courthouse this morning.

"We need to put him in the Doggy Dash!" Owen shouts.

Britt's brow wrinkles. "I don't know if Edward's ready for racing."

"Sure he is! You can come over for dinner tonight, and we can practice at our house. We can teach him how to run when the whistle blows, and he'll be the winningest dog at the fair! That's okay, Dad, isn't it?"

My son is standing beside Edward, repeatedly stroking his head with every sentence, and I glance at Britt. Her lips part, and she looks like she's searching for a way to say no.

"I think it's a great idea." I don't know about the Doggy Dash, but I definitely want Britt to have dinner with us. "I'm marinating kabobs, and I've got corn on the cob for grilling."

She places a hand on her forehead. "Edward's a good boy, but he's really hard to train."

"We can try!" Owen jumps up and grabs her hand. "Mr. Harold said any dog can join. He said they don't even have to be very fast. Miss Magee is putting Periwinkle in it, and she's just a Yorkie. Edward can totally beat her!"

"Oh no." Britt's nose scrunches. "Edward would flatten a little dog like that."

"They're supposed to stay in their own lanes," Owen explains, like she doesn't know the rules.

"That's what worries me."

Owen catches her hand. "Please, Miss Britt? Can we try?"

She looks up at me with pleading eyes, and I grin, thinking how cute she is conflicted, wanting to please my son and looking to me for help. It's a dynamic I haven't had in a long time, and I didn't realize I missed having a partner to share Owen's energy.

I put my hand on her shoulder. "Why don't we head over to my place, have dinner, and do a practice run. If Edward isn't interested or doesn't want to cooperate, then we'll know."

"Yeah!" Owen does a little fist pump before scooping up Edward's leash and leading him out the back door to my truck.

Britt lingers beside me. "You should be a diplomat."

Sliding my hand from her shoulder down her arm, I pull her closer. "I had an ulterior motive. I like having you for dinner."

"Hmm…" She lifts her chin. "I like when you have me for dessert."

Energy shoots to my dick, and our faces are close. Our lips are a breath away from touching, and I'm ready to close that gap when Doug's craggley singing voice echoes in the hallway.

"I'm going down, down, down, down…"

Releasing her arm, I step away as she exhales a sigh. My deputy does a side step into the room, pausing when he sees us.

"TGIF and Happy Fri-yay! I'm ready to go down for the library!" He shuffles out the door, and Britt exhales a laugh as she follows him.

My mind is on that near-kiss and wondering if we'll have a chance to get that close again tonight. I should've invited Ryan for a sleepover to distract my son.

"We're ready when you are, Aiden!" Britt calls from a few feet away, where she's in a squat behind Edward, holding the side of his collar.

We're all in my backyard. I'm standing in front of the grill minding the kabobs and the corn while Owen waits at the tree line, Zander in hand, and I grin at the sight of them playing with the dog.

"Here goes," I call. "One, two, three…"

I give the whistle a long puff, and Britt releases the hound.

Owen yells at the top of his lungs. "Come on, Edward! Come on, boy! Run to your friends!"

To his credit, Edward leaps forward, running in a relatively straight line to where my son is jumping up and down, waving Zander over his head.

Britt stands watching with her hands on her hips, and when Edward reaches Owen, the two jump all around. Edward lifts his chin and lets out a loud *Rooo!* noise, which makes my son laugh and do the same. Britt grins at the two of them, glancing at me. My stomach tightens, and I smile back at her.

She walks slowly to where I'm standing, climbing the steps up to our deck while Owen continues playing with the dog, running around and making Zander hop from tree to tree.

"It looks like Edward's doing the Doggy Dash." I use the tongs to move the corn to a platter to cool. "Are you okay with that?"

Britt's brow furrows as she watches them out in the yard. "I'm not sure it's a good idea for him to use Zander as a lure. Edward might get excited and accidentally tear that zebra to shreds."

"You make a good point." Lifting my chin, I do a taxi-whistle. Owen looks up, and I motion to him. "Come here for a second."

He runs to where we're standing, and I point to his stuffed

zebra with the tongs. "You might want to put Zander in the house while Edward's here. He doesn't know the difference between a friend toy and a chew toy."

Owen's eyes widen briefly, and he nods, yelling as he runs into the house. "Be right back, ole boy!"

The hound jumps around before dashing to the back of the yard again at top speed. Britt watches him, and even though I've resolved the Zander danger, her sunny disposition hasn't fully returned.

I think about the week and take a stab at what might be bothering her. "I know we haven't made much progress on the case, but at least it's been quiet. We can get back to digging into that Kiawah lead on Monday."

She blinks up at me briefly. "Monday," she repeats, but her mood doesn't lift.

I try giving her a reassuring smile. "All cases have lulls. It's not anyone's fault if things seem to stall for a bit. We'll get it going again."

Her lips tighten, and I think she's about to tell me something when Owen bursts through the screen door, yelling as usual.

"I'm starved!" He runs out onto the deck. "When can we eat, Dad?"

"Right now." I move the kabobs onto a platter and carry them to the picnic table. Owen grabs a juice pouch from the refrigerator, and I reach over his head to grab a fresh beer, glancing back at Britt. "Can I get you a drink?"

"Sure." A weak smile curls her lips. "I'll take one of those."

The nights are growing warmer, and as the sun sets, Owen hops up and turns on the twinkle lights lining the columns. I light the citronella lanterns, and we're surrounded by a soft yellow glow as the sky turns from yellow to orange-red, pink, and purple.

The scent of grilled vegetables combines with the late-evening scent of sweet olive, and a tempting thought enters my mind—this might be perfect.

"You live over the Star Parlor?" Owen is on his knees at the table, picking the meat off his stick with his fingers.

"I do." Britt nods, using a fork to do the same.

"Dad said that place is a bunch of hogwash." My throat tightens. Perfection slipping. "Ryan said you took him there when he was a little boy, and there's lots of candles and incense. He said it's a magic place where you do card tricks to read the future."

Britt cuts worried eyes to me. "Um, well, you see... Ahh..." She blinks a few times, looking at me again as if waiting for me to help.

"It's okay." I shrug, glancing at my plate.

Her family is what it is. Her past is what it is, and if this thing between us is going to go anywhere, we can't hide it from Owen.

She exhales, speaking slowly as if she's choosing her words. "It's not actually magic, but it's not card tricks either."

"What is it then?" Owen wrinkles his little-boy face picking up his corn and chewing on one side.

"Tarot cards were invented hundreds of years ago, back when people didn't have a lot of tools to help them make sense of their world or their lives. Each card has a different picture on it, and the pictures can have lots of different meanings. Fortune tellers say they can predict the future using them..."

My son's eyes grow wide. "Did you ever predict people's futures?"

She answers quickly, shaking her head with a little laugh. "No."

"Did your mom?"

This time her answer isn't as fast. Her eyes blink down to her plate, and a hint of frustration filters through my chest.

When she finally answers, she's again choosing her words. "Some people think she did, but my mom has a gift."

"A magic gift?"

My hands are on the bench beside me, and my fingers tighten as I wait to see what she'll say, and how I'll deal with it.

"No." She shakes her head. "She has a strong sense of empathy, which means she's really good at reading people's emotions. She'll ask a lot of questions, and get an idea of what's bothering you. Then when she deals the cards, she reads them in a way that gives you comfort."

Owen's brow furrows, and he looks up at me. "That sounds kind of nice."

Britt jumps in immediately. "It's very nice at first. The problem is people start believing she really is reading their future, then they start living their lives by what she says, then they depend on magic to make all their decisions, and when bad things happen, because bad things always happen, they don't understand why it all came crashing down when they believed…"

Her voice breaks off, and she puts her fingers on her mouth, blinking up at me guiltily. I see she's still struggling with oversharing, and I give her a consoling smile. My urge to hold her hand is strong.

Owen nods in a knowing way. "It's like when I thought I was going to get a puppy for Christmas, and I believed Santa Claus was going to make it happen, and it didn't happen and now I don't believe in Santa Claus anymore, but dad says I can't say that to my friends because some little kids still believe in him, and their parents will get mad at me if I say he's not real."

I sit up straighter, clearing my throat and feeling unexpectedly thrown under the bus. "It's not the right time for a puppy, Owen. Dogs are a lot of work, and our schedule is too tight."

Britt's eyes flicker with amusement, and she jumps in to save me. "It's exactly like that, Owen. You're very smart."

"My teacher says that." He nods, hopping off the bench and running around to where Edward is lying on the deck at Britt's feet. "It's okay, because Edward's a great dog, and I think he's going to win the race tomorrow."

"I hope so." A gentle smile curls her lips, and I hesitate, watching them from where I sit.

The two of them play, and I long to pull Britt into my arms

in the growing twilight. We made it through that little eddy, and the idea of us together grows stronger in my chest.

Britt reaches down to scrub her fingers lightly in Owen's hair. "You need to find an old T-shirt or socks to lure Edward instead of Zander. I'd feel terrible if something bad happened to your friend."

"He wouldn't hurt Zander. Would you, boy?" Owen cups Edwards jowls, leaning forward to touch their noses.

Britt glances up at me, and I give her a supportive wink. "Britt's right, little man. Even if he didn't mean to, Edward could still hurt Zander pretty bad."

Britt exhales a cough as she sips her beer, then she stands. "I've had such a good time with you guys. Dinner was delicious, Aiden. Owen, I can't wait for the race tomorrow, and I hope Edward wins." She's moving quickly as she speaks, and I'm confused by this sudden change. It's like something went wrong, and I missed it. "I have to work in the morning, so I'd better get on the road before it gets too dark."

Her fingers twist together, and I don't like this one bit. Closing the space between us, I slide my hand over hers gently. "Hey, I'll drive you and Edward back to town. You don't have to ride."

"Oh, no!" She pulls her hands away, running them down the front of her jeans. "Thank you, I mean. You're so sweet to offer, but it's a nice night. I think Edward would like the exercise, and I've just been sitting on my butt in front of the computer all week."

Owen hops up as Edward rises to his feet. "I can't wait to see you win, boy!" His voice is high, and he throws his little arms around Britt's waist. "You were right. I love your dog!"

Her shoulders relax slightly, and she leans down to return Owen's hug. "He loves you, too. You're his new bestie."

She attaches the leash to Edward's collar, and Owen and I follow her down the porch steps out to the garage where the bike waits. Frustration twists in my stomach, and I don't like her leaving this way.

Owen is oblivious to the sudden change in mood. "Get some good sleep, Edward ole boy! You've got to run tomorrow."

While he's distracted with the dog, I take the opportunity to pull Britt to my chest, leaning closer. "You okay?"

She blinks up to meet my gaze but quickly blinks away again like she looked into the sun. "I'm just tired, and you know, morning comes early."

She's trying to sound upbeat, but I've spent enough time with her to know when the sunshine is real. This isn't, but I can't force her to talk to me.

"Text me when you get home, okay?"

"I will."

Owen is still playing with the dog, and I catch her chin, leaning down to slide my mouth lightly across hers. Heat tightens my stomach, and I pull her lips with mine. Her palm flattens against my chest and she melts into me.

"I miss you." My voice is soft against her lips, and she drops her forehead to my chest.

"I miss you, too," she whispers.

"I wish we could do more."

"I know." Her chin lifts, but her eyes don't meet mine. "You can't leave Owen."

"Maybe I could." I glance across the street, wondering what Vanessa's doing on a Friday night.

My thought is cut short as Britt pulls away. "Get some rest. I'll see you tomorrow."

Reluctantly, I release her fingers. "Goodnight."

Chapter 20

Britt

ALL NIGHT, I HAD A STOMACH ACHE. FRUSTRATION WITH MY mother burned in my chest along with frustration with me. I can't blame Mom for everything. I'm the one allowing her to keep secrets.

Aiden's sweet text made my heart ache more. *Did I say something wrong?*

He thinks it's been a quiet week. He thinks we have no new developments in the case, and when he said that about Edward hurting Zander, my anxiety spiked. I almost started to cry.

I'd already overshared with my "don't believe in magic" speech, and the risk of doing it again was enormous. It tingled on my lips and burned in my throat. I was so close to breaking down and telling him everything I know, everything that happened, but the fear was stronger.

My feelings for Aiden are scary-strong, and I adore Owen. Being with them is everything I've ever dreamed of having, security, stability, a family, and I'm terrified of destroying it the way Edward could shred a stuffed zebra.

Not at all. Dinner was wonderful. Just tired. Big day tomorrow. I'm sure he saw right through my defenses, but he didn't push, which made me want him even more.

It's one more day.

One day.

If Mom is telling the truth, if she could put the man in my hands on Sunday, we could close the case and have the answers we need. It's like Aiden said, trying to find him on our own would be like searching for a needle in a haystack.

Viewed in that light, I'm actually helping us by keeping this secret. It's a good thing.

My mother would never cooperate with Aiden Stone. She might cooperate with Gran, but she might not even cooperate with me. She would certainly never forgive me for breaking her trust, for "siding with the enemy." For betraying my dad.

I shake my head. She sure knows how to play me.

I thought if I left Eureka, I could change. I thought if I went to college and got my degree and learned to do something based on facts and evidence, I would be different. Instead, it's the same old adage. Wherever you go, there you are.

Aiden's words about Raif Jones are in my head, *When push comes to shove, he'll be loyal to his family. His kind always are.*

Am I his kind?

So I ie down on the couch next to Edward on his blanket, gently petting his head.

"Things are so good for me right now." My voice cracks slightly. "Can I make it through one more day without ruining everything?"

His droopy eyes slowly close, and after a long time, mine do the same. Still, I could feel the water rising around me, and I was kicking with all my might, trying not to go under.

"You ready to run, Edward?" Owen is on his knees in front of my dog, his little-boy hair a tousled mess. "Here's what I've got for you!"

He pulls a pair of black athletic socks out of his hoodie pocket and holds them for Edward to give a good sniffing. Edward rises to his feet at once, activated and ready to go.

"He pulled those out of the laundry." Aiden laughs. "They're from lacrosse practice."

"That should work." I smile, holding Edward's leash at the starting line of the Doggy Dash.

After managing a few hours of sleep, I finally gave up and got out of bed at six this morning. I spent some extra time getting ready, touching up my hair with a curling iron and applying a little makeup.

It was so strange to be in the courthouse completely alone. I left Edward at the apartment, figuring I'd walk back and grab him before Aiden came to get me. I didn't have much guidance on what to do by myself.

Answering the phones seemed an obvious task, but other than that, I was at a loss. Walking over to Holly's desk, I lifted her headset then put it down again. I passed Doug's desk, frowning at the hand-written notes on his blotter. *Kiawah Veterans Care, discount caskets, Sy Needleman.* I didn't recognize the name.

Returning to my desk, I woke my computer and typed in *Sy Needleman* to see what came up. The picture showed an older man in a white coat with a mustache and salt-and-pepper hair. He had mostly good reviews online, and he died several years ago.

"No help there," I muttered to myself.

Searching again for the veteran's clinic only turned up another dead end. It closed before Dr. Needleman died. Leaning back, I chewed on my pen wondering what Doug or Aiden would do next.

I confess, it made me feel a lot better about the deal I made with my mom. If she actually names our suspect tomorrow as she says she will, it'll save us a lot of time. I hope Aiden will see it that way, too. It'll be a means to an end, which you have to do sometimes on cases.

It actually eased the pressure in my chest.

The rest of the morning, I puttered around, read a few online articles about crime scene photography and capturing evidence. Finally, it was time to go and take Edward for a walk and get back to meet Aiden and Owen.

Now I'm drinking in the sight of my sexy companion for the day. I don't think we're calling this a date, and I know it's too soon for him to be my boyfriend. Aiden framed it as us making a show of support for the town, getting in the mix and letting them know we're here for them.

Still, I changed into the blue dress I wore to El Rio with a white cardigan tied around my waist in case it gets chilly. Aiden is hot as ever in a chambray shirt with the sleeves rolled to show off his muscular forearms. The shirt is unbuttoned over a simple white tee, and he's wearing faded jeans with brown cowboy boots. His dark hair is styled in a messy way, and his beard is trimmed. Exhaling a sigh, I really want to kiss him again. He's such a good kisser, and I was too tense last night to enjoy it.

"It's bigger than I expected," Aiden observes quietly near my ear, and I peruse the lineup of doggy racers.

It's a group of about ten townsfolk with dogs ranging from dachshunds to hunting dogs to plain old Heinz 57 mutts.

Terra Belle is two dogs down from us with her rat terrier Sparky. Terra has been cordial if a little impatient with the progress we've made on her case. She wants "the pickle murderer" punished, and she's happy to remind us all the time. Sparky is wearing a white, pickle-patterned handkerchief around his neck, and he's hopping all around. I don't want to tell Owen, he's a shoe-in to win. Rat terriers are fast little dogs.

Sarah Magee walks over to speak to Owen. Her little Yorkie

has a pink rhinestone collar, and she's so tiny, I'm worried she's going to get trampled.

Raif Jones saunters past us on his way to the other end. He's leading a decent-sized hunting dog, and he gives me a little nod. I smile cautiously, glancing up at Aiden.

"Afternoon, Sheriff," he says, and Aiden straightens, crossing his arms.

"You realize this is a race for charity?" Aiden's voice is level.

Raif drops his chin, running a hand over his mouth, as if to hide his grin before answering. "I support the humane society." Then he cuts his blue eyes at me. "Good luck, Miss Bailey. It's nice to see you again."

"Thanks." My voice is quiet, and I move slightly behind Aiden's shoulder.

Aiden steps forward. "Where's your brother today?"

The younger Jones shrugs. "You know Bull. He's not much for town gatherings."

"I hope he's staying out of trouble." Aiden's demeanor is pure dominance, which is brutally hot.

Raif glances at his tan boots, exhaling a shew-noise. "I hope he is."

Harold's voice cuts through our discussion. He's on a ladder at the side of the track with a megaphone to call the race to order. Raif ambles to the end of the line, and I turn from him to our little team.

"I'm going to get in my position now!" Owen jumps up, giving Edward another scrub around the ears. "You got this, boy! You gotta come get my socks."

Owen's so excited, I wish we'd practiced a few times last night using his socks instead of Zander. Now I'm worried Edward only has eyes for stuffed zebra.

When I glance at Aiden again, his square jaw is tight, and he's watching Raif at the other end of the group talking to a skinny girl holding a package of hot dogs.

"They're not supposed to use food." A growl is in his voice.

"It's okay." I tug on his arm, pulling him back to our trio. "It's just a fun run. It's probably going to be a big mess anyway."

When his gray eyes meet mine, his brow relaxes. "You're right." He smiles and a little thrill sizzles in my stomach. Then he leans forward, speaking low. "I hope Edward wins."

"Me too!" I give his bicep another squeeze before squatting down behind my dog, getting ready to unhook his leash.

Harold is back on the megaphone. "We're keeping it real simple, people. All dogs must run to their second team member to finish the race. If they don't get to the second team member, they don't finish. The first dog to make it to the second team member is the winner. All good?"

A resounding affirmation rises from the group, and a moderate-sized crowd has gathered on the sidelines to watch the spectacle. Gran is there, and she gives me two thumbs up.

I wave to her, chewing my lip and wondering if Owen and I ought to switch places. "Too late now," I sigh. "Don't let us down, Mr. Ed."

I give my dog another good scrubbing around the neck, and Owen jumps up and down at the opposite end of the track waving his socks over his head and yelling, "You got this, ole boy!"

Harold's amplified voice prepares us to start. It's nothing like when I kicked off the fun run. In that case, all I did was blow an air horn and everybody took off. I didn't have to make any speeches or explain the rules.

"Everybody ready? We're doing this on three," Harold calls, and I hear the noise of growling and a little yip at the other end of the line.

Looking down, I see Raif's dog is nose-to-nose with the feisty little dachshund. Harold doesn't waste any time.

"One… two… three!" The whistle blows long and loud, and I release Edward with a whispered *Go!*

For a moment, all the dogs hesitate, and the Team 2 members start yelling and jumping up and down at the same time.

"Come on Edward! Come on, boy!" Owen is waving his socks wildly.

Edward zeroes in on him at once and starts loping down the track. He's not too fast, but he's focused.

Sarah Magee's helper has a squeaky toy, and she's squeaking it furiously while calling for Periwinkle. The teeny-tiny little dog takes off running like a rabbit in the grass, which just leaves Terra of our friends. Her Number 2 has a pickle with a bell on it, and she's waving it wildly.

Sparky takes off fast, and my stomach twists. The other dogs towards the end of the line start running for their team members as well, until the skinny girl with Raif yells, "Porkchop!" and waves the hot dogs over her head.

"The dog's name is *Porkchop*?" Aiden frowns at me, and we're both distracted by her jumping up and down in her cutoffs and tube top with a package of hot dogs.

All at once, the six dogs on their end of the track see what she's holding, and all of them change course midway, making a beeline right at her.

"Oh!" I gasp. "That's not good."

The girl screams at the mob of dogs barreling in her direction and bolts away. Even Sparky forgets about the pickle with the bell, plowing over Periwinkle in his haste to run down the hot chick waving hot dogs.

"Periwinkle!" Sarah cries, running onto the field to retrieve her dazed pooch. "Are you okay, baby?" She scoops up the Yorkie who nestles her little head under her owner's neck, no longer interested in racing.

It's utter chaos, and I'm laughing so hard, tears run down my cheeks. I'm not the only one. Raif's girl finally gives up, throwing the hot dogs over her shoulder at the mob of dogs before dashing into the ladies restroom and locking the door. The entire crowd of spectators roars with laughter, and rising above it all is a loud *Rooo!*

I sniff, looking down at the end of the track, where Edward

is jumping all around with Owen, who's letting him play tug-of-war with his black athletic socks.

"And we have a winner, ladies and gentlemen!" Harold is back on the megaphone. "The winner of the inaugural Founder's Day Doggy Dash is our very own Edward Bailey, owned by Miss Birgitte Bailey and handled by Miss Bailey and Owen Stone. Please make your way to the winner's table to collect your medal."

I'm still wiping tears from my eyes, and even Aiden has a huge grin on his face.

"That played out better than I expected," he chuckles, putting his hand on my back and walking with me to where Harold climbs down the ladder to award our gold medal.

Piper meets us at the table with Ryan at her side. She's holding a camera, and her eyes dance with laughter as well. "I have to hand it to you, Harold. That's the funniest thing I've seen in a long time."

My bestie gets on one knee to take the photo of me beside Owen hugging Edward, who's proudly wearing his medal.

"I guess we're going to be in the paper now." I lean forward, putting my hand on Owen's shoulder. "Everybody in town will see what a smart dog we have."

"I get it!" He turns, hugging my waist before dropping again to hug Edward. "Everybody in town's going to know you're the best dog! Even when hot dogs are on the line, you're still going to win the race."

Heat warms my eyes, and I stand, giving Piper a hug.

"Now that's my kind of race." Adam Stone's voice joins us, and I turn.

"Adam!" Stepping forward, I give him a hug. "I haven't seen you since I got back to town. You look so good!"

He really does. Adam was always the wild child in the Stone family. He looks just like his older brothers, with the dark brow and the panty-melting muscles, but he's so easy-going and loose. He's the kind of guy you could trust with anything.

"Hey, man." Aiden steps up behind me, placing his hand on my back, and I lean into him, remembering what he said.

I guess because we were friends in high school, Aiden got the crazy idea I wanted to date Adam, but as much as I adore him, there's only one Stone brother I'm interested in.

"Are Mom and Alex here?" Aiden asks.

"Nah, I came on my own." Adam clasps his brother's hand.

Then he does something that surprises me. Adam looks at Piper in a way that I don't think she notices. I've never noticed it until this second. He looks at her like she's a wave he's never been brave enough to ride, but he really wants to.

"I had to check out this Doggy Dash," he continues with a laugh. "I figured Pip would be here covering it for the paper."

"You figured right." Piper grins, tugging on his arm, and I cut my eyes from him to her, wondering.

Adam catches my eye, and he smiles. "Why don't I take Edward and the boys to the kids area? I've heard the corn maze is actually hard this year."

"If you're shorter than five feet," Piper clarifies.

Adam gives me a wink, and I realize we're on the same team. I want to mouth a *thank-you*, but I don't want to draw attention.

"Can we, Mom?" Ryan pulls on Piper's arm, and Owen dances all around, taking Edward's leash from my hand.

"Edward's the best dog! He can figure out any ole maze." Owen's still going. "You won the gold medal, didn't you, boy? He ran straight to me when all those other dogs ran after that girl."

"He's the coolest dog I've ever seen," Ryan agrees.

"Is it okay, Miss Britt?" Owen looks up at me, gray-blue eyes worried.

Edward seems a bit confused by all the small-human attention, but I can tell he likes it. He stands, ready to follow the little guys, which is plain adorable.

"Of course!" I shake Owen's shoulder. "Make sure he gets some water every now and then. Y'all have fun."

"We will!" Owen cries, taking off with Ryan and Adam in the direction of the kids' area.

Piper goes with Harold to get the details of the race and the charity recipient for her story, leaving Aiden and me facing each other.

"Alone at last?" He cocks a grin, and a bubble rises in my chest.

Stepping forward, I hug his arm. "At last."

We leave the racetrack, heading into the thick of the festival. We stroll through the antique car show, and I marvel at the pristine condition of the hundred year-old Fords and coupes.

"I should find out who does their restorations and get them to look at my truck," I joke.

"I'll take a look at your truck." Aiden puts his arm around my shoulder, pulling me closer to his side. "I still don't trust those brakes."

"So protective." I snuggle close, loving the feel of being tucked into his side, safe from all the craziness in my life.

Townspeople walk up to him as we stroll along the booths. Everyone wants to speak and shake his hand. I know most of the people in Eureka, but not as many as the sheriff.

The pie-eating contest is in full swing when we exit the car park, but I can't watch it. "Those contests make me feel like I'm going to barf."

We continue on to the food tent, and I try the authentic Terra Belle's Pickle Pizza (too salty), and the fried fudge (too sweet). We make our obligatory stop at the dunking booth to try and sink Doug.

His heckling game was not too bad. Sitting on the plank over a tub of water, he smiled and waved as I threw three balls and missed.

"Losing your arm, Britt?" He called, then Aiden threw three more balls and sank him.

Doug came up laughing, but Aiden leaned into my ear. "You missed on purpose."

His eyes narrowed, but I only shook my head. "I must be out of practice."

We walk down the midway to the livestock pavilion, and I drag Aiden to the winner's tent where I present the blue ribbon to Holly's prized pig.

"Like you didn't know Myrtle was going to win," I tease, elbowing him in the side as we finish the last of my duties. "She's smart as a dog."

"I know, I know." Aiden holds up both hands like he's under the interrogation lamp, and I lean forward, laughing as I push his shoulders.

His hands slide around my waist, and we're in each other's arms, right here in front of God and everybody.

"What are we doing?" I can't help asking, lightness floating around me.

He looks down at me, his gray eyes warm. "Getting too close."

My lips are heavy with need, and when I slide my tongue out to touch them, his gaze darkens.

The sky is turning a pretty red-orange, and a purple ribbon lines the horizon. Twilight is my favorite time of day, and Aiden threads my fingers, leading me in the direction of the Ferris wheel.

"We don't have much time," he murmurs, pulling me close to his chest. "I can't leave Owen with my brother all night."

"I don't know," I sigh, threading my fingers in the fabric of his shirt. "He has Edward and Ryan to keep him company."

A lusty groan comes from Aiden's throat. "Don't tempt me."

Tickets are in our hands, and we move through the nonstop line to get on the slow-moving wheel. It's enormous, and one rotation is all we get. Still, it's a long way around.

Climbing into our seats, the guy closes the door, and we rise two cars before pausing. The breeze is stronger up here, and I take my sweater from around my waist, pulling it over my shoulders.

Aiden wastes no time pulling me into his side. "I've been waiting all day for this."

Heat floods my stomach, and I slide my hands up his strong arm, moving my body closer to his. "Me too."

His beard scuffs the side of my cheek as his soft lips press to my ear, my temple, the side of my head. "It's been a long week."

He traces his nose along my hairline, inhaling deeply, sending chills down my arms. Then he kisses my head one more time before lifting his chin and grinning down at me.

"You're so fucking pretty." His blue eyes light my entire body. "How is it possible I never saw you before?"

Tracing my finger along his jaw, I try to imagine if he had seen me before. I'd have passed out from surprise. "To be fair, I was a lot younger back then."

"But you were friends with my brother. You were over at my house." He shakes his head. "I had my head up my ass after Dad died."

"I understand that." My fingers curl in the hair along his collar. "My mom was pretty messed up after my dad died. Still is…"

The thought of her sours my stomach, so I put her right out of my head again. It's not hard to do when Aiden lowers his hungry gaze on me.

"I see you now." It's a deep vibration that clenches my core. "I haven't seen enough of you this week."

We're halfway to the top, and he catches my jaw in his fingers, covering my mouth with his. I exhale a whimper, melting into his soft lips. His kiss is what I want more than anything. It's salty-sweet popcorn and rich, luscious fudge.

Soap and sweat and cedar surround me, and I reach up to hold his neck. With a rough scoop, he hauls me onto his lap in a straddle, and I'm so glad I wore a dress as his hands move higher on my thighs, under my skirt to cup and squeeze my bare ass.

Heat floods my panties, and a whimper slips from my throat. I hold his face, hungrily pulling his lips with mine, nipping them with my teeth, smoothing them with my tongue as the sensations filter through my inner thighs.

He groans, moving his hand over my leg and sliding his thumb beneath my underwear, firmly circling my clit.

"Oh, fuck…" My mouth breaks away on a gasp, and my hips start to rock.

Orgasm races to life in my core, and I need more.

"You gave me a taste of this sweet little pussy." His beard scuffs my neck as he drags his lips across my collarbone. "I've been starving for it all week."

"I love your filthy mouth." I kiss his forehead, his temple.

"Feel what you do to me." His hand is on mine, and I slide my palm over the straining erection in his jeans.

Fumbling to his waist, I want to open them. I want to slide my hands all over him and put him inside me. At the same time, his fingers unfasten the buttons on the front of my dress, pushing the fabric aside.

"Watch this." With two fingers, I open the front clasp of my bra, allowing my breasts to spill out.

His brow relaxes with a lusty grin. "Perfect."

My nipples are tight and tingling, and his mouth covers one, biting and sucking. His thumb doesn't stop massaging between my legs, and when he slides two fingers inside, I rise in the air with a moan.

He groans, kissing his way from one breast to the other. "God, you're so wet. I want you on my cock."

"I want that." I curl my fingers in the waist of his jeans.

Soft lips followed by rough beard scuff my skin, and I'm lost in sensation. Where we are, who might see us, none of it matters as he feasts on my body, as I strain for his touch.

Our eyes meet, and I dare to ask, "Could we?"

Desire floods his gaze, and he glances around us. We've passed over the top of the wheel, slowly descending to Earth. I'm hot and wet and achy for more, and his hands are still on me.

"We don't have time." His voice is rough. "When we get down, I'll take you to my truck."

"Yes." I nod, slipping off his lap to the side and fastening my bra before buttoning the front of my dress.

He buttons his jeans, turning to face me and sliding his hand beneath my skirt again. His palm is warm against my inner thigh, and his voice is possessive. "I'm ready to get off this thing now."

I lean forward, stretching higher to cup his cheeks and kiss him again. As we glide lower, we take another nip of the lips, another slide of his tongue against mine. Our clothes are restored, and on the outside, we appear calm and collected. On the inside, I'm a raging inferno of lust and desire.

Two cars below us, a couple steps out appearing slightly disheveled as well. I glance at Aiden, and he gives me a little grin. "It's what you do at sunset on the Ferris wheel."

"When in Rome." I lean closer, my chin touching his shoulder.

The next car goes down, and the tension twists hotter in my stomach. We're almost off the ride, and I wonder if it would be noticeable if we ran all the way to the parking lot.

It's almost our turn to exit when a loud roar of people echoes from the direction of the kids' area to our left.

Aiden's brow furrows, and he looks over my shoulder. "What the hell?"

The change in his tone startles me, and I turn to see what's the matter. A crowd is surging, carrying their children and rushing away from the hay maze, panic on their faces. Aiden's body tenses, and he grips my hand tighter. Our car is at the bottom, and as soon as the door opens, he's out, helping me across the deck quickly.

"Looks like something happened in the hay maze." The kid operating the Ferris wheel stares in the direction of the mob.

"Stay close to me." Aiden's voice is at my temple briefly as he leads us straight into the swirling crowd.

Half the people are running away while the other half are running towards the maze. Some are parents with desperation in their eyes, and my stomach drops.

"Owen and Ryan!" I grip Aidens arm, and we're both moving faster.

My chest is tight, and sickness filters through my stomach. Aiden's doing his best to make a path through the bodies. His brow is lowered, and tightness holds his jaw.

"Adam is with them." Authority is in his tone, but it's laced with fear.

I struggle to breathe when we look up, and our eyes meet golden hazel.

"It's them!" I cry.

They're moving towards us as quickly as we're closing the gap to them. Owen breaks ahead, running to meet us with Edward at his side on the leash. Ryan is right behind them, and Aiden drops to his knees, scooping his son into a firm hug. My heart aches with relief. I've never been so frightened, and I've definitely never seen Aiden afraid.

"What happened?" He looks up to his brother.

"You'd better get Doug and call the guys from Beaufort." Adam's face is lined with worry. "There's a dead body in the back of the corn maze."

Chapter 21

Aiden

"**W**HO DISCOVERED THE BODY?" I LEFT OWEN WITH MY brother, and Britt is by my side leading Edward.

We both switched directly into work-mode, and Dave Watkins, supervisor of the kids park, gives us the details as we walk straight through the chest-high corn maze.

"Thankfully, it was a parent." Dave pushes the corn stalks aside as we walk. "His toddler had thrown a ball outside the maze, so he was searching for it deeper in the rows when he discovered the body."

We reach the back of the grid, and a man is standing to the side with his chin tucked, holding a little girl with a mass of dark brown curls all over her head. Another man is beside him with his arm around his shoulders, and it appears they're a couple.

"Where are they from?" I glance at Dave.

Eureka's so small, I'm pretty sure I'd know them if they were locals.

"Drove up from Hilton Head. Read about the festival online and wanted to visit the area, take in some small-town charm."

"Shit," I hiss under my breath. "That's all we need. News of this spreading into the tourist areas."

"They actually seem pretty cool about it. They're from Brooklyn."

Nodding, I stop where the man is bouncing his little girl. "Hi, there, ah…"

"Rocky." He's a slim-built man with dark hair wearing horn-rimmed glasses, skinny brown pants, and a navy sweater.

I shake his hand, giving him a tight smile. "Sorry you had to deal with this on your vacation."

"I'm just glad I found him before Sofia… or anyone else did."

His partner holds out a hand. "Steve Lambert. Any idea who it is or what happened?"

"Not yet. Is there anything you noticed when you found him? Anyone around?"

Rocky shakes his head, frowning. "I was trying to find Sofia's squiggle ball, and then he was just… there. I called to him—I thought maybe he was asleep or had fallen. When I touched his arm, I realized he'd been dead a while."

"At this point he's a John Doe." Doug steps through the bent corn stalks, coming back from where I assume the body is located. "He's been there at least twenty-four hours, and you need to take a look at this, Sheriff."

Holly comes running up, her curly hair frizzing around her face. "I just heard what happened. What can I do?"

I motion to Rocky and Steve. "If you would, please take their statements. Rocky here found the body."

Holly nods, leading the family away, and I hesitate, putting my hand on Britt's arm. "You ready for this?"

"Of course." Her gaze is leveled on the passage through the corn stalks. "There's a lot of people on the scene. I wish I had my camera, but I can use my phone for now."

The Beaufort County Sheriff's Department is setting up

spotlights on poles to illuminate the area, and two state troopers are standing to the side with their hands on their gun belts.

"They got here pretty fast." Doug's hair is damp, and a towel is around his neck.

"That's why I had them on call." I greet the additional officers.

We step carefully through the corn stalks, doing our best to avoid contaminating the scene. Britt uses her phone's light to get close then snaps pictures of the ground, the broken stalks. Edward is with us sniffing everything. We get closer, and my stomach tightens.

I glance over at Britt in her pretty blue dress with the white cardigan over it. She tied her hair back in a ponytail, and her long bangs are tucked behind her ears. I can't help wanting to shield her from whatever we're about to find, but I have to push those feelings aside. Britt came here to do this job, and she can handle it, even if I don't like it.

"Victim is a male appearing to be in his early to mid-sixties…" Doug tells us what he knows as we get closer. "Apparent gunshot wound to the chest."

The first thing I see is gray hair sticking out from under a beige fishing cap. Thick gray scruff is on his cheeks. He's lying on his back, so we can see he's wearing blue jeans, a chambray button-down, and a brown corduroy blazer. Britt's snapping pictures of everything, getting on one knee, closer than even I'd want to be. She lifts the lapel of his coat and photographs the small red dot where the bullet entered his body.

Blue and red lights cascade around us, and an EMS truck slowly backs to where we're standing. Stopping at his feet, I notice he's wearing one dark brown work boot. My eyes immediately go to his other foot, and…

"Is this what I think it is?" My voice is quiet, and Britt's a step ahead of me.

"Our John Doe is missing half of his leg, but he didn't have a prosthetic. Or he wasn't wearing it." She rises from her squat beside the body as EMS workers approach the scene.

Nodding, I motion to Doug. "Tell the coroner we need ballistics, and I want a toxicology screening. I want the works, DNA, everything. We need to find out who this guy is and why he was terrorizing our town."

"Yes, sir!" Doug hops around, wrapping police tape all over the area.

I return to Britt, who's carefully walking the perimeter.

"A pair of crutches is over here in the corn." She walks back to where the body was found. "But he was dumped here."

"How can you tell?"

"No blood." She shines her light on the spot where they just removed the body.

She lifts her chin, and our eyes meet. I'm about to ask when Edward scares the bejesus out of me by breaking into a loud as fuck *Rooo!*

Britt's eyes widen, and she goes to where her dog is sniffing all around the ground where the dead body's head and shoulders had been. But instead of focusing on the place where he lay, he goes the opposite way, into the stalks before coming back.

"He recognizes the scent." She takes pictures of the ground above the body where Edward is moving back and forth.

I straighten, putting my hands on my hips. "We've found our suspect?"

Her lips press together, and she's focused on the ground. "I'd like to think so."

Straightening, she crosses her arms, gazing at the empty hollow on the ground. Her brow is furrowed, and instead of looking satisfied, worry lines her pretty face.

Stepping carefully around the crime scene, I go to where she's standing. "Is it a suicide or is it foul play?"

My voice seems to rouse her from her thoughts. She blinks a few times before placing her hand on my arm and smiling up at me. "We have to find the weapon. Then we have to find out who he was."

"The coroner should have what we need tomorrow. We've pretty much done all we can do here. Let me drive you home."

Edward is at her side, and she slides her hand over his head. "Sounds good. Then you need to take care of your little man. He's had a scary night."

Owen. I nod, giving her a smile, falling for her a little more for worrying about my son. "I'll keep you posted."

"You can't hold me here without a charge." Bull Jones is in the single-cell jail we have in the back of the courthouse when I arrive the next morning.

I'm walking through the back door, a box of Krispy Kreme donuts in hand for when Owen's done with Sunday school, and the last thing I want to see is fucking Bull Jones.

"Who put you in there?" My brow is furrowed, and my tone is less than happy.

"One of those Beauford County assholes." Bull scowls at me from behind the bars. "Said he had reason to believe I wasn't where I was supposed to be yesterday evening. What kind of *Usual Suspects* bullshit is this?"

My throat tightens, and as much as I despise Bull Jones, as much as I don't trust him or his family as far as I can throw them, I also don't believe in putting people in jail on a hunch.

"Where were you last night around eight p.m.?"

"I don't know." Bull's tone is defiant. "I ain't no freakin' court reporter."

"Were you anywhere near the festival grounds?"

"Fuck, no. I don't like all that hypocritical bullshit. Nobody in this town likes me, and I don't intend to act like I like them. I was down by the water, picking up chicks."

Squaring off, I put my hands on my hips as I face him in

the cell. Our eyes clash, and the urge to punch this dirtbag in the nose is so strong.

Only, I want to do it for the right reason.

"I don't like you, Bull. But I'm a man of the law, and I don't believe in holding someone without a reason." I take the key out of the cabinet beside the door and walk over to turn the lock on the small cell. "Hear this." I lean forward, lowering my voice. "Don't give me a reason."

Bull's eyes narrow, and he sizes me up. "You think you're so clean and proper. You're one bad turn from being just like me."

"Nope. I'm not." Catching him by the elbow, I escort him to the back door, kicking it open and shoving him through it into the parking lot. "Get on, and keep your nose clean."

Dusting my palms together, I scoop up the box of donuts and carry it to the breakroom where Doug is just arriving. "We got an ID on the body!"

"That was fast."

"Coroner found a wallet in the inside pocket of his over-coat." Doug places a printout of a driver's license on the table in front of me. "Gary Blue. His address is on Route 109 in Rockville."

Not in Kiawah, but near it. I'll need to get a warrant to search his place. "What about ballistics?"

"Well, it's Sunday, so we'll have to wait a day."

I'll get my warrant, but pretty much everything else will have to wait until Monday. "We can let Terra know it appears the pickle murderer has been murdered."

"I'll be sure to get right on that, Boss." Doug smiles, taking a donut from the box. "I'm still getting the water out of my ears."

"Morning, fellas, what do we know?" The sound of Britt's voice lifts my chest, and I turn to see her striding in, wearing a denim skirt and a thin yellow sweater.

Her hair is in a ponytail over her shoulder, and she wakes her computer and plugs in her phone. "I'll upload the crime scene photos for you to see. I found some very interesting markings where Edward was focused."

A smile lifts the corner of my mouth at her dedication to the case, even on her day off.

"We've got a name and an address, but that's as much as we can do today." I walk over to where she's pulling up the photos on her large screen.

"Check this out." She uses a pen to circle the area above where the body was found. "Tire tracks. But they're different from what we've been seeing."

I lean closer to see the narrow trail. "Looks like a trailer or a wagon."

"Which could be pulled by a three-wheeler." She straightens, putting our faces close.

I smile, glancing down at her lips, thinking how easy it would be to cover them with mine.

"Ah, I think the water's out of my ears." Doug's voice interrupts our moment. "I think I'll run over and give Terra the good news then I'll see what I can find out about those tire tracks."

My eyes meet Britt's, and hers warm with a smile. I squeeze her arm, glancing over my shoulder to see Doug pumping his elbows as he hustles down the hallway to the break room exit.

Turning back, I slide my hands over her waist. "Hey."

"Hey." Her voice is soft, and she lifts her hands around my neck.

It's enough. I seal my lips to hers, and a little sigh slips from her throat when our mouths open, and our tongues curl together. My hands are on the bare skin between the top of her skirt and her sweater, which has risen with her arms. I'm about to slide them higher when a voice rings through the empty room.

"Hey, bro!" Adam's call is loud, almost like a warning, and we step apart as he finishes. "Church just let out, and I figured you'd need some help with Owen."

Britt turns, smiling brightly as she pulls the sides of her sweater down. "Good morning. Or is it afternoon?"

"Almost, but not quite." He holds the door, and Owen trots in dressed in his khakis and white shirt with a tie and navy blazer.

"Where's Edward?" He looks from me to Britt, and her nose wrinkles.

"Hello to you, too!" she teases. "He's in my apartment, but it's okay with me if you want to go check on him. He might even need to go for a walk."

"I have a better idea." Adam walks over to where we're standing and sits on the edge of my desk. "It's Sunday, the water's perfect. Why don't I take them out to the beach?"

Owen jumps up and down in place. "Can we take Edward?"

Britt's lips form a little O, and she looks up at me. "I'm okay with that?"

I nod, looking up at my brother. "I was planning to drive over and see what I could find in Gary Blue's house, so that would really help me."

"I'm on it. I'll see if Piper and Ryan want to tag along."

"I bet Piper would love that." Britt's encouraging tone makes me feel like I'm missing something.

My brother exhales a laugh and looks down almost like he's embarrassed. He points at her and mutters something on his way out the door with Owen, and I'm certain I missed something.

It only takes a few phone calls to get the search warrant, and I catch Britt's hand. "Want to take a ride with me to Kiawah?"

She smiles and even with this dead body hanging over us, she seems back to her usual, light self. Maybe it's because we found our suspect, although his death raises more questions than it answers. All of which I hope to find when we search his house.

"Sure, let me grab my gear."

Making our way from Eureka to Rockville requires navigating a labyrinth of country roads through the marshlands between the islands. It's a cool day, and the windows are down. Country music plays softly on the radio, and Britt threads her fingers in the passing breeze as we pass mile after mile of red cedars, live oaks, loblolly pines, and palmettos.

I think about yesterday at the fair and today in the courthouse, and I exhale a laugh. "I think my brother's trying to wear me down."

She looks over at me. "How so?"

"I think he's being nice, offering to keep Owen, so he can trick me into going to church with him."

Her cheeks lift with her laugh, and she leans her head against the back of the seat. "Why would he want to trick you into going to church?"

My hand rests on top of the steering wheel, and I look out over the tall grasses growing thick in the marsh.

"After our dad died, he got really into all that stuff. He likes to give me a hard time because I don't believe." Exhaling heavily, I look down at my lap. "Mom's right there with him, saying Owen needs dreams and magic in his life."

Britt turns in her seat to face me. "Your mom said that?"

"Yeah." I lift my chin with a bitter laugh.

"My mom would never believe anyone in your family felt that way." I can't comment on the topic of her mom, and she continues. "Your dad fought so hard to keep my gran from being mayor. Mom still hasn't forgiven him for it."

It's a sting from our past, and I'm not sure how much it bothers her. "He realized he was wrong about Edna. The two of them were actually friends before he died."

"I know." Her voice is quiet, and I reach over to take her hand.

"She cares about the town, and my dad learned it from working with her. He thought she would be irresponsible and run it into the ground. He thought she'd turn Eureka into a laughingstock." Sliding my thumb along the side of her hand, I say what I'm not sure he ever did. "He was wrong."

She lifts her chin, looking up at me with so much

vulnerability, her small hand in mine. "Sometimes you can be wrong about people."

Her words settle around us like a blanket, until the GPS system interrupts, telling us we're almost to our road. I give her hand a squeeze and return mine to the wheel. We take a narrow dirt road like so many others in this area, leading deeper into the forest, to a tiny cabin under a copse of pine trees.

Pulling up to the place, I shift the truck into park and kill the engine. We're quiet for a moment, waiting to see if anyone will emerge. When no one does, I take my gun out of its holster and glance over at Britt.

"Wait here while I make sure it's empty."

Her eyes are serious, and she takes out her phone, holding it in her hand. "I'm ready to call for backup if we need it."

Without another word, I slide out of the truck and close the door, walking slowly towards the porch. The windows are dark, and the only sound is the birds chirping overhead, the insects buzzing on the ground.

My boots thump on the wooden planks, and I knock loudly on the front door. "Anybody home?"

I wait, listening closely for the sound of shuffling or voices. Still, only the noise of birds and insects answer. Reaching out, I put my hand on the doorknob and turn it slowly. The door is unlocked, and it falls open easily, thumping against the wall.

I look back at Britt, whose eyes haven't left me. Giving her a nod, I take a step forward, through the door, looking all around to see if another human is on the premises.

When I'm sure they're not, I step onto the porch again and signal to her it's all clear. She opens the door and slides out, carrying her camera as she trots up the stairs.

"That was intense." A shaky laugh is in her tone.

I give her arm a squeeze. "You can never be too careful. People move out here because they don't trust anyone. They'll meet you at the door with a shotgun."

"I hear that."

Stepping through the small space, it looks like any other old hermit's shack. There's a couch and a reclining chair in front of a flatscreen television. The kitchen has a spindly wooden table and chairs, and the gas stove is ancient.

Britt takes a few quick photos then touches my arm. "I'm going to look around outside."

"Be careful." I walk to a desk in the corner, where a few of the drawers are open and the contents spilled out. It looks like someone was searching for something.

An old photo album is open on top, and stepping closer, I see it has newspaper clippings mixed with photographs.

"The Great Stantini?" I read the headline softly.

Curious, I take a closer look, and I see faces I barely recognize in a few of the pictures. Tapping the light on my phone, I get closer. It's Gwen and her husband, taken years ago.

Lifting the thin newsprint, I read, "Escape Artist Roswell Accuses Bailey of Theft." The next reads, "Roswell Vows Revenge," and another, smaller article reads, "Psychic community abuzz in the wake of Bailey drowning."

I'm about to call Britt inside when I slide the album off the desk and a letter falls to the floor. Picking it up, my eyes scan the longhand quickly. It's written to Gary, and the signature tightens my throat.

It's from Gwen.

I know you want to stay off the grid, but you don't have a choice now...

It's the closest I've ever been to catching him. Don't let him get away with all he's done, even to you. Let's set the record straight...

Stay strong, Gary. We're so close. This time we'll expose him...

I've spoken to my daughter, and she won't say anything until I tell her.

My lungs grow tighter the more I read, the anger in my chest intensifying with every word. I've only felt this sensation once before, sitting in the closet of my bedroom, looking at page after page of my wife's betrayal.

When I get to the final sentence, I'm at maximum rage.

Footsteps thump on the wooden floors behind me, and Britt's bright voice enters the room.

"Sure enough, I found them! The same ATV tire tracks are all over the place out there, and even narrower ones that might belong to a trailer. The only problem is, it's gone. There's not a single vehicle out there. That's weird, right?"

She walks over to where I'm standing, holding her camera for me to see. My jaw is tight, and I can't look at her for fear I might grab her by the shoulders and shake her. She hid this from me. What else is she hiding?

Grinding my jaw to stay silent, I lift my phone to take my own photos of the scene on the desk. I slide the letter into my pocket, then I turn for the door.

"Let's go." My voice is rough. "We've got another stop to make."

Chapter 22

Britt

"**D**ID YOU FIND SOMETHING IN THE CABIN?" MY VOICE IS SMALL in the large truck.

Aiden doesn't answer. He doesn't even look at me. His brow is lowered, and the muscle in his jaw moves back and forth. He hasn't said a word since we got on the road, and the knots in my stomach are making me sick.

The radio is off, but the windows are cracked and the wind roars around them intensifying my anxiety. We're headed back to town much faster than when we left. It's possible we might be speeding, but I don't know why.

I hold my camera in my lap to keep my fingers from twisting. I feel so small, like I felt when I was young and afraid, and I had no one to hold my hand. I'm in that place again, and I don't know why or how to stop it.

We were so happy this morning. I was relieved we had our guy—I didn't need my mother anymore. Now we could put all our attention on why Gary was burglarizing the town and how he died, whether at his own hand or the hand of an accomplice. I was convinced we'd find our answers at his house.

I should've known it would never be that simple.

We're driving through town, and when we pass the courthouse, I look to Aiden again. "Where are we going?"

Again, no answer, and the knot twists tighter in my gut. Angry Aiden is scary as fuck, and as we drive past town, out to the neighborhood I know so well, my fear intensifies.

He pulls into my mother's driveway and slams the truck into park before killing the engine and getting out. The door closes, and this time, he doesn't come around to my side. He walks right up to the front porch without waiting.

Grabbing the handle, I slide out of the seat and hurry to catch up. I'm having trouble filling my lungs with air, and by the time I reach him, he has already knocked on the door once.

His fist rises, and he's about to pound on the door when I hear a noise from inside.

"Coming!" It's my mother's voice.

The door flies inward, and Aiden's fist is still raised. She lets out a little yelp and starts to close the door again, but Aiden puts his palm out and stops it.

"It's time to talk." His deep voice is ominous.

Her eyes narrow at Aiden, and she only holds the door, not opening it. "What's this about?"

"I'm sure you know we found a dead body in the kids' park at the festival last night."

"And I'm sure you know I was working in the tarot tent all day yesterday."

"The body was dumped sometime Friday night, and I have reason to believe you were working with the deceased."

Mom's eyes fly to me, and I'm blinking fast. "You said you would wait."

My eyes widen, and I shake my head no.

Past the lump in my throat, I manage to whisper, "I did."

Aiden bristles at my side, and fear locks me in a straitjacket.

His voice has an edge when he speaks. "Your daughter kept her word to you. We were just at Gary Blue's house in Rockville, where I found this letter with your signature."

He pulls a folded sheet of thick, cream paper from his pocket and holds it out to her.

Mom recoils. "I don't know what that is."

"Let me help." He begins to read, his voice stern. "Stay strong, Gary. We're so close. This time we'll expose him." He folds the paper, leveling his stormy eyes on her. "Expose who, Gwen?"

"I'm not speaking to you about this. It's a family matter you couldn't possibly understand."

"A criminal is dead, and you're the last one we know who communicated with him." Aiden returns the letter to his pocket. "So perhaps this is a family matter, and you're the prime suspect."

"Don't be rude, Aiden Stone." Mom pulls her jewel-toned, paisley-patterned silk robe tighter around her body. "My family has never been criminals."

She's dressed in black leggings and a black tank top, and her curly, curly hair is full around her head. She looks every bit the eccentric fortune-teller I told Owen she isn't, and my stomach has a lead weight in it.

"Of course." Aiden exhales a bitter laugh. "You just take money from desperate people and claim to predict their futures."

"That is not what I do." Her hazel eyes flash.

"I don't care what you do. I want to know what you know about Gary Blue."

Mom exhales, opening the door. She walks up the hall to her kitchen, and Aiden walks straight inside after her. I rub my hand over the pain in my stomach and follow them to where my mom takes down a coffee mug and pours herself a cup.

"Britt, would you like a cup of coffee?" Her voice is clear, confident, and I'm terrified of what she's about to say.

As usual.

"No, thank you." I keep to the perimeter of the room, still

hoping I might be able to salvage things with Aiden. as hopeless as it appears.

"I'd offer you some, Sheriff, but I don't like you." Mom turns, walking to her small table. "Have a seat."

"I'd rather stand." Aiden's expression is stoney, and he clearly doesn't give a shit about the coffee snub.

"Suit yourself." Mom sits, taking a sip of her coffee and beginning, like she's doing a reading. "Gary Blue assisted an escape artist and magician named Stan Roswell back in the day. He was Stan's helper, meaning, he was the guy who recruited ladies to sit in the audience and volunteer to be sawed in half. Gary and Stan parted ways years ago. I heard they'd had a falling out, and Gary went off the grid. I was one of a very few who knew how to reach him. When the petty crimes started, and Britt told me about the prosthetic leg, I went to find him. Gary didn't commit those petty crimes. He didn't break into my house. I have an idea who did, but I wouldn't expect a Stone to understand or administer justice."

"When was this alleged break-in?"

"Wednesday, and it is not *alleged*. My daughter and her hound were here checking out the scene. Birgitte can verify it."

Aiden inhales deeply, crossing his arms, and I feel dizzy. He still won't look at me.

"Where is Stan Roswell now?"

"If I knew that, you wouldn't be here."

"What is that supposed to mean?"

My mother slaps her hand on the table and stands. "Stan Roswell is behind all of this. He probably killed Gary, and I'm more convinced than ever he killed Lars. I don't know what he's after, but you should stop wasting time with me and start searching for the real criminal."

Aiden lowers his arms, but the fury hasn't left his features. "I'm not putting you under arrest, but you are definitely a person of interest. Don't leave town."

I'm right behind him. He has to take me with him. We have to talk.

Mom calls after us, "Don't blow another murder, Sheriff Stone. If your father had investigated my husband's death thoroughly, Gary Blue might still be alive."

Aiden turns on his heel at the door, eyes blazing past me. "If you'd come to me when all this started instead of sneaking around, Gary Blue might still be alive."

With that, he turns and slams the door. I grab the handle, pulling it open and running after him.

"Aiden, wait." My voice is breathless. "Please."

His truck door is open when he stops, and I blink fast to keep the tears out of my eyes. This hurts so badly.

"You lied to me." It's a flat accusation.

"No! It wasn't like that!" I reach out to put my hand on his arm, but I stop, pulling it back and crossing my arms over my waist. "I told her I was going to tell you. I was on my way to tell you, but she begged me to give her time. I know, it sounds bad, but she said it was connected to my dad… She said she would give us the suspect, and I thought if it would help us—"

"So you chose your mother over telling me the truth." His voice is so angry, my chin drops in defeat. "Did your mother kill Gary?"

"No!" I shake my head. "She would never do something like that. She's odd, but she's not a killer."

"How do you know?" His jaw tightens, and when his stormy eyes finally meet mine, I see pain there. It slices me in two. "Why should I believe you? I thought you were different from them, but you're not."

"I am!"

"When it suits your purpose."

"That's not true. She's my mother, and I wanted to give her a chance. She said…" I can't even say it.

She won't put dad's death behind her, and neither will I.

Exhaling slowly, he looks into his truck. "I lived with a woman who lied to me for six years. I'm not doing it again."

"Aiden, please." My chest collapses as I watch him climb into the cab. "Don't go."

"I can't see you anymore." He slams the door and starts the engine.

Trembling hands cover my mouth as he backs out of the driveway without another word. My legs weaken, and I lower to my knees watching his tail lights disappear. Red dots turn to red smudges as the tears flood my eyes, as the water rises past my neck.

I'm right where I started, in a straitjacket and drowning.

Chapter 23

Aiden

"**I** CAN'T WORK WITH HER, EDNA. SHE WITHHELD CRITICAL information about the case, which resulted in a man's death." It's Monday morning, and I'm sitting across from the mayor in her office with the door shut.

I spent the rest of yesterday chopping wood in the backyard, cleaning limbs off the top of the house, mowing the lawn with the old push mower, basically anything I could do to burn the anger, the frustration, the *ache* out of my body.

It wasn't only in my chest this time, it was everywhere. It was in my hands that had touched her, my lips that had tasted her beautiful skin, my ears that wouldn't stop hearing her broken voice begging me, *Don't leave...*

Adam brought Owen home from the beach with Edward, and he took one look at my face and offered to return the dog to Britt. I managed to hold it together as I listened to my son tell me all about his fun day with "the best dog ever" at the beach.

I did my best not to show that it was like nails driving into my chest hearing his little-boy voice so happy and in love with another woman who ripped my trust to shreds.

Then, when he finally went to sleep, I polished off the rest of the Stone Cold single barrel I'd been keeping in the cabinet.

Now my head is pounding, and my anger is back full-force, and the last thing I want to see is a bright little blonde with a sexy little backside and a sunshine face who says I'm safe with her that she's different, when in reality she's just like them.

"Aiden, I know you're emotional." Edna leans back in her chair, folding her hands. "But we don't know enough about the case to make a causal connection."

Of course, her grandmother would take Britt's side.

"Don't patronize me, Edna." Ice is in my tone, and I'm done playing nice. "I want her off my team."

"You need to remember your place, Sheriff." Edna's steely gaze clashes with mine. "I'm the mayor. I signed Birgitte's contract. We have a dead body on our hands, and we need to find out who did it. She can work with Doug and report to me."

Frustration climbs up my shoulders. I know the chain of command. Edna is my boss, even though she's elected and I'm not. Still, she's the CEO of the town, and I'm her first in command. Can't change the facts.

"Fine." My jaw is set, and I stand. "I'll keep you informed of developments in the case, and I'll converse with Doug about what I need done."

I snatch the door open and stride out into the office area, keeping my eyes away from the corner where her desk is located. Doug, as usual, is hanging around Holly's desk laughing and eating a donut.

"Doug." My voice is clipped, and he hops to attention, hustling over to where I'm standing.

"Morning, Boss." Doug has that permanent smile on his face. "What can I do you for today?"

"You're working with Britt now. I want you to take her to

Gary Blue's place and process the scene. Take the dog, and see if he picks up any scents."

"Yes, sir." He polishes off his donut and wipes his hands with the paper napkin.

I'm headed back to the fairground to see what I can find in the corn maze. In the meantime, we're waiting on ballistics. Pausing at the back hall, my eyes are drawn to Britt at her desk, collecting her camera and supplies.

She's dressed in simple khaki pants and a green sweater. Her hair hangs down her back, and her long bangs obscure her eyes. Still, I can read her body language. Her lips are tight, and her shoulders are rounded.

If she feels bad, I don't care. She should feel bad.

Anger tightens my throat, and I redirect my eyes to Doug. "Also, collect Gwen Bailey's firearm for ballistics testing."

I feel her eyes snap to me, but I turn on my heel and leave the room. We've got work to do, and if she has a problem with it, she can talk to her grandmother.

Workers are dismantling the remainder of the festival equipment when I arrive at the fairgrounds. It's odd doing this alone. In the past, I had Doug with me to inspect a crime scene, then I had her.

Now, walking down what was the midway, I'm assaulted by memories of strolling hand in hand, stopping at the booths, dunking Doug. Her mood had been mixed leading up to the day, and I'd been worried it was something I had done. My chest heats when I remember texting her, asking that very question.

It wasn't me.

A loud noise overhead draws my attention, and like a gut punch, I see the remainder of the Ferris wheel slowly being dismantled. I don't want to remember her straddling my lap, my face buried in her tits, her hips rocking against my hand. I don't want to think about how good it felt to have her in my arms. I believed we had something real, but it was only hormones and chemistry.

Steeling my resolve, I continue to what was the corn maze. Now it's an empty space roped off with yellow crime scene tape. Most of our documentation is complete, but the scene is still ours for a few more days to investigate.

I walk to the spot where the body was found, and I inspect the area behind it, where Edward had picked up the scent of the boot we found at Terra's. A flat path disappears into the stalks, and just as Britt said, a trail of narrow tire tracks leads towards the road.

I can't tell if they were made by a car or a trailer, and it doesn't take long before they're lost in the mix of tracks from all the vehicles used to haul in the equipment for the large children's area.

Whoever dumped Gary's body planned it so we wouldn't be able to follow him or her. I'll ask the Beauford guys to inspect the tracks and see if there's any way to make sense of them. I'll tell Doug they need to come out here and be sure every little detail is documented.

I think of Britt carefully examining Terra's field and studying the alley behind Holly's house. I was so impressed by her thoroughness. I have to trust she'll be as thorough again, knowing I've got my eye on her mother.

My jaw tightens, and I know she will. I'm angry that I know she will.

I've done all I can do here, and I'm walking back to my truck. We'll know a lot more once we have the coroner's report and ballistics. I need to take a long lunch so I can get a workout at the gym or go for a long run. I need to burn this tension out of my chest, then I'll see what I can find out about Stan Roswell.

Being so close to this, with how much it's linked to her family, feels like I'm walking through the past, reliving my dad's frustration with Gwen and her persistence about knowing every detail of Lars's case.

Lars Bailey attempted a stunt where he was bound in a

straight jacket and locked in a metal trunk then dropped into the ocean fifty yards from the shore. Boats and emergency workers were all on hand, but he was an escape artist. The point was to let him escape.

A huge crowd was gathered on the shore watching the performance, and a screen was erected to give them a close-up view of the surface of the water where the black metal coffin-shaped box was lowered. It sank all the way to the bottom.

He was supposed to be free in less than two minutes. I remember it so clearly.

Lars had always fascinated me with his tricks, and he always had a new one every Memorial Day weekend. I was seventeen, just graduated high school, watching with my dad on the sheriff's boat.

Five minutes passed, and the surface of the water remained quiet. We all strained our eyes, waiting for him to break through the currents, arms extended in a triumphant *V* over his head, like always.

I remember looking over at the boat where Gwen and Edna waited, and straining my memory, I try to remember seeing a little girl. She would've been ten… I was way too focused on the dark blue water, a sick feeling in my stomach as another minute passed, as silence held the spectators on shore, as the tension grew stronger.

At the seven-minute mark, my dad said to call it. Lars's team said to wait. He should have been fine. He was in a sealed box. At the ten-minute mark, Dad insisted something was wrong, too much time had passed, and they finally relented.

I'll never forget the chains raising the box from the water. It was too heavy, they were getting too much resistance. When it finally broke the surface, streams of water gushed from the broken seals. Everyone gasped, a woman's screams turned to wails, and a pit was in my stomach.

Lars Bailey was dead.

By Friday, we've ruled out Gwen's gun as having fired the shot that killed Gary Blue, and we've verified he had no alcohol or drugs in his system. We were also able to establish his time of death as late Friday night.

Doug and Britt thoroughly documented the scene at his cabin and at the fairground, but even with all this information, we're left with as many questions as answers. They're all focused on what's missing.

We can't find Gary's prosthesis, and there are no signs of a three-wheel ATV anywhere. Holly's chickens haven't been recovered. We haven't even found signs of chickens, which are pretty hard to hide, and we found no trace of white boards or paint.

For that matter, I'm starting to think the mysterious signs are the work of a different person altogether, and considering they're relatively harmless, I'm taking them off the table.

Suicide is still on the table, but after all Gwen said, I'd like to find this Stan Roswell and question him.

I've managed to keep all of this out of the press. The last thing we need is a swarm of reporters and social media types sticking their noses in everything and getting in our way. The worst are "true-crime detectives," also known as meddling amateurs.

Of course, Piper Jackson, Eureka's very own Lois Lane, has been at the courthouse snooping around since Day 1. When I told her no comment, she immediately drifted to her bestie's area. It provoked the one word I've said to Britt all week. A solid *no*.

Her green eyes blinked wide with surprise, but she nodded, cutting her eyes to her friend and shaking her head.

"Are you helping solve crimes, ole boy?" Friday also means Owen is with me in the office, and the sound of him playing with Edward at Britt's desk is like tiny knives stabbing my stomach.

"You're wishing you could win another race, aren't you? Are you coming over to our house tonight, Miss Britt?"

"Ahh… not tonight." I can tell she's not sure how much he knows.

Nothing. He knows nothing.

I turn slightly, speaking to him. "You're headed to Gram's tonight, Owen. Ryan and Pinky will be there. In fact, we need to get going."

"Okay." His enthusiasm dims slightly. "I haven't forgotten about you, ole boy! We'll play together real soon, don't you worry."

He hops up and gives Britt a hug. I try not to notice her squeezing him back because it fucking sucks to feel this angry at her and still know she cares about my kid.

Driving Owen the short distance to my mother's house is a little like water torture. Slow drips driving me insane.

"Edward's such a good dog. I'm sure he misses chasing after my socks. Are we going to have them over for dinner again? Maybe we could get together at a park or I could go to Miss Britt's and play while you're at work. Maybe I could take Edward for a walk again, or we could see what else he can find…"

He doesn't stop talking, and I'm starting to wish Santa and I had gotten on the same page at Christmas and got him a damn puppy.

"We'll see." Is as much as I say.

Mom is thrilled to have "her babies" at the house for another Friday night. I hang around the door, wondering what I'm going to do alone in my empty house with my son gone for the night. It took less than a month for me to get used to the possibility of her.

"Hey, there's the old Aiden face I know and love." My youngest brother drifts over to where I'm shadowing the door of my mother's house. "Why the scowl?"

"I'm not really in the mood, Adam." My voice is flat, and I couldn't be more honest.

"Feel like having a drink with me? Just because Alex is out of town doesn't mean we can't open the tasting room."

I hesitate a moment. Hanging with my brother is a recipe for annoyance. At the same time, I don't want to drink alone tonight.

"Sure. Let's go."

He follows me out, and it's not long before we're seated on polished wood barstools at the reclaimed oak and brass bar inside our family's distillery.

"A little single barrel for you." Adam pours two fingers in my glass. "And some special reserve for me."

I lift the tumbler, clinking it to his, and we take a sip of the smooth bourbon whiskey I've been using to kill the pain for the last five days.

"Talk to me, bro. What happened with you and Britt?" He leans on his forearms.

"She didn't tell you?"

"Not a word. She just thanked me for bringing Edward home and said she had a headache, which in my experience is always code for something else."

I decide I don't care. I'm tired of carrying this alone.

"She's just like them." It's as much as I'm able to get out.

My voice is thick, and the weight of emotion pressing down on my chest catches me off-guard.

"Them... who?"

Taking another sip, I'm able to continue. "The Baileys. They're all tricky con artists, bending the truth to suit their purposes. I thought she was different, but she's not."

Adam's brow furrows, and he rubs his finger over the lip of his glass. "We're talking about Britt Bailey?" I cut my eyes at him like *don't play with me*, and he holds up both hands. "Just checking because I'm pretty good friends with Britt, and that doesn't sound like her at all."

Pain twists in my stomach, and I polish off the rest of my drink. He's quick to pour me another inch. "She lied to me. I was going along, thinking everything was great, and the whole time, she was keeping secrets and lying… just like Annemarie."

"What did Britt lie about?"

"Gwen." It comes out a growl. "Gwen knew who our suspect was. More importantly, she knew *where* he was, and when Britt found out, she didn't say a word. She went a whole week smiling to my face and going behind my back."

My brother nods solemnly, pouring himself another shot. "That shit with Annemarie was fucked up."

"It was." I clink my glass against his.

"A whole year, sneaking around, sending letters. I mean, who even sends letters anymore? It's like she wanted to get caught."

He's saying the words, and my stomach tightens along with my jaw. "What's your point?"

Blue eyes lift to mine, and if he says what I think he's about to say, I might punch him.

"I remember this one time when we were in school, and Cass wanted Piper to write her English paper for her. Even then, Piper was killer at writing. Always got the *A*."

It's not what I thought he was going to say, and my jaw relaxes. "Okay?"

"Britt wouldn't hear of it. She told them it was cheating and if they did it, she wouldn't be their friend anymore. Ultimately, they didn't do it."

I don't like the sting of pride fighting with the anger in my stomach.

He takes one look at my face and finishes. "I've known Britt a long time. She might be vulnerable to her mom's games, but what she did is not the same as what Annemarie did. It's not even in the same universe."

"It's the lie, Adam. We spent the whole weekend together, and she never said a word." I think about how she acted those days, the way she left so abruptly Friday night. "She knew she was doing wrong."

"You've heard that saying, 'To forgive is divine'?" He squints up at me.

"And you've heard the saying, 'Fool me once'?"

His lips press together, and he nods. "Yeah, but Britt's not like Gwen, and she's definitely not like Annemarie. She's sweet, she's serious, and she cares. If anyone deserves a second chance, it's her."

I finish my drink, ready to be done here for the night. "I've had enough of second chances."

"So you're going to lose a girl, one who made you smile for the first time in five years, because she didn't rat out her mom?"

Standing off my stool, I point at him. "Saying it that way makes it sound like it's no big deal." He chews the side of his lip, but to his credit, he doesn't say it. "I'm not going to hold somebody in my arms, trust her with my son, if she can't be honest."

"Everybody makes mistakes."

"Some mistakes are harder to forgive than others."

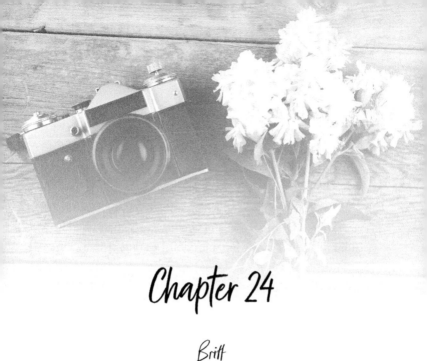

Chapter 24

Britt

"I THINK I'M GOING TO DIE." I'M LYING ON MY COUCH WITH MY head in Cass's lap. "Everything hurts. It's like a sinkhole has opened in the middle of my chest, and it's swallowing me whole, crushing all my bones."

Six days ago, my life was practically perfect. I had a great job, my own place, I was home again, and I had a gorgeous man to hold my hand, calm my fears… and give me incredible orgasms.

Then on the seventh day it all went to hell.

I can still feel his soft hair in my fingers, his lips on my breasts, his mouth claiming mine. I can still feel the warmth of his palm against my inner thigh as we descended from heaven on the Ferris wheel.

We should've stayed in Eureka on Sunday and had sex. We should've gone to the beach with his brother and Owen.

I should've told him when I had the chance.

Every day this week Doug has been upbeat and cheerful, expressing amazement at my work and complimenting me on how smart I am for putting together a theory based on all that's missing.

Then every night, I would come home and lie on the couch and cry. Or eat. Or drink.

Finally, this afternoon I went to Gran and told her I should go back to Greenville. As expected, she forcefully rejected the idea.

"You're going to stay right here and do the job I hired you to do. A killer is on the loose, and you have to help us find him."

Blinking down to my lap, I fought the sting of tears in my eyes. "I hurt him, Gran."

My voice was just above a whisper, and she was out of her chair, circling her desk to pull me into a hug before the first tear could fall. Resting my cheek on her shoulder, I closed my eyes as the pain twisted my chest.

"I've always tried to make the right decisions. I was the good girl, the straight-*A* student."

"You made a mistake, child." Her soothing voice did little to ease my pain. "Love can be tricky when family grudges are there. But I made peace with Andrew Stone. His son is a good man, if a bit closed-minded, and I bet you can help him with that."

"I can't help anything. I only screw everything up."

Holding my shoulders, she smoothed her hands in the sides of my hair. "It was your first time being put in that situation, but you're learning."

"He won't give me another chance."

"He will."

"You don't understand. He's been hurt before. I didn't think what I did was the same, but I guess from his side, it feels that way. He'll never forgive me."

"He might." She gave me a little smile. "I think he'd be a fool not to."

I hugged her, wishing she could be right.

Confiscating my mother's gun turned my misery into anger.

I almost let Doug do it himself, because I wasn't sure I could see her without letting her have it.

In the end, I was a professional and did my job.

"What does Aiden Stone want with my gun?" she groused, unloading it and packing it in her case. "He's wasting time as usual and leaving me unprotected."

"He's following procedure." I couldn't keep the edge out of my voice. "Hiding evidence makes you appear suspicious."

"You think I killed Gary?" Her eyes flashed to me.

"No."

She pushed her hair over her shoulder, lifting her chin. "At least he hasn't turned you against your family."

"He's actually not even speaking to me now. Happy?"

Silence fell around us, and when she answered, her tone actually sounded contrite. "No, I'm not happy if you're sad. It's possible Aiden might be good for you in some ways. At least he sounded good in one way."

"That's it. I'm leaving." I picked up her gun and put it in my bag, starting for the door where Doug waited patiently, smiling like the conversation didn't take an awkward turn.

"Waste all the time you want." Mom followed me slowly to the door. "I'm doing my own research."

My eyes blinked closed, and I was almost afraid to ask. "What does that mean?"

"It means I'll find Stan, and when I do, I'll make him confess he killed Lars and Gary, and I'll make him tell me why he's doing all this. That'll show the arrogant Sheriff Stone."

"You're not to leave town, and if I find out you did, I *will* tell Aiden this time, and he'll probably put you in jail."

Holding up both hands, she turned towards the kitchen. "I heard. I'm not planning to leave town."

"Then how are you going to get his confession?"

"I pulled out the spell book and did it the old-fashioned way."

"You cast a spell." A growl rumbled in my throat, and I couldn't deal with her another minute.

I motioned to Doug, and we brought her gun to the station where not surprisingly, it wasn't a match.

Now it's Friday. A whole week has passed, and this separation, this intense regret has formed an aching pit in the center of my chest. My two besties organized an emergency intervention, armed with Ben & Jerry's.

"You're like the house at the end of *Poltergeist*." Piper sits at the other end of the couch, a pint of Chunky Monkey in her hand. "Where it all crumples together and disappears into thin air. That was sick."

I push her with my foot. "You're not helping."

"Sorry!"

"Hang in there my sunny little BB." Cass hugs my shoulders while holding a spoon of Cherry Garcia for me to nibble. "He'll come around. You guys were too good together for him to ditch it over a misunderstanding."

"It was more than that. He's only said one word to me all week."

"What was it?"

"*No.*"

"I was there for that!" Piper calls with her mouth full. "I'm pissed at him for it, too. He won't give me anything for my story, and the town has a right to know what happened. People are scared. They want to know they're safe."

"They're safe." My voice is muffled by another spoonful Cass swooped into my mouth.

"Can I quote you on that?"

"No." Tucking my face in my bestie's lap, I'm not getting over this. "What am I going to do, Cass?"

"Say you're sorry." Cass nods, taking another bite of ice cream.

"I want to." I sit up, shoving my bangs behind my ears. "I want to tell him I know I was wrong not to trust him with this when I trust him with everything. I want to tell him I won't let my mom guilt trip me ever again. I've learned my lesson. I want to tell him I love him…" My voice breaks, and my chin drops as the pain rushes in like a storm surge, knocking the wind from my lungs.

"You love him?" Cass's voice is a soft whisper.

Nodding, I touch the tears off my cheeks. "How can I apologize if he won't even speak to me?"

"Let's see." She scoots around on the couch. "What would Shania say…"

"She gal darn gone and done it?" Piper suggests.

Cass shakes her head. "What about 'Any Man of Mine'?"

Curling my nose, I shake my head. "I'm on the wrong side of that equation. I need something where she screwed up and sings about loving him so much she'll never, ever, *ever* do it again."

I add the emphasis on the last *ever* from the depths of my soul.

Piper shakes her head. "Shania never sang a song like that. You're thinking of something from waaay back. You need Waylon Jennings."

Frowning, I try to think of which song she means. "The Dukes of Hazzard?"

"Ahh, that would be… *wrong*." She puts a spoon of ice cream in her mouth before getting on her knees and leaning closer.

In a flash, I know exactly the song she's talking about. "No."

A warning is in my voice, which she completely ignores. "Wrong!" She growls in her best Waylon Jennings impersonation before falling back on her butt laughing.

Cass presses her lips together, her eyes widening comically like she's about to burst.

"Don't you dare," I push her with my foot.

Her brows squench, and she clasps both hands over her mouth and nose. "That song is so funny."

"You should've known it all along," Piper continues, and I move my foot to her hip, pushing so hard she falls off the couch. It doesn't stop her.

"You are evil and you must be destroyed." I say, quoting my all-time favorite character from my all-time favorite film—Ouiser from *Steel Magnolias*.

She only laughs more, and Cass caves, belting out in her own growly impersonation, "Wrong!"

"You are both pigs from hell." I grab a pillow and flop hard on it, turning away from them snorting and laughing.

They only crawl closer to me singing that dumb song even more. I sit up hard, slapping the pillow on my lap when I notice my phone is lit up on the coffee table.

It's probably a text from my mother that I have no desire to read. Still, I grab it at the very least to get them to shut up.

When I see the screen, my heart jumps to my throat, and my mouth goes dry.

It's a text from Aiden. **Would you be willing to meet at the Little Sunbeam Park tomorrow afternoon? Owen wants to play with Edward.**

I grab them both, and they crowd around me reading what he wrote.

My fingers shake so hard I have to retype my message three times to fix the typos. Finally, I settle for a simple **Sure!**

I get a one-word reply. **Thanks.**

Piper puts her arm around my shoulder and squeezes. "Looks like you've got your chance to say you're sorry. You'd better make it good."

I hope she's right.

Chapter 25

Aiden

"GOOD THING WE DIDN'T WASH THESE SOCKS!" OWEN BOUNCES in the backseat of my truck, holding Zander and waving his dirty socks around. "Edward loves the smell of my stinky socks. He's so weird."

"He's a dog." My voice is flat, and I'm having second thoughts about this idea.

It feels like a visitation, and we were never even officially a couple—even if the whole town seemed to know about us. I just couldn't keep listening to Owen talk about Edward, and after I saw Britt hug him at work, something cracked inside me.

I still meant every word I said to my brother about her, but lying alone in my bed staring into the darkness, that day on the boat seventeen years ago haunted me, the way Gwen screamed when the metal box was pulled out of the water, when we all realized at the same time something had gone terribly wrong.

I thought about losing my own dad four years later, and while I didn't scream and wail, my insides made the same sound she did.

I'm not ready to let my guard down again, but I'll let Owen play with her dog.

When I pull into the parking lot, my mom's bike is already parked beside a post, and Britt's inside the park with Edward. She's wearing a long-sleeved white tee and cutoff blue jeans with her cowboy boots, just like the first day she crashed into my life.

A low growl vibrates in my throat, and I'm pissed at how much I still feel for her. I'm pissed at how fucking pretty she is and how fucking weak I am when it comes to her. One look, and I want her.

"Edward!" Owen is out of the truck before I've killed the engine, and I sit for a moment watching him run to her.

I watch her lean down and hug him tight. A smile breaks over her pretty face, and all the charitable feelings I had on the drive over twist into frustration in my stomach. Something about her is different. Maybe it is a kind of spell she casts—which I'd considered that night so long ago on the back porch.

All I know is I've never felt this way for a woman. She could hurt me in a way no one ever has, and I don't like it.

Climbing from the truck, I walk slowly to where she stands watching Owen run all over the park waving his socks as Edward bounds and *Rooos* beside him. She pushes her long bangs behind her ears, and the closer I get, I see her eyes are red. She's smiling, but it's sad. The sunniness I'd grown to love about her is missing.

"Thanks for doing this." My voice is rough, so I clear it. "He hasn't stopped talking about Edward all week."

"Edward misses him, too." She blinks up at me and her bottom lip slips inside her mouth.

I put my hands in the back pockets of my jeans to head off any temptation to touch her. "How's it going with Doug?"

"Good." She nods, looking down and pushing her hair behind her ears. "He's so upbeat and positive all the time."

"I think it's the donuts."

She exhales a smile, and Owen and Edward charge back to where we are, circling her.

"Did you see our picture in the paper for winning the race?" His little voice is loud and happy, creating a sharp contrast to the mood between us.

"I sure did." She scrubs her fingers through the top of his hair. "I cut it out to save."

"Dad did, too." He drops to his knees, hugging Edward's head, and I shift my stance when her eyes flicker to me. "I wonder if I could teach him to play hide-and-seek. Can you play hide-and-seek, old boy?"

"I'll hold him and count to twenty if you want to try." She takes a knee beside the dog, putting her hand on his collar. "I think he'll probably find you pretty quick."

"I'll hide in a really hard place." He lifts his arm and rubs it under Edward's nose. "Ready to find me, boy?"

"Go ahead, and yell when you're ready."

Owen takes off running towards the tree line at the back of the park.

"Don't go too far," I call after him, and he does a little wave over his head.

We wait a few minutes until Owen yells he's ready, then Britt releases the dog. "Go get him!"

Edward lunges forward, sniffing all over the ground in the direction my son ran. We watch as it takes less than two minutes for Edward to find him. He stands at the base of a live oak tree, lifting his head and *Rooo*-ing loudly until Owen finally drops to the ground laughing. He rolls around in the grass as Edward sniffs him all over.

"Those two." I exhale on a breath.

Britt blinks up at me, and her brow furrows. Her lips part, and she seems about to say something, then it seems she changes her mind. "I have a new theory about the case if you'd like to hear it."

I straighten. "Okay."

"I was actually taking Edward for a walk when I discovered Mom's break-in." My brow lowers, and she pushes past that part quickly. "When we went inside, Edward started carrying on like he recognized the scent the same way he did when we found the body in the corn maze. Only, if you remember, in the corn maze, he wasn't howling at Gary's body. He was howling at the trail behind it."

She has my attention now, and even if I'm frustrated with her, I can't deny her instincts are good. "What are you saying?"

"Gary wasn't wearing his prosthetic when he died, and we haven't been able to find it in his cabin. He also doesn't have a three-wheeler, or it's missing as well." I nod, and she continues. "What if it was Stan the whole time? What if he used Gary's prosthetic to frame him, or to divert the attention to him?"

It's an interesting idea. "But why would he do that?"

She shakes her head, looking down. "Maybe so we'd be searching for Gary instead of him?"

"You think Stan was planning something bigger?"

"I don't know, but my mom is trying to find him. This time I'm telling you everything. I told her not to leave town, but she never listens to me."

Noted. "Have you found any evidence of Stan Roswell being with Gary?"

Again, she shakes her head, and her brow furrows. "We only have the photo album in Gary's cabin and Mom's story. You know, where she believes Stan is behind everything."

"Yeah, I know." Gwen has been a thorn in our side for years, but I wonder how long I'd pursue it if I thought someone had killed my dad.

Silence falls between us, and she looks out at Owen, chewing her lip. Her brow is furrowed, and I want to slide the lock of hair out of her eyes. I hate what's happening between us, but my stubborn heart restrains my hand.

Owen and Edward come running towards us again, and I've stood here with her, maintaining my distance as long as I can. Her brains mixed with that cute little ass and the wrinkle in her nose is what got me last time.

This time I'm keeping our relationship purely professional.

"You can do better." The stern note returns to my voice. "Come back when you've got something I can use."

She visibly wilts, and I tell myself it's the same thing I'd tell any of my officers. Except for Doug, because I'm not sure he could. It doesn't matter.

I motion to Owen, and he gives Edward another hug before running to Britt and hugging her waist. "Maybe y'all can come over for dinner again one night!"

"Maybe." Her voice is quiet, and I turn away, stalking to my truck.

I put Owen inside and close the door. My door is still shut when I look back to see her leading the bike to where I'm standing.

"I should probably return your mother's bike." Her voice is quiet, and a surge of protectiveness rises in my chest.

"I still haven't checked the brakes on your truck."

She blinks up at me. "You're still going to do that?"

"I'm still concerned about your safety, if that's what you mean."

"Oh, Aiden." She parks the bike, taking a half-step forward. "I'm so sorry for not telling you about Gary. I didn't think about how it would make you feel. I should have. I should have trusted you to help me. Can't we please talk about it?"

Mist is in her pretty green eyes, and my muscles tense with the war raging inside me. She's so close I catch her faint scent of flowers and the ocean. She twists her hands together, and her voice breaks on the last words. My brother said if anyone deserves a second chance, it's her.

"I'm not doing this." I shake my head, turning away. "Keep the bike for now. I'll figure it out later."

With that, I climb into my truck and put on my seatbelt, leaving quickly without looking back.

Chapter 26

Britt

IT FEELS LIKE A ROPE IS TIED AROUND MY HEART, AND WHEN HE DRIVES away, it rips through my ribcage, falls to the ground, and bounces over the rocks and stones on the asphalt as he drags it behind him.

Leaving the bike beside his empty space, I walk slowly to the swings and sit. My hands are in my lap, and I lower my chin as a tear traces its way down my nose.

Edward sits in front of me waiting, but I don't want to move. I don't want to ride back to town. I imagine sitting here forever and letting that be my punishment.

No, I don't think even that would ease this pain.

So I sit.

I don't know how much time passes before the crunch of feet on gravel sounds from near the road. A small footpath leads from the park to town, and I glance up to see Adam running in my direction, then slowing and taking a turn to walk over to where I'm sitting on the swings.

"Hey, girl." He's breathing hard, and a sheen of sweat covers his shirtless chest. "What are you doing out here?"

"Playing with my dog." I look at Edward, who is now lying on the grass in front of me.

He puts his hands on his hips, frowning. "Is that so?"

"Owen was here, so he's tired. I'm letting him take a break."

"Owen was here?" He walks over and sits in the swing next to me. "Does that mean Aiden was here, too?"

My chin bobs up and down, but I don't want to talk about it. He seems to understand and doesn't press. He only sniffs, looking forward and swaying slightly back and forth. We're quiet, and his running shoes make a soft rustling sound in the rubber mulch.

Adam is a comforting presence. We never dated in high school, but I always enjoyed his friendship. He's observant and quick, and I remember how he was my ally for a little while, taking Owen and entertaining him so Aiden and I could be alone. I never thanked him for it.

I lift my face, and when our eyes meet, I feel the urge to confess. "I was falling in love with him."

"I know." His voice is quiet, and his damp hair sticks out in sweaty waves around his face. "I was going to suggest we go for coffee, but now I'm thinking you might need something a little stronger."

My nose wrinkles. "You're a mess."

That makes him laugh, an attractive smile spreading across his handsome face, and the family resemblance is so strong it hurts. He stands, turning to face me in my swing and holds out his hand.

"Come on." I reach out and allow him to pull me to my feet. "I'll meet you at the distillery, and we're going to figure this out."

"I knew from the start it was a mistake, but I didn't realize how bad it would hurt him." I'm sitting at the glossy wooden bar in

Stone Cold distillery with Adam across from me, talking to him like I'm giving my confession.

A tumbler of their single barrel bourbon is in front of me, and it reminds me of my first night at Aiden's house, when he invited me over for burgers then took me home and destroyed the possibility of me ever being with any other man.

After we parted ways on the playground, Adam ran back to his place. I biked home to deposit Edward, then I changed into jeans and a long-sleeved sweater and rode out to meet him here at the bar.

"I knew he didn't like my mom, but I thought ultimately he'd understand my predicament."

"What was that?" Adam sits across from me in a short-sleeved, navy V-neck sweater and jeans.

He has his own glass of bourbon, and he's listening intently. I lower my hands to my lap, lacing my fingers together. Talking about my mom always makes me itchy and uncomfortable. I know how it sounds.

"My mom is kind of obsessed with my dad's death, and she's convinced what's happening now is connected to it somehow." Exhaling, I add under my breath. "She's always convinced everything is connected to his death."

Adam takes a sip of his drink, squinting one eye at me. "So what's your predicament?"

"She said the reason I had to give her time was for my dad. She said she was so close this time." Lifting my glass, I tilt the tumbler side to side. "Then she did this reading, and I totally fell for it. God, I'm so dumb."

"For caring about your family?"

"For getting sucked into her crazy again. When I moved back, I insisted on getting my own apartment for that very reason. So I wouldn't be inundated with her nonstop beliefs and suspicions twenty-four seven."

"Maybe she's right."

I set the tumbler on the bar a little too forcefully. "Don't do that."

"Hey, I'm just playing devil's advocate," he laughs, and a deep dimple appears in his cheek.

It reminds me of how all the girls at school would follow him around like love-sick puppies. I never felt that way for Adam, but he's definitely sexy and playful, and he has an understanding nature that could charm the panties off a nun.

Sitting straighter on the barstool, he slides both palms down his dark jeans. "I think he overreacted."

Shaking my head, I disagree. "He's been hurt before. I should've been more sensitive to his wounds."

Adam's brow furrows and he studies my face. "He told you about Annemarie?"

I nod, aching at how blind I'd been. Of course it's where Aiden's mind went.

"Wow." Adam lifts the tumbler and takes a sip. "He does love you."

My eyes slide closed, and I ache with wanting to believe it's true. "He barely looks at me now."

"He's angry. He's on the defense, but there's a big difference in cheating on someone and holding back information for your family. He'll come around."

"I don't know." I study my hands, missing him so much.

"Listen, I've seen my brother in more than one romantic relationship, and he's never been like he was with you. He was happy. Hell, he actually smiled and gave out compliments."

"You make him sound so mean."

"He was mean. He was a grumpy asshole until you."

"He's not an asshole!"

A warm smile curls his lips, and he reaches out to cup the side of my neck, placing his forehead to mine briefly. "You are so good for him. He's going to get his head out of his ass. Just don't give up on him, okay?"

I reach out and hug him back. "Thanks for making me feel better."

"You've always been a good friend to me, and I think you'd make a great sister."

That makes me smile, and real warmth soothes my insides. "I think you'd make a great brother." Sliding off my chair, I check the large clock over the door. "I'd better head on back before it's dark."

"If you don't mind hanging around while I clean up, I can drive you. That old beach cruiser will fit in the back of my Jetta."

"Don't you always have a surfboard in the back of your Jetta?" I wink at him, and he shakes his head.

"I took it out last weekend. It needs sanding and a fresh coat of wax."

"It's okay." I squeeze his muscled arm. "I actually like riding in the twilight. It's magical."

"Hold up. I thought you stopped believing in magic." He's teasing, and I almost laugh.

He really has made me feel better. He's given me hope.

"Maybe there's no magic, but there might be a little pixie dust."

"That's the spirit. Ride safe, and text me when you get home."

"I will." Leaving the bar, I realize I forgot to ask about the secret he's been keeping, specifically with regard to my bestie Piper.

"Next time," I say to myself, unlocking the cruiser from the bike rack.

A gorgeous full moon is just rising as I take off down the narrow road leading from the distillery back to town. It's a little farther out than the neighborhoods, but it's still only a few miles from my apartment.

My mind is full from our conversation, and I'm actually smiling again. Of all the people who've tried to encourage me,

Adam is the one who actually helps me believe I could end up with Aiden again.

Exhaling a sigh, I long so much for his strong arms around me. If I ever get the chance to be there again, I swear I'll never mess it up. Lifting my eyes to the starry sky, I say a little prayer that it might happen. It can't hurt, right?

The sound of tires approaching from behind makes me stop pedaling so I can coast to the shoulder, out of the way. I expect it to be Adam finished early, since we're both heading in the same direction, and I'm surprised when it's a light blue Ford I don't recognize. We're pretty far off the beaten path.

It slows to match my speed, and I see the passenger side window is lowered. Inside, an older man looks over at me and smiles. His face is wrinkled, but his hair is dyed dark brown. He even has a thin mustache on his upper lip.

"Nice night for a ride." He smiles in a way that makes my heart beat faster.

A touch of evil is in his tone, and I don't answer. I focus on the road and pedal faster, pulling out ahead of him.

He gives his truck a little gas, and he's easily keeping time with me. "Not very friendly, are you?"

My chest tightens, and my stomach quivers as I strain to get closer to town. Out here on this lonely road, no one is around to help me, but we're so close to Eureka. I pump my legs harder, standing on the pedals.

"Why are you running?" His voice is too calm, like he has a plan, and he's just waiting for the right moment to execute it. "I need directions."

Roaring is in my ears and little gasping noises come from my chest as I push harder. The truck gets ahead of me and suddenly whips over in front of my bike, causing me to veer onto the shoulder and lose my balance.

With a little scream, I fall to the side, but the bike doesn't go all the way down. The truck door opens and slams shut, and

I walk the bike backwards as fast as I can to get away from him and get out of here.

I'm not fast enough, and he straddles the front wheel, grabbing the handlebars. "You're Lars Bailey's daughter, aren't you?"

Realization washes over me, and I'm ready to scream and kick and fight and run.

"I haven't seen you since you were a little girl." Stan lowers his chin, leveling his eyes on me from under his brow. It's a sinister look, and it triggers a memory from deep in my past. "I'm going to need you to get in the truck and come with me."

"I'm not going anywhere with you." I push off the bike and turn to run in the direction of the distillery.

My hope is Adam is on his way, and I'll meet him on the road. I only make it a few steps before he's on top of me.

Jerking my elbow back, I land a hard blow to his torso. He lets out an *Oof*, but it's not enough. He's surprisingly strong, and he grips my arms, jerking my back to his chest. Then he loops one arm across my shoulders, holding me tight. I try to scream, but it's lost in the cloth he presses over my nose and mouth.

Three panicked breaths, and everything goes dark.

Chapter 27

Aiden

"**D**O YOU THINK MISS BRITT MIGHT NEED SOMEONE TO WALK Edward?" Owen is buckled in the back seat, wearing his little navy blazer on the way to Sunday school.

I've been restless ever since our meeting in the park, and the way I left her. I had to get away from her presence, but her presence won't leave me.

I miss her.

As she told me her new theory about the case, I missed working with her. I missed her instincts and intelligence. She's smart as a fucking whip.

When her eyes flooded with tears as she spilled her heart to me, I wanted to pull her into my arms and forgive everything. I missed tracing my nose along the line of her hair. I missed holding her body next to mine and hearing the little gasps and whimpers that lace her breathing when I touch her.

Stubbornly, I ran away, but after passing a sleepless night fighting with my brother's words, I've reconsidered my hard line.

"Ryan's mom said her friend Miss Cass walks dogs for

money." Owen's still working on his plan for seeing his new bestie. "I'd walk Edward for free!"

Glancing in the rearview mirror, I give him a smile. "Sounds like an offer she can't refuse."

He grins so big, my heart swells. Seeing how much Britt loves him is another crack in the wall I've built. *Everyone makes mistakes…* Damn Adam.

Owen's out of the truck and jogging up to meet Ryan as soon as we reach the church, and I decide to stop by the courthouse. I know she's there, because I have her work schedule.

In two turns, I'm pulling into my reserved parking space. Hopping out, I plan what could be the reason for my unexpected visit after saying I didn't want to see her again.

We need to discuss her new theory on the case. What could Stan be planning? Where is he? She told me straight up her mother is doing her own sleuthing, which shows she's trying to make up for her mistake. It's another blow to my defenses.

Reaching out, I grasp the metal handle on the door, but it doesn't budge. My brow furrows, and I lean forward, cupping my hand over the glass. The room is dark. The door is locked. Nobody's here.

I dig in my pocket for the key and unlock the door, flipping on the lights as I pass Holly's and Doug's desks on my way to hers. It looks the same as it did when she left on Friday. Pausing, I pull up the schedule on my phone, and I wasn't wrong. Her name is down for today.

Sliding my hand behind my neck, I hesitate, thinking. Then I swipe my thumb across the screen, and tap out a short text. *Sleeping in?*

It doesn't make sense for her to not be here. She's not the type to ditch work.

Returning to the glass doors, I gaze across the square in the direction of the Star Parlor. Without giving it a thought, I push through the door and head across the street. I'm only going to be sure the cruiser is there. I won't go upstairs or bang on her door or anything overbearing-boss-ish like that.

At the speed I'm moving, it doesn't take long to reach her building. I step inside the glass door and go to the space behind the stairwell, where I know she parks the bike. A bad feeling moves through my chest when I see it's empty.

Dragging my fingers through the scruff on my jaw, I rationalize. She probably went for a ride… on the day she's scheduled to work. I might have passed her on my way here… across the wide-open square. She could've gone for donuts.

Donuts! I exhale a laugh. Fuck. I'm acting like a paranoid caveman, and she's probably on her way to the courthouse right now with a box of Krispy Kreme.

I turn to leave at the same time the door to the Star Parlor opens, and Gwen stops short with a little yelp.

"Aiden!" Her voice is breathless, and she presses a hand to her chest. "What are you doing here? Birgitte said you two aren't speaking."

"We're not." My tone is flat, and I continue for the door when she stops me.

"If you're not speaking, why are you in her stairwell?"

"It's her day to work, and she's not at the courthouse. I was just checking on her."

Gwen's eyes whip to the empty space where the bike is normally parked then to me again. "Something's wrong."

A fist knots in my chest, but I push back. "She's probably just getting donuts. We always have Krispy Kreme—"

"My daughter hasn't eaten a donut since she was a child." Gwen closes the space between us quickly. "I'm telling you something's not right here. I can feel it."

"Don't start that with me."

"Even if you don't believe in magic, there are proven instances of a mother's intuition being correct. You have to send out an APB or an Amber Alert or whatever you people do to get everyone searching."

My stomach churns, and of course, I would do all of those things. "I can't call a search party until we're sure she's missing."

A low barking from upstairs sends another flash through my chest. "Edward." I grab the railing, taking the steps two at a time.

The door is locked, but Gwen is right behind me pulling a set of keys from her pocket and opening the door. We both enter to see the dog hasn't been fed. Her bed is made, but it hasn't been slept in. A knot forms in my throat as I scan the small apartment. No signs of dinner, no dishes in the sink or on the drying rack.

"She hasn't been here."

"Oh, God!" Gwen clutches her stomach, dropping against the wall. "Not her. Not my girl."

"Stop it," I bark. "We have to keep calm. When was the last time you saw her?"

"The day you sent her to get my gun." Her eyes flash to mine. "Which I still don't have back."

"You'll get it back." Anger is in my voice, in my veins. It's the only way to fight the growing fear. "The last time I saw her was at Little Sunbeam Park yesterday afternoon with Edward. She obviously came back here after that."

My phone is out, and I see an hour has passed. "I've got to pick up my son from church."

I start for the door, and she grabs my arm. "What can I do?" Panic is in her voice, and I look around the room.

"Take care of Edward." I put my hand on her arm, calming my tone. "Give me your number, and I'll text you when I've found her."

Her lips tighten, and for whatever reason, she's struggling with this simple request. This simple olive branch.

"You love her."

My chin pulls back, and I hesitate. *Fuck it.* "Yes."

"You'll search until you find her? You won't give up?"

Pressure is in my chest at her words. I don't like this line of thought. We have to stay positive. We're going to find her riding back to the courthouse with a box of donuts, and she's going to smile her cute smile and ask if I'm being over protective again.

A sliver of fear pierces my insides at the thought. "Give me your number."

She finally relents, and when she passes my phone back to me, I'm out the door, jogging down the steps and heading to the church.

Owen is on the lawn playing with Ryan, and I decide to wait and see if Piper knows anything when my brother strolls out the door.

"Hey, bro! What are you doing at church?"

"Picking up Owen." My tone is clipped, and his smile fades when he reads my expression.

"Is something wrong?"

"I don't know. Nothing, probably. Britt wasn't at work this morning, and when I went to her building to check on her, her bike wasn't there."

"She didn't text me." His voice is urgent, and my eyes snap to him.

"What was that?"

"I ran into her at the park yesterday looking like she was about to cry, so I invited her to Stone Cold. We had a few drinks, and she took off on her bike headed home. I told her to text me when she got there, but she didn't. I figured she just forgot."

I'm jogging to my truck while he's still speaking. "Watch Owen for me."

Silence fills the cab, and I grip the steering wheel as I fly up the narrow road in the direction of my family's distillery, straining my eyes as I scan the shoulders. A bad taste is in my mouth. I need any shred of hope I can find.

If she had an accident, she'd have used her phone to call for help—unless her phone was broken.

If someone hit her, I want to believe they'd have done the right thing and reported it. I want to believe they'd have done the better thing and taken her to get help. But what happened to Annemarie burns in my memory. It tightens my lungs, making breathing difficult.

My knuckles are white, and my eyes ache from searching. I'm halfway to the distillery when it all goes to shit. My stomach drops, and I pull to the side of the road with a squeal of tires.

There in the small ditch is the beach cruiser. I'm out of the truck, running to where it lies, and I see the contents of her purse spilled beside the basket—including her phone.

"Fuck," I growl, gripping the sides of my hair and looking up and down the road.

Nothing is out here, and at night, no one would've seen. Whipping out my phone, I text Doug to get out here ASAP, then I call the Beaufort guys I know for backup.

My insides are in knots as I slowly retrace my steps to the shoulder, scanning the ground for anything, any footprints or tire tracks or lost items. The thick grass obscures everything except in one spot where it's slightly uprooted, where a vehicle might have pulled off the road.

My next text is to Gwen. *Found the bike, no Britt. Need Edward.*

There's only one way off this road, but after that, they could've gone anywhere. Britt's new theory about the case is in my head. We were trying to find a reason Stan would hide behind Gary. Maybe this was it.

Chapter 28

Britt

NTENSE SUNLIGHT SHINES ON ME, AND I SIT UP TO FIND I'M IN A SMALL tower room overlooking the ocean. My mouth is so dry, and a metallic taste is on my tongue. I squint against the sun, trying to get my bearings.

In front of me, a door leads to a balcony, and I run to open it, rushing out into the brisk morning air. It's more of a widow's walk, and a briny wind whips steadily against my face. Spinning all around, I try to figure out where I am. I don't see a single house. My only surroundings are the ocean straight ahead and shrubby wax myrtles spreading out on each side.

Taking a deep breath, I yell for help as loud as I can, but a gust of wind hits me in the mouth, stealing my breath and muffling my cry.

Returning to the small room, my heart beats too fast. A set of stairs is against a back wall, and I rush down them only to find a locked door at the bottom. It's dark at the bottom of the stairwell, but I beat on the door, yelling for anyone to let me out.

Silence is my only reply.

Walking up the stairs again slowly, I see a wet bar with a small sink in the opposite corner. I pour myself a glass of water and sip it as I look around for a restroom. Nothing. Sitting on the bed, I rub my fingers over my eyes trying to remember what happened.

The man who kidnapped me knew who I was. I didn't know for sure, but I'm certain it was Stan Roswell. *Why is he doing this?* Aiden's question is the same as mine, and I still don't know the answer.

A scuff of footsteps coming up the stairs tells me I'm about to find out.

Keys rattle as the door is unlocked, and the stepping resumes, climbing higher. Fear tightens my throat with every tap, and I back slowly to the balcony door. A dark head appears, and he turns on the landing, leveling his eyes on mine and giving me an unsettling smile.

"Good. You're awake." His voice is even with a touch of an accent I can't place.

"Who are you?"

"You don't remember me?" He places a hand on his chest, feigning sadness. "You hurt my feelings." Closing the space between us, he drops the pretense. "I guess it has been a while. Hold this."

Shoving a copy of the *Eureka Gazette* in my hand, he positions it under my chin. Lifting his phone, he snaps a photo and turns like he's about to leave.

"What do you want from me?" My voice is a panicked cry.

"Nothing." He's back on the stairs, walking down quickly.

I don't understand, but it might be my last chance. "I need to use the restroom!"

The top of his head is all I can see when he stops, and he lifts his eyes to mine, studying my expression. I imagine I look pretty wild, but I hold steady. Turning, he walks up the stairs again, crossing the room to where I'm standing.

His hand shoots out, and he grips my chin so hard, I yelp. "At this time you have value to me. But if you become a problem, I will get rid of you. Understand?"

I don't understand at all, but I nod quickly. He releases my face and turns away again. "Follow me."

Hesitating, I watch him start down the stairs again. He's near the bottom when he stops. "Last chance."

Moving quickly, I go to the stairs and follow him to the door. When we're on the other side, he grips my arm, guiding me along a wood-paneled, wood-floored hall lined with pictures of people I don't know to a small bathroom.

He pushes me inside and pulls the door shut. "You've got five minutes."

Looking all around, my shoulders drop. No windows, no indication of where I am. It's a simple half bath with a bar of soap and a towel beside a small sink. My face is pale and dirt is on my cheek when I look in the mirror, so I take a minute to splash water on my face and scrub it away.

I take the full five minutes to use the restroom, clean up as much as possible, and try to calm my nerves. I'm a pawn, but I don't know the game we're playing.

"Time's up." A loud banging on the door makes me jump, and I reach out to turn the knob with trembling hands.

The door shoves inward quickly, and he grips my upper arm again, dragging me into the hall and in the direction of the stairs to the balcony again. He doesn't speak, and I decide to take a chance.

"Stan?" I sound so small, and he doesn't flinch. "Are you Stan Roswell?"

We're at the door, and he pulls it open, shoving me inside. Our eyes meet at the last minute, and the black evil holding my gaze freezes my bones.

"The one and only." He slams the door shut, turning the key in the lock.

"Wake up and eat." The sharp voice jerks me awake, and I scramble across the twin bed, pressing my back to the wall.

A plate of fried eggs and toast sits on the bedside table, and my stomach growls. I haven't eaten in twenty-four hours, and I'm desperately hungry.

Stan's back is to me, and he looks out the glass balcony door at the ocean.

My voice is so dry I can barely speak. "How do I know it's not poisoned?"

He exhales a huff, turning to me. "I still need you."

It's not very reassuring, but I reach for the glass of water beside the food and take a sip. My stomach turns painfully, and I lift a triangle of toast, carefully nibbling the corner. If this is my last meal, I want answers.

"Why did you kill Gary?"

Stan's lips purse, and he considers my question before answering. "I caught him communicating with your mother." His black eyes are on mine again. "He betrayed me, so he had to be killed."

His easy confession scares me. He doesn't care if I know the truth, which means he doesn't expect me to survive this imprisonment. It shakes my confidence so hard, I almost drop the plate.

Roaring is in my ears, and I struggle to calm my survival instinct, my need to run or scream. I have to think like a scientist. I have to summon my training and force my brain to think through what I know, to remember what I've learned about these types of situations.

Breathing slowly, I tell myself to be calm. *Think, Britt...*

I can't escape this room. The door is bolted below. I'm too high for anyone to hear me if I scream, I don't have my phone, and I didn't see a way to climb down.

He could leave me here to die, and no one would ever find

me. Only, reflecting on his actions up to now, that isn't his style. Stan Roswell is a showman, and when he's ready to kill me, he'll turn it into a production, the same way he did with Gary.

My only hope is to buy time. I don't know if he sees me as a human. I don't know if it would matter if he did. If my mother can be believed, this man has pursued his vendetta against my father for decades.

"Why did you terrorize the town and frame Gary for it?"

His eyes are on the ocean again, and he answers absently. "To create a distraction."

"You broke into my mother's house. What were you trying to find?"

"Her." He turns, looking down at me. "When someone steals your life's work, knows every trick you've ever done down to the last detail, they keep a record. The proof is in her possession, but Gwen is very clever. She's hidden it too well."

Realization flickers to life in my chest with every word he speaks. Like the sun breaking across the ocean at dawn, the truth flashes in my brain. I thought she was obsessed, but all along it was him.

Stan Roswell murdered my dad, and he's been hiding ever since.

"Or it doesn't exist because he never stole from you." My voice is calm, my fear slowly being replaced by the need for justice.

Stepping forward, he rips the plate from my hand. "Don't test me. I'm happy to let you starve."

He strides to the stairs, taking the plate as he descends quickly, slamming the door and locking it behind him. Gazing at the piece of toast in my hand, everything shifts. I have to make it out of this. I have to survive to tell what he did.

This time it really is for my dad.

Chapter 29

Aiden

"THIS JUST CAME THROUGH ON MY EMAIL." GWEN CHARGES INTO the courthouse, where we've assembled a full investigative team.

Edna is combing her network of magician friends to see if anyone has any information on Stan Roswell, the state troopers are combing the area for all vehicles on the distillery road the night Britt went missing, and the Beaufort deputies are combing their criminal database for information on Gary Blue that might lead to our suspect.

I'm on my feet, meeting Britt's mother halfway and taking the computer printout from her hands. When I turn it over, it's a punch to the gut. Britt's face is in black and white, and she's holding a copy of the *Eureka Gazette* dated today.

"When did you get this?" My voice is hoarse.

"It was sent an hour ago from a Gmail address I don't recognize. I suspect it's a fake account."

"Still, we can track it down using the IP address. I don't have the equipment for it, but the guys in Beaufort do. Will you allow them access to your computer?"

She lifts a black messenger bag, sliding out a Power Book. "Can they find it using my laptop?"

"Maybe." I'm already texting them as she speaks. "I don't know."

"I have more." She powers up the computer and logs into her account, pulling up the message and turning the device so I can read it.

You will stop your pursuit of your husband's killer. You will go live on social media and confess Lars stole my act, and ultimately he got what he deserved. No one can perform my feats but me, the Great Stantini. You will give me the evidence you have of him studying my routines, the details, the mannerisms, the words, the costumes…

"He's insane." I muse as I read.

"He's a murderer." Gwen's voice is ice. "He's not getting off with an insanity plea. He's going to pay for what he did."

I finish his message, and my entire body is tense. The more he wrote, the more unhinged his mental state appears to have grown. It's the ravings of a madman, and he has Britt.

She's smart but she's small, and I'm tormented by thoughts of her bound or caged. The thought of her hands trembling, and not being able to cover them with mine… the possibility he might hurt her sends frustrated rage across my shoulders.

With every passing second, it grows worse. "Do you think he might hurt her?"

Gwen's eyes press closed, and her head bows. "I don't know. He's using her for leverage. As long as he thinks we're cooperating, we have hope."

Exhaling a frustrated growl, I snap. "Why didn't you ever tell me any of this?"

Incredulous eyes land on mine. "You've got to be kidding me. I said over and over—"

"You said Lars was murdered, and I watched my dad

investigate the case. Despite what you think, he cared about the truth. It's why he called in the guy from Charleston."

"Your father said Lars had a risky profession, and he had to assume the risk of death was always part of it."

"He was trying to help you move on."

"Help me?" Her voice goes high.

"We had proof his equipment failed. You never gave us any proof or any reason to believe you weren't simply a grieving widow unable to let go."

"I never had proof. I only had magic."

"So why now? What provoked Stan to lash out now?"

"I don't know." She lifts her hands and lets them fall. "I only know magic is always at the right time."

The right time. "This time he has Britt, and I don't know how the fuck to find her."

"I have an idea." She nods to Edward. "Bring the dog. We're going back to Gary's."

When we reach the small cabin, it's roped off with tape and small cards are dotted everywhere indicating Britt's processing of the scene. I can see her carefully picking apart the details, photographing everything as her mind solves the puzzle, turning the pieces, testing how they might fit. Desperation claws my insides. I've got to find her.

Edward's nose is to the ground, and he runs all over the place sniffing and tracking. He goes out to the carport where ATV tire tracks cover the soft dirt.

"Britt said he could pick up a trail as old as two weeks." I'm in a squat holding his leash, feeling more helpless than I ever have in my life.

"Good thing. This trail is at least a week old, maybe more."

The dog gives me a pull, and I stand, following him as he leads us further into the scrub brush surrounding the property.

Gwen is with me, and it's the first time I've ever seen her in jeans and hiking boots. Her hair is tied back in a single, thick braid, and she actually looks like a normal person.

We're both straining, following as Britt's dog traces an invisible line, back and forth, side to side, pulling us deeper into the marsh.

"Think he's onto something?" Gwen's voice is quiet as we follow, as if any noise might distract him.

"I've never worked with dogs, but this is what it always looks like."

He breaks into a run, pulling me with him, and I pick up the pace, splashing through briny water, anticipation gripping my lungs. Gwen is right behind me running as well, and I'll be damned. If you'd told me three weeks ago, I'd be working with Gwen Bailey, trusting her and accepting her help with a case, I'd have said you were crazy.

With a high-pitched yelp, Edward breaks through a stand of cattails, me right behind him, and when I see what he's been tracking, my grip loosens. He takes the opportunity to dart away from me, but he doesn't go far. He runs right up to the red three-wheeler and lifts his head in a long *Rooo!*

"Shit," I exhale a mixture of satisfaction and frustration. "He found it."

It's not what we were hoping for, but at least it proves he's doing his job. Dropping to one knee, I recover his leash, scrubbing my hands in the sides of his head the way Britt and Owen always do.

"Good boy, Edward." I scrub him some more, and he lifts his head like he's nodding. "You're a good tracker, ole boy."

Gwen frowns, crossing her arms and looking all around the area. "There's nothing out here for miles. It's all marsh."

"I'll have the guys sweep the area and see what they can find on this vehicle. I doubt it's registered anymore, but maybe we can figure out who purchased it and where they lived."

"Thirty years ago."

She's saying what I'm feeling. It's a longshot, but I have to keep my spirits up. It's all I've got. "Let's head back to Eureka and see if they've found anything on your laptop."

I won't sleep tonight if we don't make some kind of progress.

I'm on my second day of no sleep. Owen is staying with my mom, and she agreed to keep Edward as well. We told my son Britt had to take a trip and needed him to watch her dog, and he was as happy as if we'd found a pack of wild zebras for him to ride.

Meanwhile, it's 6 a.m. at the courthouse, and I'm going quietly insane trying to find anything that might lead us to where Stan Roswell is hiding, where he's holding my girl.

I'm leaning forward with my forearms on my knees, and Edna places a mug of coffee beside me on the desk.

"Looks like none of us are sleeping these days." Her voice is weary, and I glance up to see dark shadows under her eyes.

"It's like trying to find a needle in a haystack." The words have just left my mouth when I remember saying the same thing to Britt when we were searching for Gary Blue.

Dropping my face in my hands, I groan as understanding flashes through me.

Gwen promised her she'd give us Gary, so Britt waited to see if her mother could do it. Sitting here, wracked with frustration over the impossibility of finding her, I know why she did it.

"She wasn't trying to betray me." My voice cracks. "I was so fucking self-defensive, so wrapped up in my own head, I couldn't see it."

"You see it now. That's what matters." Edna's hand is on my shoulder.

"What matters is finding her before it's too late."

Pushing off my knees, I walk slowly in a line from my desk

to the door of Edna's office and back. How can we not have a single lead?

"We're going to get a breakthrough." Edna walks to where I'm standing in front of her door. "We have to have faith."

Shaking my head, I look down. "I lost that years ago."

She places her hand on my arm, giving it a squeeze. "It's not too late to find it again." Passing me, she walks into her office and turns on her computer. "I've put out feelers in a few online groups. Something's going to turn up. It's impossible to hide in this community, especially for someone as flamboyant as Stan Roswell."

I hope she's right. I hope one of the million things we're trying turns up a lead. Doug has spent the last two days with EMS, sifting through rural addresses from Hilton Head to Charleston. The guys in Beaufort traced the email Gwen received to a coffee shop near Rockville.

All we can do is hope for something to pop, and the waiting is torture.

The front door opens, and Holly walks in with a box of donuts. Gwen is behind her, and when I'm not pissed at seeing her, it hits me how much our relationship has changed.

"Anything new?" She comes to where I'm standing, and I shake my head no.

With that one word, her legs seem to give out. I catch her, helping her sit in Doug's nearby chair, and when I see tears streaming down her cheeks, it hits me unexpectedly hard.

"We're going to find her." My voice is rough, and I close my eyes, summoning every lost bit of faith I can find. Trying again with more force, I repeat. "We are going to find her, Gwen."

"I thought the reading was for him." Her hands tremble as she uses a cotton handkerchief to blot her cheeks. "I thought it was for Gary, but it was for her."

Holly walks over with a glazed donut in a paper napkin. "Donut?"

Gwen shakes her head, but I catch her shoulder. "What are you talking about? What reading?"

"The day she came to talk to me, I did a reading for Gary, for what was coming. It said chaos, betrayal, and death, and I interpreted it to mean his life was in chaos, he betrayed Stan, which led to his murder. I was wrong. It was for her. Eureka was in chaos, and I convinced her to betray you. Then—"

"Stop." My voice snaps, fueled by desperation. "Britt is not going to die. We're not going to let that happen. We're going to find her."

"Yes, we are!" Edna rushes into the room, and we both turn to face her. "I've got a lead. Gwen, do you remember Belinda Laurent?"

"The lady in the box?" Her lip curls in disgust. "I thought she moved to Tampa."

"She did, but she's in Charleston this weekend. She agreed to meet me at the Starbucks on Highway 17 in Green Pond."

I'm on my feet. "Let's go."

A line of cars wraps around the lone Starbucks in the tiny community named after the algae in a nearby body of water. They're all waiting for the drive-through, but we park and head inside where a woman in a large, burgundy wig, a white lace shirt, and a black leather biker jacket, sits with a cup of tea at a small table.

Her eyes lift to us, but they immediately narrow when they land on Gwen.

"I thought I was meeting with Edna." She sounds like a longtime smoker, and her large bosom stretches her shirt as she stands.

"She couldn't make the drive, so you're meeting with me." Gwen's tone is sharp, and I can tell these two have a history.

"I'm not wasting my time talking to crazy people." Belinda scoots between the chair and the table, attempting to leave.

"What's a few more minutes?" Gwen taunts, sitting across from the chair Belinda vacated. "You spent years working with one."

"Can we take it down a bit?" I glare at Gwen as I reach for Belinda's elbow. "We came all this way, would you at least talk to me?"

Her gaze to this point has been narrowed on Gwen, but she looks up at me now, and her brown eyes widen. They circle my face before tracing down my chest to my waist and lower, and I feel pretty much objectified. Whatever it takes to find Britt.

"Why, I suppose I could spare a few minutes for you, sugar." Her throaty voice turns to pure honey.

"I really appreciate it." I give her a smile, and she exhales a laugh, batting her lashes.

"How can I help you?"

Holding her elbow, I escort her to her seat, taking a chair beside her. "What are you drinking?"

"Just an Earl Grey tea." She reaches into her bag and gives me a peek at a silver flask. "We can make it Irish if you want."

"From what I remember, you make everything Irish," Gwen quips, and I nudge her foot under the table.

"Thanks for taking the time to meet with us." I double down on the charm. "We're trying to find Stan Roswell, and Edna seems to think you know where he is."

"Stan and I've kept in touch." She blinks, suggestively, then she lifts her teacup, daintily taking a sip while holding out her pinky finger. "But I don't like betraying my friends without a good reason."

Gwen mutters something under her breath, but I push on. "We think he's involved in a kidnapping. It would really help us out a lot if you could give us any idea where he might be hiding."

Her brow rises. "A kidnapping?" She lowers the teacup and places her hand against her ample bosom. "My goodness. Who did he kidnap?"

"My daughter." Gwen's tone is flat.

"Oh." Belinda shakes her head, holding up one hand. "That Roswell-Bailey feud is as old as Methuselah. It's as old as her." She nods at Gwen, who is fuming. "I'm not getting in the middle of it. I've never been able to tell who was telling the truth."

I cut Gwen off before she blows. "What if I told you he killed Gary Blue?"

Belinda's eyes widen, and she sits back in her chair. "Gary's dead?"

Reaching across, I touch her arm lightly. "I'm sorry. I didn't know you were close."

Shaking her head, she lifts a napkin to her nose. "We weren't that close, but he was always so kind. He wouldn't hurt anybody. He was a veteran."

Gwen leans forward, her voice low. "Stan stole his leg, framed him for crimes he didn't commit, then dumped his dead body in a corn field. Still want to protect him?"

Belinda's mouth curls in horror. "Stole his leg? That's just low."

"Please help us find him before he hurts anyone else." My tone is gentle, and I slide my hand over hers. "Help me, Belinda."

She sits up a little straighter, circling her eyes over me again before melting into a smile. "Of course, handsome, I'm happy to help you. Do you have a map?"

Chapter 30

Britt

THINK I'VE BEEN HERE THREE DAYS. MAYBE FOUR, BUT I DON'T KNOW how long I was here before I regained consciousness from the drugs. Maybe it's been longer.

Three times a day, Stan escorts me down to the small restroom. Twice a day, he delivers meals. Every time, he's stern, quiet, not giving me any more information or updates.

I've stood on the balcony for hours, scanning every inch of the roof, the gutters, the shrubbery below, trying to find a way to escape. I'm at the very top of a three-story house, and nothing is between me and the ground.

From this height, I wouldn't survive the jump, but I can take the bedsheets off the small twin bed, tie them together, and make a rope to climb down as far as possible. Obviously, I'll have to do it in the middle of the night, when I'm somewhat sure Stan won't walk in and catch me. Then hopefully, I can steal a car or run to get help before he realizes I'm gone.

If my makeshift rope doesn't slip. If I don't fall and break anything or make too much noise on the way down.

A short bookcase against the wall holds a variety of books. I don't recognize most of the titles, but a hardcover edition of *Daddy* by Danielle Steel is tucked behind a biography of John Adams. It's not as racy as I'd hoped based on the title, but the ridiculous, twelve-hour lovemaking session is enough to keep me distracted from the fear prickling at my skin while I wait for time to pass.

The day wears on, until judging by the position of the sun, it's getting close to dinnertime. I hear Stan's footsteps climbing the stairs, and I toss the book aside, placing my hands in my lap and doing my best to appear non-threatening.

Instead of dropping off a plate of food, however, he studies me from the top step. "Would you like to come out of this room now?"

My heart leaps, and I cautiously lift my eyes to meet his. "Yes, please."

Maybe if he lets me go downstairs, I won't have to risk my life climbing down with bedsheets. Maybe I can slip out a side door when he isn't looking and run like a house on fire.

"I've prepared a nice dinner." He's watching me. "It would be nice to have someone to share it with."

"Thank you." I stand, keeping my hands clasped as I walk slowly to where he waits on the stairs.

He turns, and I follow him down, past the small bathroom, to another flight of stairs until we enter an open space with a large living room that flows into the kitchen and dining area. It's all brilliant white with navy ticking, and the view of the shore is breathtaking. The scent of grilled steak and buttery potatoes in the air makes my mouth water.

"Don't I have a beautiful home?" He lifts his chin proudly.

I want to say no, but he'll see I'm lying. So I opt for a true question. "How can someone like you afford a house like this?"

"I have my ways." His smug grin intensifies my hatred. How dare he live in luxury after he destroyed my family?

He strolls to the kitchen and opens a bottle of red wine. "Your mother must not love you. She's not cooperating."

"My mother will never smear my father's name. She loved him too much."

"More than she loves you?" He drives the knife into my chest so casually as he hands me a glass of wine.

Maybe? I sip the dark red liquid, unsure how to answer his question. It tastes like cherries and pepper with a slight metallic undertone.

"Do you like the wine?" Again, he's fishing for compliments.

"I don't know much about wine."

"This is a 1998 Barolo from the Monfortino region."

Shrugging, I turn away from him, walking to the glass doors facing the beach. My posture is casual, but I scan every inch of the outdoors, making mental notes of potential escape routes. I strain my eyes to where his blue Ford is parked, but I don't see what I'd hoped to find. I don't see a three-wheel ATV.

"Kiawah isn't the prettiest beach I've ever visited, but it's secluded, private." He walks up beside me, and I take a step away. "Nobody comes here without an invitation, and if they do… alligators."

He cuts his eyes at me, and they're dancing with an evil glee.

I curl my nose in disgust. "Alligators don't attack humans. They're usually afraid of them unless they've been fed human food. You're thinking of crocodiles, which are aggressive and will attack."

"Aren't you the expert?" He's sarcastic, and my head is dizzy.

I think I've had too much red wine on an empty stomach. "I don't like things being accused unfairly."

"Like your lying dad?"

"You're the liar!" My voice rises, and I'm definitely a little tipsy. "You're a murderer and a criminal, and you're going to get what you deserve."

"Shut your mouth, stupid girl." He's on the ropes, and the fire in my chest roars hotter.

"My dad was younger and better looking, and he had more stamina. He could do the tricks you were too old or too scared to try."

At that he snatches my jaw in his fingers painfully, lowering his face so his nose touches mine. "Shut up, or I'll put you in a weighted box and drop it in the middle of the ocean. If they ever find you, there won't be anything left to identify."

Fear tightens my lungs, and I remember what Mom said about Dad having dreams and premonitions. I think of my own dreams of drowning. Were they premonitions or my subconscious longing to be with my dad?

Satisfaction gleams in Stan's eyes when he sees he's frightened me.

He releases my face with a flick of his wrist, and I walk to the couch and sit, heaviness pulling me down. Reaching out, I place my wine glass on the coffee table, where I see a large amethyst crystal the size of my fist.

Amethyst is a protection stone. It represents reunion and connection to spiritual beings. Reunion, spiritual beings… I could be reunited with Aiden. My dad's spirit could be protecting me. It's only a hope, but it strengthens my resolve. I imagine a voice telling me, *You're not going to die here.*

Maybe it's the wine and the fact I haven't had a decent meal in four days. Either way, a sensation of calm settles over me. Cass read my tarot, and I'm married to Aiden. We have babies.

Closing my eyes, I believe he's searching for me. I believe he's as desperate to find me as I am to be found. I believe the fear of never seeing me again is as unbearable for him as it is for me, and it burns like the sun in my heart. *Find me, Aiden. Find me…*

My nose heats, but I won't cry in front of dickhead Stan. I want to know how much time I have left. I need to know if tonight's the night I attempt my escape, and if it is, no more wine.

"So you brought me here to kill me?"

"Not initially. I had hoped your mother would play along."

He exhales with a shrug. "It appears she won't, and I have to go to Plan B."

"Plan B is to put me in a box and drown me like you did my dad?" It's strange how alcohol dulls the emotions. How I'm even able to ask this question without a tremor.

"Your father put himself in that box, as you well know." From the sound of his voice, I think Stan might be getting a little drunk himself.

It gives me an idea. Crossing to the kitchen, I take the bottle off the bar. "You know, you were right. This is very good wine. Let's have more." I give him a generous pour while giving myself a little splash. "Do you know Penn & Teller? They explain how magic tricks are done, but they mix it with comedy."

"They're idiots." He lifts his nose, taking another sip of wine as he settles into the plush, white sofa.

"I think they're funny." I take a seat beside him. "You can be like them. Tell me how you did it."

His eyes narrow, and he studies my face like he's looking for signs of deception. I smile, blinking innocently.

"You're a strange girl." His tone is disgusted, but it's better than sinister. "I don't care to have this discussion with you."

"Why not? You'll never let me go. How did you manage to kill my father when you were all the way in Europe? You must have had a helper. Was it Gary?"

"Of course not. Gary didn't have a leg. He could barely get through a show without tripping over something." Stan blows air through his thick lips, and my throat tightens.

"But you did have someone."

"I didn't need anyone. Your father was so trusting, once he procured that box from the vendor, he never examined it again. It was incredibly easy to slide a knife between the seal and the metal. Once it was compromised, I only had to board a ship and set sail across the Atlantic."

Anger roars in my chest, defying the wine and the calm I'm trying to project. My trembling hand tightens into a fist, and I wish I had my phone to record his confession. As it is, I'll have to believe my word against his is stronger.

"So you admit you tampered with his equipment?"

"It was the least I could do." Black eyes level on mine, and he smiles like the devil.

Fire burns at the corners of my eyes, and my skin hums with electricity. Standing, I walk slowly to the kitchen, placing my wine glass on the bar. A wooden block holding a set of knives is directly in front of me, and I zero in on the largest one.

One step, and I hear a sound that freezes me in place. Somewhere far, far away, so far, I might be imagining it, I think I hear the faintest sound of a dog barking. My heart tightens in my chest… *Edward?*

Turning quickly, if I'm right, I know what to do. "Do you like music?"

"What?" He frowns, looking up to where I'm standing.

"My favorite Shania Twain song is 'I'm Gonna Getcha Good.' Can I play it?"

"I despise Shania Twain. Her voice is like nails on a chalkboard."

This time, I'm almost certain I hear the faint yelp of a hound. My skin tingles, and my eyes mist. I want to burst into laughter, but I wait to see if Stan shows any sign of hearing it as well.

He doesn't, and I dash past him to where a large, Bluetooth speaker is sitting on top of a bookcase.

"How does this work?" I speak louder.

"It's connected to the streaming…" He's still explaining when I grab a small remote from behind the speaker.

My fingers shake as I press the buttons, and the flatscreen television flickers to life. I quickly speak the name of the song into the remote. A music app opens, and an eternity seems to pass before the song appears on the screen, and I hit play.

Guitar strains ring out, and I turn up the volume. The song floods through the room, and I sing along loudly.

"Turn it down!" Stan shouts, placing his wine on the coffee table and standing.

I run to the kitchen, straining my eyes through the glass. *Please be out there... Please don't be a dream...*

The chorus begins, and I've stopped paying attention to Stan trying to figure out how to shut off the fancy technology in his own home. I'm singing as loud as I can.

"I said, turn it *off*!" he roars, lifting the speaker and slamming it against the wall.

I spin around, and in the sudden silence, I hear the yowling I know so well.

Stan hears it as well, and his eyes flash to mine. "What have you done?"

He crosses the room quickly in my direction, and I run away, darting around the bar, dodging him. I go to the door in the center of the glass windows, grasping the knob as I try to get it open. It's locked.

"Fuck!" I fumble with the bolt, trying to slide it back. It's stiff, and it slips between my fingers.

Stan stops me with a loud snarl. "I wasn't planning to kill you tonight."

Looking over my shoulder, I see he's holding a gun, and it's pointed right at me. Ice filters through my veins, and I lift my hands over my head.

"Okay... I stopped." Moving away from the door, I step closer to the couch thinking I'll dive behind it if I can.

"It's too late..." Stan starts, but Aiden appears on the other side of the glass behind him.

Our eyes lock, and relief hits me so hard, I clasp my hands over my mouth to keep from screaming. Stan turns, firing his gun wildly at the window, shattering the glass.

The scene erupts into chaos. Aiden pulls Edward away, dashing around to the front of the house. Stan spins in place, directing his gun to the front door now, and I grab the large amethyst off the coffee table, plotting as I crouch beside the sofa.

The front door explodes inward with Aiden's kick. Stan fires another shot at the entrance, and I scream.

"We've got you surrounded!" Aiden's deep voice shouts. "Drop your weapon and get on the floor with your hands behind your head."

"You can't possibly have us surrounded. It's too remote, and I've got the girl."

"Don't be a fool, Stan!" Mom yells from the direction of the kitchen. "Get on the ground."

Stan swings wildly towards her voice. "I'll kill you, Gwen."

He fires repeatedly, stepping slowly her way. I stand, gripping the amethyst tightly in my fist and preparing to bash it over his head. Aiden storms into the room with his gun leveled on Stan, and I stop.

Our eyes meet, and Stan swings around, firing directly at Aiden. Three shots, and Aiden slams violently against the wall before landing on the floor. My stomach plummets. He's lying face down, not moving, and I scream, as I run to him.

Stan is on me fast, and the small hairs on my skin rise as he raises his gun again. Before he can get the shot, a staccato *Pop!* sounds from outside the house, and his chest jerks forward.

He drops to his knees in front of me, and I recoil closer to Aiden's side, covering him with my body.

"Aiden…" It's a shaky whimper, tears blurring my vision as I carefully move my hands over his body. "Aiden, no…"

Footsteps crunch on broken glass, and I look up to see my mother in jeans and heavy combat boots storming across the room to where Stan lies on his back, looking up at the ceiling. His gun is still in his hand, and a gurgling noise comes from his throat as he tries to lift it again.

Mom puts her boot on his wrist, standing directly over him and pointing her gun at his head. "You will never take anyone from me again." Her voice is eerily calm as she confronts the man lying at her feet. "This is for Lars."

Another sharp *Pop!*, and Stan's head flips to the side. My

heart is beating so fast, but I don't have time to think about what I just witnessed. Tears coat my cheeks as I tug on Aiden's arm, rolling him so his face is up. His eyes are closed, his skin pale.

"Aiden?" My hands tremble as I lift them over his beautiful face, touching the line of his hair lightly.

Sitting back, I scan his chest, searching for a bullet hole, but I don't see blood. I don't see anything. Not knowing what to do, I struggle to unfasten his buttons with shaking fingers.

"Help me!" My voice is broken, but my mom doesn't move.

She's oblivious to the beautiful man, the love of my life, dying in front of me. I can't breathe. I'm gasping and crying, and with a shriek, I fall back when his arm lifts. His eyes squeeze, and he lets out a loud groan, turning onto his side.

"Fuck, that hurts," Aiden growls, putting his hand on the floor and pushing himself up to sitting.

"Wait…" I scoot closer, running my hands from his shoulders to his chest. I don't know where to apply pressure. "You've been shot."

With a gasp, he straightens against the wall, pulling up the bottom of his shirt.

"It's okay," he gasps, squinting.

"Kevlar!" I scream, diving forward and wrapping my arms around his neck. "You're wearing a vest."

My shoulders wobble, and I collapse, sobbing and holding him. Strong arms encircle my waist, and he pulls me flush against his body, burying his face in the side of my neck.

"Don't cry, beautiful. I've got you."

I slide my hands across his cheeks, kissing his brow, his eyes, a touch of salt is on my tongue.

Lifting my head, my voice breaks. "Are you crying?"

"Are you?" He smiles, and joy explodes in my chest.

Our mouths collide, and my fingers thread in his soft hair. Sealing my lips over his, they part, and our tongues curl together. Heat floods my body, and fresh tears fill my eyes. Lifting my chin, I pull him closer.

"You're here." I sniff, hugging him tighter. "You came for me."

"I've been going out of my mind trying to find you." He speaks against my neck, dragging his lips behind my ear before covering my mouth with his again.

A whimper slips from my throat, and his hands fist in my sweater at my waist, dragging me closer. I can't get enough of him. Happiness is a drug in my veins, and I'm desperate to hold him until our bodies melt into one.

A loud *Rooo!* comes from Edward right beside us, and I jump with a little squeal. Then I collapse into laughter, wrapping an arm around my dog and scrubbing his neck.

"Good boy, Edward! You were perfect!"

Mom stands over us, holding his leash. Her eyes glow as she looks down at me straddling Aiden's lap with my hand on his shoulder and my arm around my dog.

"I hate to interrupt, but a lot of people are waiting to hear if we found you. We need to let them know…" She casts a glance in the direction of Stan's dead body. "And there's that."

"I'll take care of it." Aiden bends a knee, groaning as he starts to rise.

I hop off his lap, holding his arm. Once he's standing, I wrap my arms around his waist, and his strong arm is over my shoulder.

"Did you drive?" I look up at my mom.

"We actually got here by boat. Once we knew where you were, it was the best way to sneak up on the house."

"No alligators?"

Her brow furrows. "Are there alligators?"

"I'm sure there are." Aiden finishes tapping out a text then nods to the driveway. "We'll drive that Ford back to Eureka. I just messaged Doug and Edna we're on our way." Warm gray eyes hold mine, and he slides his thumb down the side of my cheek. "We're bringing you home."

Chapter 31

Aiden

THE COURTHOUSE IS LIT UP LIKE A CARNIVAL WHEN WE GET BACK TO town. Everyone who's been working on the case is waiting, and as soon as I pull into my reserved space, Edna runs out to greet Gwen and Britt with hugs and cries of joy.

Mom walks out with Owen, and Edward lunges forward to meet his little friend.

"You did it, boy!" Owen drops to his knees and hugs the dog. "You helped Dad find the bad guys. Didn't he, Dad? Did Edward help you solve the case?"

"He sure did." I scrub my hand on the top of Owen's head, looking up to where Doug and Holly wave from the entrance to the courthouse.

Stepping past the Brewer-Bailey reunion, I go to where one of the Beaufort deputies and a state trooper are watching, arms crossed and almost smiling.

Waving for them to head inside with me, I quickly fill in the team on what we've been able to piece together, from what we knew going in and the things Stan confessed to Britt while he was holding her captive.

It appears he'd originally planned to kidnap Gwen and force her to say all the things he wrote in his deranged email live on some social media platform. The vandalism and the thefts were distractions to send us hunting for Gary Blue instead of him when she went missing.

"But why kill Gary? It blew his whole cover." Piper sits on the edge of Doug's desk, quickly making notes for the Tuesday edition of the gazette.

"He told Britt it was because he caught Gary conspiring with Gwen." My jaw tightens. "He thought killing Gary would send Gwen a message. Then he decided taking Britt would scare her into compliance."

When we've finished documenting what happened, Doug calls the coroner's office, and a crew is sent to recover Stan's body and process the scene.

With the case wrapped and Britt safe, exhaustion hits me hard. I'd like to talk to her some more. I'd like to do a lot of things with her, but when I walk to the door and look out, she's still surrounded by Gwen and Edna.

Owen yawns, and my mother hugs him to her side looking tired herself.

"We should head home." I pat my son's little back. "It's late, and you've got school tomorrow."

We walk Edward out to where the three women are rehashing everything. Owen skips forward, hugging Britt around the waist. "Edward missed you while you were out of town, but I took good care of him for you!"

"Thank you, Owen." She bends down, hugging him tight. "I know you did a good job."

She looks up at me, and my jaw tightens with all the things I want to say to her. I love seeing her here, safe, hugging my son, and I loved having her in my arms again, even if it was too brief and we were flying on adrenaline.

"Thank you again for rescuing me." She's so pretty.

My arms can't get enough of her, and I want to surround her body with mine and never let her go. Still, I can see the exhaustion lining her eyes as well.

"Get some rest. We can talk tomorrow."

Her smile dims, but she blinks it away. "Okay."

Taking Owen's hand, I help him and my mom into the truck. Hesitating, I watch her with her family. The aching pain in my chest is healed. The world is right, and magic or faith or whatever you want to call it has restored her to me.

For the first time in years, I can imagine something bigger than us, something I can't see or feel, that protected her from a madman and put her safely in my arms again.

Or maybe I'm simply exhausted from a long week of tension and fear and the successful conclusion of a desperate search. My son and my mom are waiting for me, and I have to get them home. Then we'll rest and see how it all looks tomorrow in the light of day.

I'm out of bed before Owen, showered, dressed, and ready to head to the courthouse. When Owen's finally up, I help him get dressed and brush his hair before grabbing a go-gurt and hurrying us out the door.

The mob at the courthouse has dispersed, and today it's the usual crew, Edna, Doug, and Holly. Doug is leaning beside Holly's desk holding a donut, and it's almost like nothing happened. Except Britt isn't at her desk, and Gwen is leaving Edna's office.

She's back to wearing her wildly patterned silk kimonos and scarves on her head with all the rings and bracelets and shit, but on her way past me, she stops.

"Mom said you stated for the official record Stan was killed in self-defense."

"That's exactly what happened." I sit at my desk, opening my laptop. "He fired multiple shots at Britt, you, and me. You were well within your rights to defend yourself and your daughter. Hell, you defended me."

"Thank you." She puts her hand on my arm briefly. "You stayed until the end, and you brought my daughter home."

"We both did."

I'd leave it at that, but the weight of the past is on my shoulders, and the unspoken words hanging between us need to be said.

"I owe you an apology, Gwen. You were right all along about Lars. Dad couldn't see past the facts, and I couldn't see past what had gone before. But you never gave up. You knew he was murdered, and I'm glad we were finally able to call it what it was and find his killer."

"We have closure," she says quietly before squinting at me. "Perhaps magic does bring justice?"

"More like criminals always return to the scene of the crime."

"Maybe it's a bit of both." Edna walks up to join us. "Have you seen my granddaughter today, Sheriff?"

"I was actually going to ask you the same thing. Is she taking the day off?" I wouldn't blame her if she did, although I'll be disappointed not to see her.

"She's at her apartment. I saw her when I left," Gwen says.

Edna arches an eyebrow at me. "I think you might want to check on her. She told me something about her work here being done, and I couldn't seem to change her mind."

I'm on my feet at once, heading to the door. "I'll have a talk with her."

"Take your time," Edna calls. "Take as long as you need—all day if necessary!"

Passing through the door, I hear her say to Gwen, "I picked the wrong brother."

Britt is standing in the small foyer guiding the beach cruiser to the door when I enter her building. Her hair is down, and she's wearing the light blue dress she had on the day of the fair. Energy tightens in my chest when I remember her on my lap on the Ferris wheel, the unfinished business between us.

"Aiden…" She blinks up at me when I step through the door.

"What are you doing with that?" I nod to the bike.

"Returning it to your mom. I don't need it anymore."

Standing between her and the door, I put my hand on the handlebars to stop her. "Why not?"

Her chin lowers, and her eyes drift to my hand. "I'm going back to Greenville."

"Like hell you are." My impulsive response is out before I can stop it.

Her pink tongue slips out to wet her bottom lip, and I'm this close to catching her face and kissing the idea right out of her pretty head.

Putting her hand on her hip, she looks up at me. "The case is closed, Sheriff. We found our bad guy. It's the reason Gran asked me to come here, and now it's done."

"We have more cases. We still don't know who's putting those signs all over town."

Her slim brow furrows, and her arm drops. She shakes her head. "I can't stay here. You're… I…"

Releasing the bike, I step closer to where she's struggling with her reasons. Placing my thumb under her chin, I make her look at me. "What about you and me?"

Her pretty eyes blink fast, and her words come out in a rush. "I can't work with you anymore with the way I feel. I can't see you everyday, knowing that I can never…" She exhales heavily. "You're a good man, Aiden. You're strong and good, and you deserve someone who won't hurt you. You deserve someone who knows who she is and isn't susceptible to her family's pressure."

She's so fucking adorable, and the emotions burning in my chest make it almost impossible not to smile, not to pull her into my arms. "I haven't met anyone who isn't susceptible to a certain amount of family pressure."

"Yes, but my family in particular." She shakes her head. "They're—"

"Not what I thought they were."

Her nose wrinkles, and she looks up at me again. "What are you saying?"

"Are you planning to hurt me again?"

Her eyes go wide. "No, I would never—"

"Are you going to come to me the next time Gwen wants you to hide something or do something that makes you uncomfortable?"

Nodding, she answers quickly. "Yes!"

"You'll come to me first?"

"Always."

"That's all I need to know. Now get upstairs and get naked. The only place you're going is to bed with me."

A smile breaks across her pretty face, and her hands fall away from the bike I'm holding. "Are you saying you still want me?"

I prop the bike beside the stairs and put my hands on her arms, pulling her closer. "I'm saying you're mine. You're staying right here in Eureka with me. Does that sound good to you?"

"Yes, sir!" Her voice is high, and a laugh slips through my lips.

"Now get upstairs. We've got some catching up to do."

She skips around me, and I park the cruiser, glancing up to see her sexy little ass bouncing as she jogs up the steps. Catching the banister, I'm right behind her, grabbing her around the waist and lifting her off her feet and over my shoulder as I climb the last two steps.

She shrieks a laugh, and I slide her down in my arms, carrying her through the door. Her legs are around my waist, and my hands grip her butt beneath her dress. With a sigh, she leans forward, planting her full lips on mine. Our mouths open, and I lick my tongue along hers, sweet and minty.

Kicking the door shut, I carry her to the bed, dropping her on her back and looking down at her as I unbutton my shirt. Her blonde hair fans around her shoulders, and her bottom lip pulls between her teeth as she watches me. Hunger burns in my stomach, and my dick is hard and ready to make her mine.

When I pull the shirt over my head, her green eyes flinch, and she climbs onto her knees fast. "Oh, Aiden!" Her fingers lightly hover over the large bruise above my heart. I catch a crystal tear on her cheek. "If anything had happened to you…"

"Look at me." Her chin lifts, and I slide my thumb under her eyes. "I would gladly take a bullet for you."

Shaking her head, she places her palm over the ugly spot. "Does it hurt?"

"Not as much as the thought of losing you."

Her mouth covers mine again, and our kisses are hot and hungry, desperate and needy. Emotion floods my chest, and the fact of us here, together, after being so close to losing each other, has me needing to hold her tight, never let her go.

"I'm not sure I can be gentle." My voice is rough.

Her hands cover mine, helping me lower my pants. "I don't want you to be gentle. I want you to love me like you almost lost me."

Both my hands are in her hair, and I thread my fingers behind her head, claiming her mouth in a consuming kiss. I slide my tongue along hers, breaking to nip her lips with my teeth before doing it again. My teeth slide along her jaw and my face is in her hair, inhaling her sweet scent as I consume every piece of her.

Little noises slip from her throat, driving me crazy. My voice is a groan against her lips. "What do you want?"

"I want your cock…" Her fingers cover my tip, and my stomach shudders at her touch.

"Feels so good."

Leaning forward, she flickers her tongue along the sides of my dick before pulling it fully into her hot little mouth, pumping her hand fast up and down my shaft.

My knees waver, and I catch the side of her cheek for balance. "Fuck, girl."

She sucks me faster, bobbing her head until I'm right at the edge. Then she rises on her knees, kissing my stomach, making her way up my chest. "I want you inside me."

Our mouths meet again, and I slide my palms over her shoulders, pushing the straps of her dress down her arms. She lifts the entire garment over her head, leaving her before me in only a thin beige bra that's practically transparent and a tiny scrap of underwear that barely covers her pussy.

"You're so fucking beautiful." I slide my palms over her hardened nipples, squeezing and lifting. "I love this body."

She palms my cock, dragging her nails over my rigid length. "Take me."

I capture her lips again, moving her back onto the bed before kissing my way down her neck. She reaches behind her back to remove her bra, and I cover a nipple with my mouth, pulling and teasing it with my teeth.

She moans and squirms, threading her fingers in the sides of my hair.

My kisses trail lower, along the curve of her waist, over her hip as I settle between her thighs. "This is mine."

"Yes…" She gasps as I hook my finger inside the front of her thong and rub it up and down against her clit.

Her hips jump and move with my hand, and I drag her panties down her legs, dropping them on the floor before returning to cover her pussy with my mouth.

"Oh, God!" It's a cracked sigh, and her knees rise.

Circling my tongue, I pull her clit with my lips, focusing my attention on her response, the movement of her pelvis. Her body rocks like a wave on the ocean. Her breasts bounce with her gasps and shudders, and I slide a hand up to cover one, lifting and squeezing, plucking and tugging at her nipple with my fingers.

Louder moans ripple from her throat, and my tongue moves faster, stroking and teasing until I slip two fingers into her slippery core. I curl them against the inside of her pussy, and she rises off the bed with a loud noise between a cry and a swear.

Her body jerks and shudders, and I smile, moving my lips to the crease of her legs before kissing my way to her navel, higher to her soft tits.

Bracing myself on my forearms, I look down at her flushed cheeks, the pink spreading across her chest. "Was that good, beautiful?"

She nods, smiling lazily, lifting her arms to my neck. "So good."

"Are you ready for me to fuck you?" Another nod. "Get on your stomach, and hold onto the headboard."

It's a low order, and her eyes widen with excitement before she flips over quickly, reaching over her head for the metal frame.

Gripping her hips, I push her legs apart with mine. Leaning forward, my mouth is behind her ear, my beard sliding against the back of her neck.

"Wider." She shivers, letting out a little moan as she obeys my simple command.

Her sexy little ass rises, and I grasp my dripping cock, sliding it up and down her core until I find her entrance. With one hard thrust, I'm fully inside her, and we both moan loudly.

"Oh, shit," she gasps.

"Fuck…" I growl as her pussy grips my cock, clenching and pulling me. "God damn…"

My forehead drops to her shoulder, and I try to catch my breath, to calm the fiery orgasm racing through my pelvis. It's been so long since I was here, I'm going to come fast.

"Hold on, baby." I'm on my knees, and I start to thrust, eager and punishing.

Our skin slaps, and she scoots forward on the bed, wailing

and shuddering. I'm lost in the swirling waves of pleasure tightening my ass and driving my hips. Keeping one hand on her waist, I slide the other around between her legs, finding her clit and massaging it fast.

Another loud wail comes from her, and she jumps, her ass twerking against my pelvis as she comes again. Her pussy convulses around my dick, and it's more than I can take. Another hard thrust, and I hold steady as my orgasm surges through me, pulsing my dick, and bending my back. Leaning over her, I groan as my pelvis jerks forward with involuntary thrusts.

It takes a minute for my body to settle, for my breath to calm and my vision to clear. I'm still buried, balls-deep inside her sexy little body, and her hands are still gripping the headboard. Her breath is shaky as well, and I kiss the back of her shoulder.

She shudders, another little clench around my dick, and I groan, pressing my lips across the center of her back to her other shoulder before giving her a little nibble.

"Fuck, Aiden," she gasps, her body shivering again.

I smile at how responsive she is to me, and I reach up to cover her fist with my hand. "You can let go now."

Her head rises, and she looks at our hands. "Can I?"

With a soft laugh, she relaxes her fingers, and I step out of the bed, going to the bathroom to retrieve a damp cloth. She's on her back when I return, and I pause, taking in her beautiful form, blissful and sated, watching me.

I'm on my knees, dragging the cloth between her legs before putting it aside and pulling her into my arms. Her cheek is on my chest, and our bodies are flush.

Threading my fingers in her hair, I kiss the top of her head. "I've been wanting to do that since the last time we did it."

She laughs softly, lifting her eyes to mine. "I thought when you left the courthouse last night, we were back to where we were that day in the park, and I couldn't bear it."

I cup her face in my hands. "We'll never be in that place again if I have anything to do with it."

She threads her fingers behind my neck, her thumb caressing my cheek. "I promise to come to you every time."

Rolling her onto her back, I cover her mouth with mine, parting her lips and sealing it with a kiss. We kiss and her legs spread, wrapping around my waist again.

It's all the invitation I need, and I slide into her still-slippery core, taking it slower this time, rocking together as we climb higher on the waves to ecstasy.

When we're finished and sweaty, I notice my phone is lit. Reaching for it, a text from Edna is on the screen. ***You've been working very hard. Take the rest of the day off.***

Britt rolls out of the bed and stands, walking to her small bathroom. "Do you have to go?"

"Your grandmother, the mayor, just gave me the day off." Sitting up, I put the phone aside, watching her walking around buck naked.

She lifts her phone, and her green eyes cut to mine. "She texted me the same thing." Then her gaze lifts over the bed. "Oh, shit!"

I'm about to question, when she dashes forward, quickly closing the windows over the bed. "We did it again!"

Her hands drop to her sides in exasperation, and I stand, lifting her off her feet and carrying her to the bathroom.

"We should get cleaned up so we can fuck some more."

"We've got all day," she laughs, and I put her down, switching on the water.

"We're just getting started."

Standing under the warm spray, I slide soapy hands all over her breasts and belly as she presses her back to me. I wash her hair, and turn her to rinse, which puts us chest to chest, which leads to more kissing. Then she drops to her knees and sucks me so good, I almost slip and fall before lifting her up and taking her hard from behind.

At noon, we're both wrapped in terry cloth robes and

nothing else, sitting on her couch beside Edward and watching *The Closer.*

"I've never worn this color." My robe is bright pink, while hers is white with little blue flowers all over it.

She grins, curling into my side. "It complements your skin tone."

I wrap my arm around her, holding her close and kissing her forehead, her temple, the top of her head. She's fresh flowers and the ocean, and I think about how cute she was in Terra's pickle patch in that ridiculous jumpsuit and those enormous, clear goggles. She impressed the shit out of me that day.

The words are right on my lips to say, when her phone lights up with a text.

Sliding forward she lifts it then hops off the couch. "Adam says your mom made us lunch. He's on his way up to deliver it and take Edward. He also says he's got Owen for the night."

"Do you think they're all working together?" My tone is sarcastic, but the knock on the door sends her hustling to get it.

"I think they are," she calls. "I'm okay with it!"

"Your lunch, milady." Adam waltzes into the room, placing a basket on the bar before calling to Edward. "Come on, boy."

My dog hops off the couch, and Adam takes the leash off the rack beside the door. "Pretend I was never here."

"You are too much." A laugh is in Britt's voice, and he returns to give her a brief hug.

"I'm glad you're safe." He kisses the side of her head before pointing at me on his way out. "Don't let me down, bro. I think pink's your color."

With that, he's gone. Our eyes meet, and I'm off the couch, going to where she stands, her eyes shining like the sun.

Cupping her face in my hands, I slide my thumbs across her cheeks. "You're the best thing that's happened to me in a long time. You changed me. You brought me back."

Her hands cover mine, and she blinks quickly. "What are you saying?"

Reaching down, I lift her off her feet, carrying her to the bed. Her legs are around my waist, and her hands are on my shoulders as I sit, holding her on my lap in a straddle.

"I never want my life to be without you. I know it's a lot. I'm older, I have a son…"

"I love your son."

My eyes hold hers, and I place my hands on her cheeks again. "I love you, Britt Bailey."

"Oh, my God…" Her voice breaks.

"The thought of you being in danger or hurt nearly killed me. I can't lose you again. I want to be your husband. I want you to be my wife. Is it possible you want that, too? Is it too soon?"

She nods and shakes her head at the same time, and tears spill onto her cheeks as she begins to laugh. "It's what I've always wanted, and it can't be too soon. I've dreamed of this for years."

"For years?" I laugh, desire sizzling in my veins.

"You were the star of all my teenage dreams." Diving forward, she kisses my lips, my cheek, my eye—any place she can find.

I'm picturing her dreaming of me when her robe loosens, falling open. I cup her breasts in my hands, lifting and squeezing them. Her mouth is on mine again with a moan, and my cock thickens beneath her. One quick lift, and I'm inside her with a groan.

Pumping her legs, she rides me, grinding her pussy against my waist as I grip her ass, doing my best to stay with her. "I love your hot little cunt."

"Yes…" She hisses, riding faster. "More…"

My lips are in her hair beside her ear. "You're so wet for me."

"Oh, God…" she whimpers, lowering her legs and turning on my lap so her back is to me.

Rocking her hips, she writhes against my chest, holding my neck with her hand as she moves up and down on my dick.

My hand is between her thighs, rubbing her clit, and looking down, I watch her breasts bounce as her ass slams against my body. "You make me so fucking hard." Another little whimper, and I bite the skin at the side of her neck. "Come for me."

Her back arches, and she moans loudly, shuddering and clenching. Flattening my palm against her stomach, I hold her as my own orgasm breaks. I strain and buck as her body tightens around me. With another slow thrust, come spills onto our legs.

Another cleanup is short-lived. Halfway through lunch, we end up feeding each other and fucking. Later on the couch, we start watching a show and end doing a sixty-nine. Even after we finally collapse into bed exhausted, I wake before dawn with a raging hard-on.

Her back is to me, her round little ass pressing against my stomach. It only takes a shift of my hips to be inside her. My fingers find her clit, and she wakes, moaning and coming.

Standing in her kitchen in my uniform at 8 a.m., I wait as she finishes getting ready for work. She emerges from the bathroom in a gray dress that extends below her knees and a pair of chunky white tennis shoes. Her pretty hair hangs in loose waves down her back, and I reach out to pull her into my arms.

"You look delicious." I lean down to kiss her neck.

Her eyes cut to the side, and she teases. "I remember when you complained about how I dressed."

"Those cutoffs and boots? Hell, you nearly had my dick hard in front of Doug and everybody."

"I like your dick hard." She grins, wrinkling her nose adorably. "I'll be walking funny all day because of it."

"I love your walk." Leaning down, I kiss her glossy pink lips.

She lifts her chin with a laugh. "I have to apologize to Danielle Steel." My brow quirks, and she explains. "When Stan was holding me hostage, I was reading one of her books and the couple had sex for twelve hours straight. I said it was unbelievable."

My lips pucker, and I nod. "Yeah, we beat that."

"We did." She kisses me again before dragging me to the

door. "You go first. I'll wait a few minutes, so we don't arrive at the same time."

"I'm pretty sure they're on to us."

"Just go."

Another kiss, and I head out the door, jogging down the stairs to where Gwen is standing at the entrance to the Star Parlor. "Good morning, Sheriff. I didn't expect to see you looking so well-rested today."

"Good morning, Gwen." *Not discussing my sex life with her.*

My hand is on the doorknob when she stops me. "I did a reading for you this morning." One backwards glance, and she waves a hand. "I know, I know, but it was very interesting. The Ten of Cups, the Four of Wands, and the Empress."

"I don't know what any of that means."

"Love, marriage, happily ever after, babies…"

Releasing the door, I nod, holding up both hands. "You're right. You win. All of that is correct."

She responds with the first genuine smile she's ever given me. "Take care of my daughter."

"I intend to—forever."

The door opens above, and Britt steps out, locking it before heading down the stairs. When she sees us, she stops with a little, "Oh!"

I hold out my hand, and she shakes her head, walking down to my side. Her mother nods, and it's official, I believe in magic.

Or more correctly, I believe in love, and this girl at my side is magic. Although, now I realize love is also magic, and with enough love, you can do anything.

You can change your life.

You can even change your mind.

It only took a little taste to find the love of a lifetime.

Epilogue

Britt

Six months later

"**B**ALANCE IS THE FIRST THING YOU HAVE TO MASTER." ADAM stands behind me on the surfboard, lightly holding my waist. "Balance is the key."

"Sounds like life." My arms are extended, and my knees are bent as the small waves form under us.

"You'd be surprised. I've had a lot of insights out here riding the waves."

"I'm sure you have." The deep voice at my feet sends a thrill to my core.

"Aiden, look!" The wake from him swimming to us bounces the board, and I start to wobble. "Whoa... I think I'm doing it!"

"You're amazing. I'm coming up to help you."

"What's wrong, bro? Jealous?" Adam laughs, slowly lowering to his knees. "You got it Britt. Keep your knees soft."

He tips off the side of the board, and I let out a little yelp when it rocks. Still I manage to stay on my feet. My heart is beating so fast, and my tongue sticks out between my teeth.

"Get on your knees," Aiden orders, holding the sides of the wide, beginner board.

Keeping my eyes focused straight ahead, I do as he says, lowering to my knees and then taking a seat. He climbs up, straddling the board behind me, and I lean against his chest, tilting my face up to kiss his salty jaw.

"I'm glad you joined me." His warm skin is against my bare back, and I'm less interested in surfing now. "Maybe we can slip into the water and scare the fish."

A laugh vibrates through his chest, sending another surge of energy to my stomach. "Come on, let's try this."

Looping a strong arm around my bare midriff, we slowly make our way to standing. A gentle wave lifts the board, and I move in time with him holding me. I love Aiden's large hands on my bare skin, and surfing is like a dance.

"We should surf together every time," I yell over my shoulder. "We'll be like those old beach movies where their hair never gets wet."

A rough wake catches us, and out of nowhere a wave runner flies past us, sending a curve of water and upending the board. Grabbing my nose, I squeal and fall into the ocean. Aiden dives off the other side then swims under to where I'm paddling.

"You okay?" He's breathless, but I'm nodding as I grab his shoulders. His jaw is tight, and he grabs the board, pushing up to sit on it before helping me climb aboard. "Those assholes are inside the buoys. Someone could get hurt."

His brow is lowered, and he's studying the wave runner zipping around several feet from where we're floating. Shouts from the beach get my attention, and I look over to see Piper and Cass waving. I wave back, giving them a thumbs-up.

Owen and Ryan run past them with Edward bounding along and Pinky doing her best preschool joggle behind them.

"Let's head back to the shore. It's almost time to go."

"I'll pull you in." He kisses the top of my shoulder before

slipping into the water again, and it's the sweetest hit of dopamine.

He's about to pull me in when the wave runner circles around to where we are, slowing this time and floating closer to us.

"Hey, there!" Shading my eyes with my hand, I almost recognize the female voice. "Didn't mean to throw you just then."

"No worries," I call, giving a little wave.

I expect her to leave, but instead she gives the vehicle a bump of gas that scoots her closer to where I'm sitting. "Britt Bailey, is that you? My goodness, it is you! I've been wondering where you went. I thought you might have drowned."

The voice clicks in my memory, and I wrinkle my nose, trying to smile. "Maylynn? What in the world are you doing out here?"

"You're just never going to believe. Keekee's cousin Harold owns a popcorn place near this teeny little town. He's been begging us to come for a visit. It's where the Stone Cold distillery is located. You probably don't know anything about bourbon, but it's very prestigious."

My lips part, and I'm about to burst her bubble when Aiden surfaces beside me, wrapping a muscled arm over the board. "Everything okay back here?"

"Well, hello." Lowering her shades, Maylynn's eyebrows rise. "If the lifeguards are that handsome, maybe we all should try drowning."

She lets out a shrieky laugh that makes me cringe. "That was my worst fear," I point out quietly as Aiden's brow lowers.

"Aiden Stone, this is Maylynn Evers. From Greenville." I wave my hand back and forth between them.

"I see." He's not impressed. "Next time keep that thing outside the buoys. You could kill somebody."

"Yes, sir, handsome lifeguard." She laughs more, turning the machine and starting the engine. "We should meet up at the popcorn palace, Britt. I'd love to catch up."

With that she zips away, and I look down at Aiden, who's still frowning. "I don't like her."

His flat statement of fact hits me just the right way, and I start to laugh. The more confused he looks, the more I laugh until I lean down to kiss his lips. "Pull me in, Mr. Handsome Lifeguard."

"I'll do more than that." His voice turns naughty, and he kisses the top of my thigh, sending heat racing to my core.

"Hold that thought. I have to meet up with the girls tonight, and you're taking the kids to see a movie in the park."

"How many times can they watch *Finding Nemo*?" he growls. "That opening scene is the worst."

"But the rest is so funny and good, and you have Dorie and all her forgetting. Make a popcorn run during the beginning part."

He grins up at me, and I lean down to slide my hand along his cheek. My platinum engagement ring sparkles on my finger, and I sit up holding it with my thumb as he pulls me to shore.

He gave it to me last Friday night after dinner on the deck. Owen couldn't sit still the entire meal, but I thought it was because he wanted to teach Edward to catch a frisbee. He'd been talking about it all week.

Instead, once the dishes were cleared and we'd cleaned up, the two of them disappeared into the house. When they returned, Owen was holding a chocolate cupcake with a sparkler on top for a candle, and Aiden had a sheepish grin on his lips.

"It's not my birthday." I sat straighter, taking the gift from Owen.

"No." He shook his little-boy head, turning serious. "We have something very important to ask you." My eyes widened, and he continued. "Dad and I had a talk last night, and we decided it would be a good idea for you and Edward to live here with us. He said zebras live in families, and we should be a family, too."

My eyes flew to Aiden's, and when I saw a mist in his eyes, my breath hiccupped. "You want me to be your family?"

Owen's voice turned thoughtful. "I asked Dad if you could be my mom, and he said he asked you to marry him, so that would make you my stepmom. I think that's a good idea, but you'll be my *nice* stepmom. Not a wicked one like in the Disney movies, but a nice one like in that old movie Miss Cass made us watch, where they sang all the time."

"*The Sound of Music*?"

"Yeah. You're like that stepmom." Placing his hand on my shoulder, he looked at me with those gray-blue eyes just like his dad's. "Would you like to live here and take care of me and Dad? You make him smile more than he ever did before, and I promise I'll bathe with soap and I won't leave my dirty underwear all over the floor, and I'll take Edward for walks all the time and teach him to do tricks. I think you'll like being in our family. What do you say?"

Warmth thickened my voice, but I nodded quickly. "I would love to be your family very much."

"Woo-hoo!" He jumped forward, wrapping his arms around my neck and hugging me before pulling away. "Your turn, Dad!" Then he took off with Edward. "Come on, ole boy. We're going to be a family now! You're going to be my good dog, too!"

My nose wrinkled, and Aiden caught my hand. He pulled me to him, lowering his face to mine for a kiss. He just caught my lips with his briefly before stepping back and reaching into his pocket.

"I asked you this six months ago, but I wasn't prepared to make it official." My heart jumped, and he held out a small box. "You're the magic in my life, and I want you with us every day from now through forever. Then I want to find you again on the other side and love you for another forever, and on and on, through every lifetime."

More tears flooded my eyes as he lifted the beautiful

platinum band adorned with tiny platinum flowers around a stunning round diamond. "It's so beautiful!"

"It reminded me of you with the little flowers and the complete circle," he explained, sliding the ring onto my left hand. "Do you still want to be my wife? Be Owen's *nice* stepmom?"

Laughing, I pull his lips to mine. "More than anything in the world. Forever, and again and again…"

I'm smiling at the memory as we reach the shore. He helps me off the surfboard, and before we go, I jump into his arms, kissing him long and slow, sliding my lips across his and touching his salty tongue with mine.

Strong arms go around my waist, and he looks down at me with a bad-boy grin. "I can't get out of the water with a semi in front of all our friends."

One more kiss, and I pull away. "I was just thinking about tonight, future husband."

"Can't wait, future wife."

Hours later, I'm sitting at the bar in the distillery with Cass and Piper laughing and brainstorming small weddings.

"Do they make a Krispy Kreme wedding cake?" Cass swipes her finger over a large iPad where we're looking at wedding photos on Pinterest. "You'll have to have one for Doug."

"Dear ole 3-D," I laugh. "He does love his donuts."

"Mom says she'll attend the wedding, but she's not buying anything off your registry." Piper rolls her eyes. "She says your selections are impractical and useless in the event of an apocalypse."

"What is Martha going to do when the world never ends?" Cass leans forward on the bar, her dark hair spilling over her shoulder.

"That's something we never have to worry about." Piper takes a sip of her bourbon. "She'll be waiting for the second coming or the brain-eating fungus or the nuclear storm until her dying breath."

"I almost wish something like that would happen. Save me from the hell of dating apps." Cass turns to me, lifting my finger and studying my engagement ring. "At least you don't have to worry about it anymore."

"How's it going, ladies?" Alex is behind the bar, holding a round bottle of amber liquid. "Who wants to try this year's special reserve?"

Three tumblers slide towards him at once, and he chuckles.

"We're getting your future sister-in-law loaded while we discuss her upcoming nuptials." Cass lifts her glass, turning to me with an arched eyebrow.

Alex's gaze lingers on the bare skin of her back, exposed by the red halter dress she's wearing. It's a look that only lasts a moment, but it's a look I recognize from his older brother. My future brother-in-law would devour my bestie if he had half a chance.

It gives me an idea...

"I want all the scoop on this new line." Piper sips her drink, turning the bottle. "It's smoky with a touch of sweetness. How do you do it?"

"Wheat instead of corn, and age it ten years. Or in this case seven."

"Seven years!" Cass's eyes go wide, and she turns back to him. "You must be so patient."

"You have no idea." He lifts his glass, taking a sip, and I can barely breathe at the heat simmering in his amber eyes.

Cass seems oblivious, and I glance at Piper, but she's tapping on her phone. I'm about to ask if Alex is still looking for a nanny when an unwelcome, loud voice interrupts us.

"Speak of the devil!" Maylynn Evers is behind me, and I turn to see her standing beside a not-smiling Keekee Waters. "We were just talking about you, Britt Bailey! I was saying the last time we saw you, you told that funny story about your car stalling out at a gas station... I don't know where you get your sense of humor."

Embarrassment heats my chest, and I'm sure it's up my neck and all over my face. I don't know how to reply, and Cass jumps in to save me.

"I'm sorry, do we know each other?"

"That's highly unlikely." Keekee's eyebrow arches, and her eyes slide from my friends to me. "You live in this little town now?"

"Eureka's my home." I stand straighter, having enough of their mean-girl attitudes. "What's your excuse?"

Maylynn titters a laugh. "There you go again. *Hilarious*. I told you, we came to see this incredible facility. It's been written up in all the major publications."

"Including mine," Piper calls, holding up her tumbler.

"The best of them all." Cass taps her glass against it.

"Are you a journalist?" Keekee's gaze lands on her.

"I'm actually the publisher of the *Eureka Gazette*."

"You mean that little rag my cousin's always talking about? I saw that." Turning to the bar, she smiles at Alex. "Excuse me, sir, we'd like to sample the special reserve if you don't mind."

Alex's eyes narrow, and our eyes meet. "Are they friends of yours, Britt?"

Hesitating, I'm not sure how to answer. I think about the last time I was with these women, how Maylynn ditched me when Keekee turned her nose up at me. I remember how I sat alone in her well-appointed living room nibbling a bland cucumber sandwich and wishing the ground would open up and swallow me.

"No." I shake my head. "Not at all."

His brow arches, and he sets the bottle down, emerging from behind the bar.

"What's in the water?" Maylynn murmurs to Keekee. "I've seen more panty-melters in this little town than anywhere I've been."

"I'm sorry, ladies." Alex holds out his hand towards the door.

"We're closed tonight for a private tasting. I'm afraid you'll have to go."

"What?" Keekee's eyes flash. "There was no notice of a private tasting. We came all this way to visit this establishment."

"Well, I'm the owner, and unless you're friends with my sister-in-law here, you'll have to leave."

"What... Why, I..." She flashes her eyes at me before turning on Alex again. "Do you know who I am?"

"I do." His voice is flat. "You're the lady who's leaving my bar."

"I've never heard of such a thing!" Keekee bellows like a wet pigeon as Alex clasps her arm and Maylynn's in a firm grip, escorting them to the door. "This is not the end of this... I've never been so insulted in my life!"

Keekee is still going, but Maylynn, looks back shaking her head with a laugh. "I've never been thrown out of a bar before!"

My eyes narrow, and while I'm not sure how I feel about Maylynn Evers, I hope I never see Keekee Waters again.

"Were those the bitches from that Greenville Ladies Club?" Cass's hands are on her hips, and she's fuming, watching Alex put them outside before closing the door and turning the bolt. "I wasn't finished with them!"

She starts to follow the way they left, but I grab her arm. "Easy, Champ. Alex handled it."

"Yeah, he did!" Piper cheers as he returns to us. "Put it here, bro!"

They do a fist bump, and we spend the next hour discussing small-wedding options. I don't want to do it on the beach. I don't want to do it in a park. Then Alex offers the distillery, saying he's been wanting to add an events line, and looking around the beautiful, wood and brass facility, it feels exactly right.

Later, as I'm crawling into bed with a sleeping Aiden, I rest my head on his chest thinking how much has happened, how much has changed since the day I blew into town with no brakes. It was a bit of a metaphor, since I haven't stopped since.

My gorgeous fiancé rouses, turning and pulling me close,

pressing his lips to my brow and my cheek, sending happiness sparkling through my veins.

"Did you have fun tonight?" His voice is laced with sleep, and I trace my fingernails softly up and down his muscled arm.

"I did. Alex suggested having the wedding at the distillery, and it sounds absolutely perfect."

"Whatever makes you happy." He kisses my lips as his hands drift under my thin sleep shirt, covering my breasts. "I've got what I want."

"Mmm," I exhale a moan, moving closer to his touch. "Your brother was my hero tonight."

A low growl vibrates in Aiden's throat. "I taught him everything he knows."

It makes me laugh, and I turn onto my back, pulling him over me as heat filters through my body. "He's got nothing on you."

Our mouths collide, and we're lost in sensations, touching, holding, tasting. His clean cedar scent surrounds me, and as our lips chase, deep satisfaction fills my soul.

I've found the place where my nightmares end, and my dreams come true. Aiden says I gave him magic, but he gave me what I needed most. I don't dream of drowning now, and when my hands tremble, his strong ones cover them.

I left to try and find my life. An old vendetta, a dash of pixie dust, and a little taste of heaven brought me home. A lot of love means I'll never leave again.

That's the true magic.

Aiden

The Next Day…

Never too late to try again. The white sign with blue lettering is nailed above the entrance to the gazebo in the square in front of the courthouse.

"It's a nice sentiment." Doug stands beside me, Krispy Kreme in hand, gazing up at it.

My arms are crossed, and I'm not sure what to think. "Maybe."

Britt has her camera out taking photos of the sign, the ground around the small structure, and the bushes lining the stairs. "I don't think it's related to our last case. We got all those guys."

"As far as we know." I motion to Doug. "I want you to check this thoroughly for fingerprints."

"We never find any. Whoever's doing it must wear gloves."

"Check it anyway." Going to where Britt is carefully lifting branches, I lean down. "Find anything?"

"No." She stands, chewing her lip. "This person knows how to cover their tracks."

Scratching my fingers through my beard, I look around. Pedestrians slow to read the sign, nod or shrug, and continue on. At a glance, it appears harmless.

"It's not a bad message." She looks up at me.

Reaching out, I pull her close. I've got this girl, and she's safe. That's what matters to me, keeping her safe always. "We'll keep an eye on it. In the meantime, we have a wedding to plan."

Her nose wrinkles. "And several lifetimes to spend together?"

"Yep." I kiss the top of her head, glancing at the sign once more.

It's not too late to install security cameras, and I'll be watching over her this time if someone wants to try again.

Thank you for reading *A Little Taste*. It's only the beginning! *A Little Twist* is Alex and Cass's single-dad, nanny romance, available now.

Keep turning the page for a special sneak peek!
Also available on Audio!

Prologue

Alex

Sixteen years ago

"Patricia, I'm so sorry for your loss." Reverend Shepherd clasps my mother's hand, smiling warmly into her eyes before moving to my dad. "Andrew, Gladys and I are praying for you all."

"Thank you, Jim." My dad shakes the older man's hand, his arm around my mom's narrow shoulder as she clutches a cloth handkerchief to her nose.

I'm standing between my older brother Aiden and my younger brother Adam in a navy suit that makes my neck itch, in front of a stinky flower arrangement.

Stargazers, my mom called them when she lined us up in row. "What a lovely arrangement of stargazers," she'd observed, her nose red from crying.

Stinkgazers is more like it. They're making the pressure in my head worse. Looking over my shoulder, I notice a narrow door with a green *Exit* sign above it, and I wonder if there's any way I can get the hell out of here.

Aiden's jaw is fixed, and at twenty, he only has one year left at Annapolis, the US Naval Academy in Maryland. With his dark suit, short hair, and perfect posture, he already has the look of a future Marine, stoic and unflinching. I guess that'll be me in three more years, when I graduate from high school and follow in his footsteps.

Adam, by contrast, is dressed in a short-sleeved shirt and khakis. His brown hair is a little too long, and it curls around his ears in waves that are bleached caramel from spending all summer surfing.

He's doing his best to fight his tears, roughly wiping away any strays that make it onto his cheeks. But he's only thirteen. He can still get away with crying.

Not me. At fifteen, I'm a young man now. At least, that's what Dad said when he'd helped me with my necktie. The implication being, *men don't cry*. The only problem is when I see Pop lying in that casket, stone cold and unmoving, it pits my stomach and tightens my throat.

He's too thin. His skin is the wrong color, and he never wore suits. He said we had that in common. We'd rather be in our waders fishing in the brackish marsh.

Even when he was so sick with cancer he couldn't get out of bed, I'd sit beside him, and he'd close his eyes. He'd ask me if I could see the redfish swimming in the reeds. I'd hold his hand and say I could. He'd remind me how important it was to be patient, to wait for the fish to come to me, don't rush them. *Good things come to those who wait.*

Now he's gone.

I like to imagine he's found the best fishing hole in heaven, and he's hanging out with all of Jesus's friends, who were also fishermen—as he liked to remind me when Mam-mam would give him a hard time for fishing on Sunday instead of going to God's house. He's probably up there swapping stories and comparing lures.

Pop wouldn't want me to be here trying not to cry. He'd

want me to be out by the water, at our favorite spot, taking in the sunshine and smiling over our memories. He'd say you have to have the clouds, the overcast days, to catch the biggest fish. You don't catch anything on sunny days.

Reverend Shepherd has gone to the back of the room, and Aiden has joined my dad and our uncles around the casket. They're going to carry it out of the church. Adam has his arm around Mom's waist, and the two of them have moved closer to the aisle.

I take a step back, in the direction of that door, as the organ music starts and the men reverently lift my grandfather's casket off the stand. They take another step forward, and I take another step back. Again and again, we move until the entire group is at the top of the aisle, and my hand is on the cold metal barrier leading out of the small sanctuary.

The minute I step out into the muggy afternoon, I start to run. First Presbyterian Church of Eureka, South Carolina, population 3,002, is on the side of town closest to the old neighborhoods, where my family lives. It was designed to be "walkable," but my mom says it's too hot and humid to walk to church in heels.

I run the short distance to the house, and when I get inside, I toss my slick leather loafers in my bedroom, along with my stiff blazer and starched white shirt and tie. Slacks go next, and I snatch a pair of swim trunks off a pile of clean clothes in the corner I was supposed to put away.

In less than ten minutes, I'm riding my bike through the palmettos, out to the closest body of water. Sticking to the dirt paths, my tires thump hollowly over small, wooden footbridges, splash in shallow creeks, and crunch over wet gravel.

When I finally make it to the start of the little lagoon that leads out to the ocean, I abandon my bike and my Vans and take off on bare feet.

In the shade of the Walter pines, it's cooler. The air is still thick with briny moisture, but the pungent odor of lilies is finally out of my nose, replaced with the scent of pine straw and the ocean.

I follow the familiar path as my mind fills with memories of Pop. I can see his calloused fingers attaching the fly to his line and sharing his old stories and wisdom.

"The only place you find *success* coming before *work* is in the dictionary," he once told me.

He'd worked hard all his life as a contractor, but his true joys were his family, fishing, and the smoky bourbon he brewed in our family's distillery.

He'd just started teaching me how to make it. Looks like I'll have to figure out the rest on my own. A hot tear lands on my cheek, and I didn't realize I was crying. I only felt the knot between my shoulders, the ache at the base of my throat, the pain in my chest from longing for days I'll never have again.

The sun shines brightly past the edge of the trees, but I stop short of the water. I stay in the shadows, leaning my head against my forearm as more tears fall. I'm not ugly-crying. I'm just letting the emotion drain from my eyes, my own private memorial to the old man who was my best friend.

Cicadas screech louder. The water ripples past, and I inhale a shaky breath. I'm finding calm when I hear a voice that stills my thoughts. It's sweet and clear as a bell, and like a soothing balm, it quiets my sorrow.

Swallowing a breath, I take a step closer, behind the black trunk of a massive live oak tree to get a better look, and what I see almost knocks me on my ass.

The most beautiful girl I've ever seen is floating on her back in the clear water. Her eyes are closed, and her dark hair floats around her like a mermaid. Only, she doesn't have any clam shells, and my teenage dick jumps to life at the sight of tight, pink nipples. *Shit.*

Reaching down, I try to calm my erection. It's been happening at all kinds of unexpected and embarrassing times these days. I avert my eyes, forcing my brain to think of tobacco juice, stepping on a nail, failing algebra—anything to make my boner go away.

I should go away, but she's still singing the song I sort of recognize, and I can't seem to move.

"I believe in angels…" Her voice goes perfectly high, and it's so pure, I feel like I'm having an out-of-body experience.

I'm not at the little lagoon, I'm in freakin' heaven. Glancing to the side, I don't see Pop anywhere, so maybe it's more of a teenage fantasy. I've found a beautiful, naked angel in the water singing like a siren.

A splash draws my eyes involuntarily to the inlet. She's on her stomach now, and her hands part the water in front of her as she swims. I can't see her body anymore, thank God, and I'm doing my best to forget the sight of her perfectly small breasts and tight nipples.

Dammit. I'll never get rid of my woody this way, but I'm scared if I move, she'll see me. Still, I've got to get out of here.

I take one step, and of course, it's the wrong one. The ground gives way with the sharp crack of branches, and I slide around the oak tree I'd been hugging, splashing into the shallow water at the base.

The girl behind me screams, and I squeeze my eyes shut, not moving from where my stomach is pressed to the tree. My feet are in the water, and I listen as she scampers into the brush.

"Who's there?" Her voice is sharp. "What are you, some kind of Peeping Tom?"

Busted. I release the tree and take a careful step backwards, doing my best not to fall. "Sorry, I didn't know you were here."

When I hear her stomping in my direction, I turn carefully. Thankfully, she's clothed now, but the dress she pulled on clings to her wet body in a way that makes my stomach tight. Her wet hair hangs in thick locks over her chest, and when our eyes meet, it's a punch to the stomach.

Cass Dixon moved to Eureka to live with her aunt Carol at

the beginning of the summer. I noticed her the first day she arrived at the Pak-n-Save, and she stopped me in my tracks.

She's the prettiest girl I've ever seen with long, dark hair and almond-shaped blue eyes. She's tall for a girl, but she has an easy way of moving, like a dancer.

"Hey, Cass." I'm doing my best to be casual, but it's the first time we've ever spoken.

"What are you doing out here, Alex Stone?" Her hands go to her hips, and she's sassy. She tilts her head to the side. "Aren't you supposed to be at a funeral?"

"I ran away."

"How come?"

Shrugging, I look down, shame and guilt twisting together into a knot in my stomach. "I didn't want to be there anymore. I wanted to remember my grandpa like he always was. Not like… that."

Her full lips press together, and she nods, walking over to sit on a log moldering away at the water's edge. "I get that."

Her feet are in the water, and I walk over to sit beside her. "You do?"

We're not looking at each other. We're just sitting side by side, watching the tiny ripples of water rolling in and around the cove.

Her shoulders move up and down. "I've never lost anybody I can remember, but I think if I did, I wouldn't want to see them dead."

The word stings a little, but she's right. "It was all wrong. The flowers and the music, even his clothes—it wasn't anything he would've liked."

Our feet move like white fish in the currents. The soft ripple of water surrounds us, and insect noises fill the air. It's a comforting place, and being here feels safe, familiar. Sitting beside Cass feels familiar, even if we've never talked before. She's easy, like an old soul I've always known.

"What was he like?" Her voice is gentle.

My hands are in my lap, and I think about the old man. "He liked to fish and tell stories. He built houses and made whiskey. He asked me what I thought about things, and he really listened."

It sounds dumb, but with Aiden being the oldest, he always talks to Dad. Adam is the youngest, and everybody talks to him. Pop was the one who made a point of talking to me, like it was important to him to know how I felt about things.

A slim hand covers mine, and my eyes flash to where she's touching me. "I'm sorry he died."

Glancing up, I study her pretty face. "You have a really good voice."

She smiles, full lips parting over straight white teeth, and a pinpoint dimple is at the corner of her mouth. "Thanks. I love to sing."

"What was that song?"

"'I Have a Dream.' It's from the Broadway musical *Mamma Mia*." She tilts her head, taking her hand from mine. "Technically, it's an Abba song, but I love Broadway best."

"Have you ever been?"

She shakes her head. "Maybe one day I'll go. I'd love to see *Phantom* or *Wicked*… I wish I'd gotten to see *West Side Story*, but it's gone now."

Nodding, I'm not sure how to respond. I've never known anybody who knew so much about Broadway shows. "Why are you living with your aunt?" Her brow furrows, and I quickly explain. "I was just wondering what happened to your parents."

"Oh." Her voice goes quiet again. "My mom couldn't take care of us anymore, so Aunt Carol asked if I wanted to come stay with her."

"Us?"

"My little sister Jemima and me."

Again, I'm not sure what to say. I've never known anybody who didn't live with their parents. "I'm sorry."

Her chin lifts, and she smiles. "It's okay. Some people aren't cut out to be parents, I guess. That's what Carol said. As much as they try, they can't get it together. Or keep it together." She adds the last part under her breath. "Doesn't mean she doesn't love me. Or even that she doesn't like me."

My brow furrows, and I can't tell if she's pretending not to care or if she's really okay with her situation.

"I can't imagine anyone not liking you."

She bends her leg, putting her foot on the log and resting her cheek on the top of her knee. Her eyes meet mine, and her smile is back. "You're nice. Your dad's the sheriff, right?"

"And his dad before him."

Her small nose turns up at the end. "You're starting tenth grade?" I nod, and she lifts her head. "I'm only in eighth, but maybe we can be friends."

I don't say anything, but my eyes drift to her full lips. I've never kissed a girl before, and I'm having all kinds of thoughts about things I've never done. I've never been on a date, never held a girl's hand, never seen a girl naked in real life… until now.

"Don't you want to be friends?" Her voice is defiant, and I sit up straighter.

"Uh, sure… I guess." *Do I?*

She stands up quickly, practically jogging in the direction of the forest, and I jump up fast to follow her.

"Where are you going?" I hop over rocks and sticks wishing I had my shoes.

She stops and turns so abruptly, we bump into each other, and I grab her arms to keep us both from falling.

Lifting her arms out of my grip, she shakes her head. "I guess you think you're too good to be my friend. I guess you're too awesome to hang out with a middle schooler who doesn't even have a mom."

"I don't think any of that!" My reply is loud, and I blurt what I was thinking. "I think you're really pretty, and I was thinking how I might like to kiss you."

Her eyes blink wider, then her mouth closes as her brow

lowers. "You spied on me naked, and now you want to kiss me? Are you trying to cop a feel?"

Am I?

Maybe a little.

"No! I like talking to you. And listening to you sing, too."

She studies me a moment longer, her breath coming in quick pants from running. Before I can think, she steps forward and presses her full lips to mine in a closed-mouth kiss.

My heart squeezes in my chest, and heat rushes from my stomach to my groin. Her lips are so soft, and her small breasts press against my chest. My teenage dick is at it again, and I'm trying to decide whether to push it down or wrap my arms around her waist and pull her closer.

Before I can do either, she's gone, running at top speed to where a bike is parked by the path. She jumps on it and pedals away as fast as she can.

She leaves me hot all over. The water ripples behind me, and I'm fighting my second boner in less than thirty minutes—both because of the same girl.

My head is dizzy, and all I can think is one thing: I never want to be *friends* with Cassidy Dixon. Not ever.

Available on Amazon and on Audio

Acknowledgments

Kicking off a new series is so exciting and terrifying and fun and scary. Luckily, I have the most amazing team of helpers and readers and friends, and *I love you all!*

Huge thanks and so much love to my husband "Mr. TL" for his patience while I write, his encouragement when I'm discouraged, his ideas when I'm stuck, and his eagerness to read each new adventure.

Thank you to my beautiful daughters who have left the nest but still believe in me, make me laugh, and support me from afar. I love you ladies!

Thanks so much to my alpha readers Renee McCleary and Leticia Teixeira for your enthusiasm and incredible feedback on Aiden and Britt's story! Your funny notes and swoony highlights keep me motivated!

Huge thanks to my *incredible* betas, Maria Black, Corinne Akers, Amy Reierson, Courtney Anderson, Jennifer Christy, and Jennifer Kreinbring. You guys give the *best* notes!

Thanks to Jaime Ryter for your eagle-eyed edits and to Lori Jackson and Kate Farlow for the killer cover designs, to my dear Wander for the *perfect* image, and the amazing Stacy Blake, who helps me make my gorgeous paperback interiors!

Thanks to my dear Starfish, to my Mermaids, and to my Veeps for keeping me sane and organized while I'm in the cave.

I can't begin to put into words how much I appreciate the love and support of all the influencers on BookTok, Instagram, Facebook, and to my author-buds! I love you guys so much...

I hope you all adore this new world, these crazy characters, and all the love! I'm so blessed to have you. Thank you for helping me do what I do.

Stay sexy,

<3 Tia

Books by
TIA LOUISE

ROMANCE IN KINDLE UNLIMITED

THE BE STILL SERIES
A Little Taste⋆
A Little Twist⋆
A Little Luck, **coming Dec. 14, 2023**⋆
(⋆Available on Audiobook.)

THE HAMILTOWN HEAT SERIES
Fearless, 2022⋆
Filthy, 2022⋆
For Your Eyes Only, 2022
Forbidden, 2023⋆
(⋆Available on Audiobook.)

THE TAKING CHANCES SERIES
Trouble⋆
Twist of Fate⋆
This Much is True⋆
(⋆Available on Audiobook.)

FIGHT FOR LOVE SERIES
Boss of Me⋆
Wait for Me⋆
Here with Me⋆
Reckless Kiss⋆
(⋆Available on Audiobook.)

BELIEVE IN LOVE SERIES
Stay★
Make Me Yours★
Make You Mine
(★Available on Audiobook.)

SOUTHERN HEAT SERIES
When We Kiss
When We Touch

THE ONE TO HOLD SERIES
One to Hold (#1 - Derek & Melissa)★
One to Keep (#2 - Patrick & Elaine)★
One to Protect (#3 - Derek & Melissa)★
One to Love (#4 - Kenny & Slayde)
One to Leave (#5 - Stuart & Mariska)
One to Save (#6 - Derek & Melissa)★
One to Chase (#7 - Marcus & Amy)★
One to Take (#8 - Stuart & Mariska)
(★Available on Audiobook.)

THE DIRTY PLAYERS SERIES
PRINCE (#1)★
PLAYER (#2)★
DEALER (#3)
THIEF (#4)
(★Available on Audiobook.)

THE BRIGHT LIGHTS SERIES
Under the Lights (#1)
Under the Stars (#2)
Hit Girl (#3)

COLLABORATIONS
The Last Guy*
The Right Stud
Tangled Up
Save Me
(*Available on Audiobook.)

PARANORMAL ROMANCES
One Immortal (vampires)
One Insatiable (shifters)

GET THREE FREE STORIES!
Sign up for my New Release newsletter and never miss
a sale or new release by me!

About the Author

Tia Louise is the *USA Today* best-selling, award-winning author of super-hot and sexy romances. She'll steal your heart, make you laugh, melt your kindle... *and have you begging for more!*

Signed Copies of all books online at:
http://smarturl.it/SignedPBs

Connect with Tia:
Website
Instagram (@AuthorTLouise)
TikTok (@TheTiaLouise)
Pinterest
Bookbub Author Page
Amazon Author Page
Goodreads
Snapchat

** On Facebook? **

Be a Mermaid! Join Tia's Reader Group at
"Tia's Books, Babes & Mermaids"!

www.AuthorTiaLouise.com
allnightreads@gmail.com